SHERLOCK
IS A GIRL'S NAME

EDITED BY
NARRELLE M HARRIS   ATLIN MERRICK

First published by Clan Destine Press in 2024
PO Box 121,
Bittern Victoria 3918
Australia

Copyright © Atlin Merrick and Narrelle M Harris 2024

All rights reserved. No part of this book may be reproduced or transmitted in any form or by any means, including internet search engines and retailers, electronic or mechanical, photocopying (except under the provisions of the Australian Copyright Act 1968), recording or by any information storage and retrieval system, without prior permission in writing from the publisher.

National Library of Australia Cataloguing-In-Publication data:
SHERLOCK IS A GIRL'S NAME

Editors: Atlin Merrick and Narrelle M Harris

ISBNs: 978-1-922904-71-3 (paperback)
         978-1-922904-72-0 (eBook)

Cover art by Andrea L Farley
Design & Typesetting by Dimitra Stathopoulos

www.clandestinepress.net

Narrelle

To all the Sherlock Holmeses and all the John Watsons

who I have known and loved,

and all the ones to come.

Atlin

To Arthur Conan Doyle

Your detective outshone you too often sir,

but he's nothing without his writer

And to Joseph Carey Merrick, who outshone us all

Contents

Introduction		7
The Solitary Recyclist	Narrelle M Harris	9
The Case of the Love Affair	Kenzie Lappin	35
Adjectives are Forever	Verity Burns	46
The Clothes Maketh the Man?	Sarah Tollok	49
The Mystery of the Vanishing Echoes	Eugen Bacon	65
The Game is a Foot	Atlin Merrick	81
What You Think They Mean	Verity Burns	93
The Case of the Man Who Wasn't Dead	Dannye Chase	95
A Mother's Reputation	Stacy Noe	109
The Curse of the Amethyst Society	Katya de Becerra	117
The Book for the Page	Verity Burns	137
A Taste for Skulls	Tansy Rayner Roberts	139
The Conductor's Last Overture	JD Cadmon	157
Something Borrowed	Millie Billingsworth	171
The Case of the Toxic Teacake	Karen J Carlisle	173
Author Bios		190

Introduction

There are so many adaptations of Arthur Conan Doyle's famous detective.

We've seen Sherlock Holmes and John Watson go forward (and backward) in time, across continents, they've even been known to change species.

Sometimes the detective has been a woman as well, and as editors of this collection, oh did we want to read more of just how the world's most famous consulting detective would move through the world if she were female.

So you'll find here a baker's dozen *(gently fistbumps this almost-pun)* of tall tales, including Sherlock as a woman on a generation spaceship; searching for clues in Russia; 42,000 miles in the air; in 19th century London, and so much more. Her Watson may be a child or a robot; a woman or man; modern, canon, or somewhere in between.

This collection has been created with a spirit of adventure, exploring what being a woman might bring to the legend created by Arthur Conan Doyle. We've loved the Sherlocks we've met here and we hope you do, too.

Narrelle M. Harris & Atlin Merrick

Summer or Winter 2024
(Depending on your hemisphere)

The SOLITARY RECYCLIST

Narrelle M Harris

Lord Robert St Simon, of the Londinium's D Deck St Simons, was adamant that the disappearance of his fiancée was not a case of mere domestic estrangement, but deeply sinister.

'Hatty dropped her bouquet on her way into the wedding chapel. It bruised the petals! Do you have the slightest idea how much fresh, soil-grown flowers cost on this ship?'

The divinely dressed St Simon – all peacock colours, high collar, real silk and jewelled hair decorations – eyed Sherlock Holmes' plainer garb – simple black trousers and coat, sensible shoes, long black hair braided and pinned up in the manner of labourers and scientists: those who worked for a living. That look couldn't have said more clearly "you couldn't possibly understand".

Sherlock Holmes, her expression giving nothing away, and who knew exactly how much the ludicrously wealthy would pay for a bouquet of fresh, authentic white and red greenhouse roses, simply waited for St Simon to get to his point.

'I stepped into the chapel ahead of her, then turned to offer her my hand, and she was gone!'

The disappearance of Hatty Doran, the Beautiful Heiress Bride from the Wedding of the Century was the talk not only of the *Londinium*, from the upper decks to the far reaches of the waste disposal works, but the whole damned spacefleet. Her parents and abandoned groom had posted a reward, but the bride remained unseen and unreported.

'Cold feet,' Sherlock suggested, unimpressed with Lord Robert. She'd only agreed to meet with St Simon at his D Deck residence because she was avoiding Hud50n, and Hud50n was nowhere near the upper decks. 'Or a return to her intemperate ways.'

'Impossible! Hatty has left those years far behind her and is incapable now of such erratic behaviour,' said St Simon stiffly. Even his hair jewels glittered in sympathetic outrage. 'She loves me. She only wants to please me. Something happened outside the chapel. Something that made her drop that bouquet and then vanish, and I fear for her safety.'

'Very well.' Sherlock sat forward, fingers steepled, her attention snagged by several noteworthy things in the previous speech. 'What happened? Tell me exactly.'

'I don't know!'

'Your theories might assist my inquiries.'

'Poison. A threat with a concealed weapon. Mind control. How should I know? It's *your* job to find out.' Lord St Simon's expression suggested a grimace, as though Sherlock's lower-decks origins were malodorous as well as gauche.

Sherlock wondered why the snooty Lord Robert had bothered with her at all, but it was too late for misgivings. Regrettably, she had become interested in the case.

'Poison and threats are theoretically possible, although the various images I've seen of the event don't support them,' said Sherlock. 'As for "mind control" – that isn't very scientific phrasing; I hope you're not actually suggesting hypnotism or sorcery. It's a much less plausible hypothesis. A perpetrator would have to have physical access to Ms Doran's augmentations to introduce the relevant – and might I add very complex, horrifically expensive and absolutely illegal – nanites into her systems.'

Lord St Simon paled, as well he might. The personal violation inherent in such a scheme was absolutely debased and hardly bore thinking about.

'Ms Doran is fitted with the usual neuro- and optics-enhanced and comms-enabled augmentations?' Sherlock asked.

'Of course she is. Everyone is, unless they have some impairm–uh.' St Simon stammered to an audible halt. No tell-tale standard port decorated

Sherlock Holmes' temple, let alone signs of more embellished state-of-the-art augmentations.

The pale, slender woman smiled thinly at his faux pas. She didn't owe this man any explanations of her preferences. Her wristcomm, of the old fashioned, unembedded kind, blinked briefly with the notification of another unanswered message.

St Simon ploughed on. 'But she dropped her bouquet!'

Sherlock's attention became more avid. 'Why is that detail so important?'

St Simon blinked at the unexpected question, then did his best to answer it. 'Hatty had, as you suggested, a somewhat…unconventional upbringing on the mining ships owned by Doran Mining. Even after she went to the *Liberty Belle* for her education, she had almost no check on her naturally impulsive, juvenile nature. Her family struggled to rein her in. But recently she has grown and matured and become a model of elegance and poise, the envy of all, worthy of her great commercial dynasty and our splendid match,' insisted St Simon. 'In her new maturity, my darling Hatty is the personification of grace.'

Sherlock waved a long, thin hand, also the personification of grace, and she arched an equally graceful eyebrow in inquiry. 'Describe again what happened when she dropped the bouquet.'

'We had passed a crowd of well-wishers who thought it fitting to cheer and applaud our passage. I don't know who let them onto D Deck because I'm sure half of them didn't belong there. They had crowded around, taking vids and photos and cheering us on, but before we could enter the chapel, Hatty fumbled and dropped her bouquet. One of the *hoi polloi* picked it up – rather roughly I should add – and put it back into her hands. Seeing the bouquet restored, I stepped into the chapel ahead of her but she didn't follow me. When I looked back, the crowd was dispersing every which way, and by the time they'd cleared, she was gone.'

'This was two days ago. Why did you wait so long to engage me?'

'The regular Yardarm police services and two other enquiry agents have failed to find her. The Yarders found her wedding dress weighted with stones at the bottom of an ornamental lake in a D Deck public garden, and still made no progress! You're my last resort!'

'Quite.' Sherlock's teeth practically snapped shut on the T and her smile did not reach her eyes. 'Show me the film again.'

St Simon, glad the detective was finally taking this seriously, once more called up the video on his wall screen. Sherlock watched the images captured by the wedding videographer. The crowd of well-wishers. Hatty stopping suddenly, dropping the bouquet. The person handing it back to her. The camera then tracked St Simon into the chapel and, seconds later, back towards the bride, only to find the crowd swirling and then clearing from the procession area, and the bride nowhere in sight. The videographer panned back and forth, but the foaming lace of the champagne-coloured dress had blended and then vanished into a background of soft beige walls and gentle lighting.

'Well?'

'Intriguing.'

'What is?'

'Nothing I can talk about yet. Do you have any other recent images of your fiancée?'

St Simon displayed a great number of them, proud as he was of Hatty's beauty and poise, and would have continued except that, after only half a dozen, Sherlock stepped away from him.

'I'll meet you here again tomorrow, Lord St Simon. I should have some answers for you.'

'Do you know what happened to my bride?'

'I have some thoughts. A theory. Nothing more. Tomorrow.'

Sherlock left before St Simon could demand anything further.

Sherlock's wristcomm haptics hummed across her radiocarpal joint just as she returned surreptitiously to V Deck. She knew damned well what the call was about and shut down the inevitable reminder with a few taps on the unit's glowing face.

With perfectly treacherous timing, an AI 'droid in ship's livery stepped out of a service room and into Sherlock's path.

'How are you today, Sherlock?'

'Fighting fit, Hudson!' Sherlock said, looking for an opportunity to dodge by.

'Wristcomm working? You haven't answered any of my messages.'

'You know me. Busy busy.'

'Have you found someone to share your rooms with yet?'

'Very nearly,' Sherlock lied.

'Ms Victoria Trevor is definitely not returning?'

'Definitely not,' said Sherlock through gritted teeth. 'Ms Trevor and I are no longer suitable cohabitants.' Victoria Trevor had ceased playing at being a Bohemian when her mother had promised forgiveness, an increased allowance, and restoration to the family fold on C Deck. Friendship had been cast aside in less time than it took to say 'reversal of disinheritance'.

'You know the *Londinium* regulations require proper and efficient use of living space, and that sharing V Deck rooms is mandatory for otherwise unattached residents.'

'I am well aware of the regulations as they affect mid-deck residency, thank you.'

'I've done the best I can,' said Hud50n, this time in a kindlier tone. 'I know Ms Trevor left abruptly, and I've pleaded special circumstances to the Marylebone Sector Council to extend your deadline. I know you don't want another flatmate assigned by the Helm, or to be forced to return to dorm accommodation.'

Sherlock shuddered. 'I still have two days.'

'I can give you three.'

Sherlock grinned and impulsively shook Hud50n by the hand. 'Three! Excellent. I can bring this case to a close and have time to spare.'

Hud50n was not convinced, but Sherlock had now darted by and into her accommodation designated 'V Deck, Marylebone Sector – Baker Street Corridor | Room 221:B (Port side)'.

Sherlock invested a productive half hour in secured calls to a few contacts: the most sophisticated gossip-monger she knew and the shadiest trader-of-favours of her acquaintance. As a result, she owed Langdale Pike a future juicy secret in return for a thorough unofficial biography of Hatty Doran's personal, rather than public, life.

As for Shinwell Johnson, the man had a surprising set of ethics, honour of sorts, and they'd developed a good working relationship over the years. Johnson had been vital in addressing the Baron Gruner business, and Sherlock trusted his intel. He'd agreed with Sherlock's suspicions and slipped her a name of someone who might know the next link in the chain.

Sherlock, now wearing a long, battered coat over her sturdy trousers and shirt, slipped out of her apartment again. Bypassing the residential elevators, she made for the service lifts.

'Sherlock! I was hoping to see you!' St4mf0rd beamed a greeting to the consulting detective, tipping his hat to her as they entered the lift together.

Sherlock sighed. It seemed to be her day for being stopped by friendly AIs. Momentarily resigned to her fate, she complimented St4mf0rd on his new hat. 'A gift from a grateful patient, I perceive.'

'Yes it is! How can you tell it was a gift?'

'I said gift, I suspect it was payment. You're always treating your patients for pittance if they're in need, and I've never seen you wearing a hat before. But I saw a milliner in your waiting room last week and how discreetly and kindly you spoke to her. It's a logical conclusion.'

'Oh, well done. I do like hearing how you do it.' St4mf0rd tilted the hat to a jaunty angle. 'I think it makes me look distinguished, don't you?'

'Very fine.' Sherlock checked her wristcomm, suggesting she had no time for small talk.

St4mf0rd remained cheerfully unoffended. 'You might be wondering where I'm going in the service lift.'

'You're no doubt visiting a friend on the lower decks.'

'I am! And on this subject, have you found a flatmate yet?'

'Not yet.'

'I have a suggestion...'

'I'm on a pressing case,' said Sherlock quickly.

'You are always either on a pressing case or so crippled with ennui you won't leave your room,' observed St4mf0rd good humouredly. 'But I am visiting a friend who I think would suit you.'

'In what way, "suit me"?'

'They're a competent 'droid of quiet habits and with a story. You like a person with a story.'

This was very true. Nevertheless: 'I don't have the time.'

'You're heading my way. Give it ten minutes. Knowing you, you'll have decided by then if you can stand Watson as a flatmate, and if you can, that's one problem resolved.'

Sherlock regarded St4mf0rd with fond exasperation. 'You know it's cheating to use logic on me. All right. Ten minutes.'

Sherlock Holmes had made it a lifetime's study to know every corridor, vent and shaft of every deck of the starship *Londinium*, from bow to stern, from the primary helm to the meanest hold. The *Londinium* was, however, a very large generation ship; its inhabitants had bolted additions to its skin over the centuries, and Sherlock was not yet thirty. She knew more about this city-sized vessel than its original architects, but her knowledge was far from complete, and it got scrappier the further down she went.

All of which explained how she had never before strolled the corridors of ZZP deck, which was so far down in the *Londinium* that borough labels like Whitechapel Sector or The Hamlets had long since lost their meaning.

'Here we are,' announced St4mf0rd, halting before a dingy metal door. He knocked briefly before pressing his palm to the entry panel. The door slid aside and he led Sherlock into a large and brightly lit storeroom.

Stacked high to the ceiling, and along hundreds of metres of shelving, were machine parts. Body parts, really – appropriately shaped plates and articulated joints, packages of synthetic skin and hair, and obsolete versions of all the advanced technology that ordinarily formed the limbs, torsos, heads, brains and inner workings of AI androids.

Sherlock had visited the human recycling room in her youth, where the organic departed came to rest after all the human rituals were done. There, augmentations were removed and dismantled, and undamaged memory circuits returned to family members or disposed of, according to the deceased's will. Flesh and bone were divided into recyclable donor components (such as healthy hearts and corneas) and the rest went to fertilise and water the massive bio-organic farms and gardens that kept *Londinium* a thriving space-borne metropolis in the midst of a larger, thriving fleet of spacecraft.

Dead androids, after their farewell rituals, arrived at equivalent institutions, transferred over the skin of ships, rather than internally, as the cold of vacuum didn't affect them. Their remains were subjected to a final Proof of Life test and, when death was confirmed, broken down into their component parts. Robotic 'organs' considered reusable were directed to mid-decks AI clinics, like the one St4mf0rd served. The rest of the parts – memory chips, obsolete electronics and the like, were meant to be melted down for more general repurposing, though in practice much of it was stored in rooms like this for years at a time.

Ultimately, all life on board came to an end, and when it did, it went to one recycling room or another.

'Watson!' St4mf0rd called out across the rows of shelves. 'I've brought someone to meet you!'

Rows away, a whirr sounded, a metallic creak. A pleasantly modulated voice rose up. 'I'll be right with you.'

The creaking and whirring come closer, until a strange being came into view.

The AI designated W4t50n had dark synthi-skin which only partially covered the 'droid's face and skull, revealing the bright metal endoskeleton of a cheekbone and forehead. The android's mismatched mech-eyes – one blue, one brown – were dilated, taking in every nuance of the light spectrum. W4t50n's right hand was finely detailed, with dark skin over long, dextrous fingers. The left was a metal skeleton sheathed in a close-fitting rubber glove, in which W4t50n held a magnetic screwdriver. The android's trouser-clad legs appeared to be slightly different lengths, producing an uneven gait. The right leg whirred as W4t50n walked. The creaking emanated from the android's left shoulder when it raised an arm to place the screwdriver on a nearby shelf.

'Stamford, hello. And hello…?'

'This is Sherlock Holmes,' announced St4mf0rd as though producing a rabbit from a hat.

W4t50n cast an appraising, inquisitive look over Sherlock. 'A pleasure to meet you at last. Stamford said he wanted to introduce us.'

'He did?'

'Stamford hasn't told you about me?' W4t50n ventured.

'He may have tried. I've been preoccupied.'

The skin on W4t50n's face stretched in an amused smile. 'He said you were often preoccupied.'

'I often have things on my mind. I'm a consulting detective, you see. The only one in the fleet.'

The announcement prompted wariness. 'A detective?'

'A *consulting* detective.'

'He said you solved mysteries and knew things about people even when you'd never met them before.'

'I have a modest talent in that area,' said Sherlock, her tone by no means modest. 'For instance,' she continued, her grey eyes bright, 'I know that you served on the military frigate *Afghan Prince* before you were badly injured in the pirate raid that took place eighteen months ago while protecting an asteroid mining operation.'

W4t50n's eyes whirred wide. 'How could you…? Did Stamford tell you my history?'

'Not a word of it, though he hinted that you had one. I merely observe, and connect the dots of what I know.'

'Which is?'

'No other situation could explain the magnitude of your injuries, your presence on the *Londinium,* or the repairs you've undertaken using non-military parts,' said Sherlock. She seemed to realise that her crisp explanations were discomfiting to the android, and she continued in a gentler tone. 'Had you died, under the technical specifications for AI death, your body would have been recycled on the *Prince* or the nearest hospital vessel. That you've made it this far, with such significant injuries, suggests you were recovered from space or from the skin of the *Prince* and transferred to the *Pearl of India* hospital ship for assessment, possibly with someone to advocate for your survival.'

'My human partner, Murray, brought me to safety, thinking I might continue to function,' said W4t50n carefully. 'The 'droid assessment staff disagreed.'

'Murray must have argued eloquently on your behalf, and surely you must have still been capable of speaking for yourself.'

'She did, and I was,' agreed W4t50n. 'Nobody thought I'd truly recover, though; even Murray.'

Sherlock nodded gravely. 'And so you were relieved of military duty and sent to a civilian ship,' she said, then smiled brightly at W4t50n. 'Where you admirably defied the odds. And as you evidently continue to be self-aware and capable of repair, the authorities are not permitted to reduce you to components.'

W4t50n raised an eyebrow in dry humour. 'I am yet alive, within the meaning of the Act.' W4t50n's chin lifted. 'What else do you guess about me?'

'I never guess,' scoffed Sherlock, offended. 'What I know of you I deduce from your presence and your circumstances. As for your character – you are clearly a 'droid of courage and determination, to have survived in such circumstances. A swift assessment of this space indicates recent activity to organise the stock for easy use by those with older operating systems or who can't afford newer parts. Some AIs may find it distressing or challenging to work in what is essentially a very primitive hospital – yet here you work.'

W4t50n had adopted an attitude of tolerant amusement.

'In short, you think ahead, consider others, can think laterally and creatively. Yet here you live, for the time being, despite an entitlement to a residential billet, suggesting circumstances, some anxiety perhaps, that has led you to remain here instead of finding a home. Your repairs are uneven, and I know some humans, and some androids, would look askance, but it's more than that. Perhaps you are concerned about some aspect of your self-repair not fitting with the legal definition of artificial life.'

The amusement faded. 'I don't know what you're suggesting.'

Sherlock's tone softened. 'I only meant to remind you that you're not required to self-repair every injury. You know that, don't you? That narrow definition of AI life was struck down in Blair vs the Helm three years ago. If human capacity to heal can be supported through antibiotics, surgery and artificial organs, sentient android life can avail itself of similar interventionist practices. That's not illegal.'

'It isn't,' agreed W4t50n, 'but it's expensive. My army pension doesn't amount to much.'

'True, I'm sorry to say. You've suffered considerably in service to the fleet. Nevertheless, you are entitled to a billet, and I am in need of a room mate before I'm either removed to the dorms or assigned someone who's not to my taste; nor I to theirs. It's why Stamford has brought us together, after all. And he's correct. It's a marvellous idea.'

W4t50n's eyes dilated small, then large. 'You'd share rooms with an AI?'

'Why not?'

'Some people have *notions*,' said W4t50n drily.

Sherlock barked a sudden laugh, humour lighting up her otherwise severe features. 'I am not "some people".'

'Clearly not.' W4t50n's patchwork face indicated doubt, then tilted with a speculative half smile. 'I am also non-binary, which is quite ironic, considering.'

Sherlock burst out in a peel of delighted laughter. 'A pawky sense of humour, indeed. If Stamford had told me that, I'm sure I would have listened sooner. He knows me better than I give him credit for. So how about it, Watson. Will you take the billet?'

'I'll consider it.'

Sherlock's knowing smile contained a hundred unspoken thoughts, but she only said, 'Of course. If you want to see the rooms, tell Stamford and he can arrange an inspection for you with Hudson. Right now, I must fly. I have a case. Though Stamford…if I might borrow your hat?'

St4mf0rd, ever a generous soul, passed it to Sherlock, who fitted it over her braids and pulled the brim low over her eyes. Then Sherlock flew, coat tails flapping behind her.

Strangers were not unusual on the ZY Deck, but they were easy to spot. Most of the rozzers from the Yardarm always gave themselves away with their poorly concealed Yardarm ways and sightseers couldn't help gawping at the crowds or going pinch-mouthed at the smells. Gawpers and rozzers generally got the Rookeries version of The Cut Direct. The few who came on legitimate ZY Deck business weren't properly strangers and received a modicum of courtesy in exchange for their trade.

This one, though, was a mystery. Not clearly from above or below, never seen before, not ill at ease in the bustle or the odours they produced, but no-one from the Yardarm either. A cypher. And Kitty Winter was not in the mood for mysteries. She nodded for her people to *watch the joint* and prowled her way over to the unknown person sitting in a tilted chair, head resting on the wall and hat pulled over their eyes.

Kitty's augmented left eye assessed the stranger as she approached. Heat sensors picked up the normal human temperature range, so not an android; no electronics showed, so unaugmented as well. No weapons, either, and a steady, fearless heartrate. What a very peculiar visitor, indeed.

'Kitty Winter,' the stranger observed as Kitty drew near.

'Who's asking?' A two-word challenge.

'One who wishes you well,' said the stranger.

'Ain't nobody from up-decks wishes me well,' Kitty snarled.

With a long, thin finger, the stranger pushed up the brim of the hat. Large grey eyes set in a thin, pale face assessed Kitty; beneath an aquiline nose, the woman's fine mouth suggested wry humour. 'Shinwell Johnson does, and sends his regards.'

Kitty's hand flew to her face; to the synth-skin that covered the artificial bone underneath. 'Shinwell! What've yer done to him?'

'He's in the rudest of health, I assure you, Ms Winter,' said the woman quietly. 'Shinwell Johnson is an old friend of mine, too. My name is Sherlock Holmes, and he said that he would be well pleased if you'd do me a favour as a settlement of the one you owe to him.'

'That sounds like Shinwell, all right,' said Kitty. With a small gesture, she took her bodyguards off their alert. 'Always trading favours, that one.'

'I owe him a number myself, by now,' said Sherlock Holmes with a small grin.

'He'll collect when he's good and ready,' said Kitty. She drew up a chair and sat beside the woman with the grey eyes. 'What favour are y'after?'

'The work you had done, after Mr Gruner assaulted you last year.' Sherlock gestured delicately towards Kitty's reconstructed cheek, skin and eye. 'I need to know who did it for you. Not,' she added firmly, 'who you *tell* people did it. I've already investigated Dr Fordham, who is not a doctor of either biology or bionics, but a professor of philosophy.'

Kitty shrugged. 'It's not like Gruner gave me much choice. He 'ad all the best ones, and even the not so good ones, in his pocket. Nobody'd do it.'

'No, I see that,' said Sherlock Holmes. 'And, if it encourages you to confidences, I can tell you that I was able to empty those pockets of his.'

'You must have friends in high places.'

'Just one, but the right one.'

Kitty grinned. 'So where'd he vanish to, then, that villain Gruner? Is he dead?'

'No, but he's where he can do no more harm.'

'Not even to the lowest of the low?'

'He *is* now the lowest of the low,' said Sherlock, and her gaze flicked down, suggesting the decks that descended even beyond ZY Deck; or even to the scrappier vessels of the Generation Fleet that surrounded the *Londinium*.

'I'll have to be satisfied with that, then,' said Kitty. She leaned towards Sherlock, as though bestowing a chaste kiss on the visitor's pale cheek, and said quietly, 'The surgeon who fixed my smashed face and my augs is a 'droid.'

Sherlock's expression was full of satisfaction, an internal 'I told you so'. 'Does this 'droid have a name?'

'They never told me,' said Kitty.

Sherlock's piercing gaze assessed Kitty's face. 'It's excellent work,' she noted, 'unusual for restorative surgery of that nature, completed off the records.'

'I got my face back, and augs that worked. I don't care that it ain't registered. I couldn't afford the reconstruction of the mess Gruner made of me, even if I could have found someone to take it on. The surgeon who did me's a peculiar type, but their work isn't *illegal*.'

Though perhaps not entirely legal either. Kitty had not inquired too closely.

'And where can I find your surgeon?'

Suspicious, Kitty's mouth pressed into a hard line.

'I mean them no harm,' Sherlock said. 'In fact, I rather hope to prevent harm.'

Kitty had misjudged Gruner badly, but she trusted Shinwell. And Shinwell trusted this odd woman.

'I met 'em in the room they call The Clockwork Morgue,' said Kitty, lips close to Sherlock's ear so that others didn't overhear.

Sherlock sat straighter, galvanised. She grinned as though a handful of pennies were dropping at once.

Kitty began to regret sharing her knowledge, if it excited that much interest, but Sherlock leaned close again, mindful of listeners.

'Don't fear for the safety of your friend,' Sherlock said, pressing a credit chit into Kitty's hand, 'and thank you for your trouble, Ms Winters.'

Kitty considered refusing payment, but on ZY deck, you took what was going and didn't let it get about that you did favours for free.

During her exchange with Kitty, Sherlock had had the rare and delightful experience of being taken completely by surprise. She spent ten fruitful minutes on her wristcomm determining shuttle departure timetables as she took the elevator away from ZY Deck, confirming a theory. Soon she was 17 decks down again, knocking on the door of her potential flatmate.

The storeroom door slid open and Sherlock swept off her borrowed hat as she entered and performed a little curtsey. 'Watson! I'm delighted you're still here!'

W4t50n regarded Sherlock wryly. 'I live here.'

'Not for much longer, I hope. I'm certain you'll make an excellent companion.'

W4t50n ignored the statement to ask warily, 'Have you completed your case, then?'

'Almost. I have two more people to consult. Hatty Doran and her companion.'

W4t50n's face became utterly immobile. 'Who?'

Sherlock might almost have believed the AI knew nothing, except she knew better; and their blue eye whirred wider while the brown remained steady. Even 'droids had tells.

'Hatty Doran, of the *Liberty Belle*, who was to have married Lord Robert St Simon here on the *Londinium* two days ago, before she vanished.'

'If the lady had no wish to be married, I don't see how that's your business or mine.'

Sherlock admired W4t50n's stance, even though the lies wouldn't convince a child. Not with those mismatched eyes and the way the fingers of the AI's left hand twitched.

'It won't do, Watson,' Sherlock said, firmly but without malice. 'I know that you know where they are.'

'I know no such thing.'

'Your blue eye says otherwise.'

W4t50n immediately closed their blue eye, but it was much too late. They opened the betraying eye and stared, resigned, at the detective. 'How did you find out?'

'Kitty Winter and her correct use of your pronouns were suggestive, but then she mentioned The Clockwork Morgue.'

'That could have been any recycling storeroom. Any 'droid.'

'True,' agreed Sherlock insouciantly, 'but you were the only one I knew of for sure, and whose temperament matched the circumstances I am investigating, and so I came here first.'

W4t50n's eyes, blue and brown, both opened wide. 'You were bluffing!'

Sherlock eloquently shrugged one shoulder and failed again to look modest. 'Occam's Razor dictates that this is the logical place to find Hatty and her companion.'

W4t50n's shoulder and leg both creaked slightly as the android turned, hands raised in a gesture poised halfway between threat and entreaty. Soldierliness was in the movement, but also caution.

'St Simon attempted to enslave Ms Doran. Francis rescued her and I freed her. You will not interfere.'

W4t50n's admission, tantamount to confession, simultaneously rendered Sherlock highly alert yet deceptively loose-limbed and relaxed. 'I'm afraid I must. St Simon is looking for her and his other agents will track her down, as I did. More slowly, perhaps, but inevitably. Eventually, someone will deduce that it was her former lover who spirited her away from D Deck. That knowledge will make their escape more difficult.'

'Why should I trust you?'

'Perhaps my reasoning will speak for me,' suggested Sherlock. 'I was going to reject St Simon's apparently lacklustre case until, adamant that his fiancée could not have simply jilted him, he made the preposterous suggestion that Ms Doran had disappeared as a result of mind control. It was such a peculiar idea that I immediately compared his insistence of her love and loyalty to my recollection of her images in recent gossip 'casts.'

'Gossip?'

'Oh yes. In my line of work, by far the most interesting and useful 'casts to listen to, besides the Yardarm reports and the science journals, are the interfleet scuttlebutt reports. For instance, I know that Ms Doran had a reputation as something of a rebel, who shocked *Liberty Belle* society through her relationship with a sentient AI who worked in the fleet's asteroid mining vessels.'

'A human and a sentient AI is an unusual paring, but not without precedent,' W4t50n immediately protested. 'Sentience can mean capable of emotion. Of love.'

'Of course,' Sherlock agreed smoothly. 'Not even all humans are capable of that.'

W4t50n's shoulders twitched with his suppressed opinion on that, but it sounded like grumbling agreement.

'A tragedy struck, however,' Sherlock continued. 'Four months ago, the AI was killed in an apparent mining accident and Ms Doran went into mourning for a period deemed…excessive, even inappropriate, by her family.'

W4t50n stared. That was disconcerting, or would have been, if Sherlock hadn't used the technique herself from time to time.

'And then three months ago, the lady experienced some kind of troubling epiphany. She came out of mourning. She became affianced to Lord Robert St Simon, of the D Deck St Simons. A great match, if you consider society alliances of value. She became, contrary to her previous life, quiet, dutiful, eager to please. What she did not become, as far as I could see, was a woman passionately devoted to her husband-to-be. In fact, she had become dull, mechanical and almost expressionless. Characteristics that an expert might more likely diagnose as consistent with artificially suppressed mental and emotional wellbeing. The use of such nanites without specific medical authorisation and patient consent is an indictable offence. They may even have been administered with specific, consensual medical supervision, if it weren't for the events at the wedding procession. Ms Doran saw someone in that crowd of well-wishers who was known to her, and who she did not expect to see.'

W4t50n's stare got wider. 'Who would that be?'

'Only one person's presence would be shocking enough to produce a surge of adrenaline of sufficient strength to override the nanites controlling her mind and emotions via her augmentations; to shock her enough that he had time to introduce counteracting nanites through her skin when he pushed the bouquet back into her hand. Francis. The sentient AI she loved and had lost, she thought.'

Finally, W4t50n blinked.

'His body arrived here a month ago, flagged as not requiring the Proof of Life test, but I could see that his positronic brain was deactivated, not defunct. I reactivated him and have been helping to repair him. Francis and Hatty had been married under common law, though they knew her parents wouldn't approve. When the St Simon wedding was announced, and we could see what had been done to Ms Doran, Francis and I began to plan how to free her. I asked some of those I've aided in the past to help.'

'That remarkably organised rabble of well-wishers. You've done incredibly well. But you'll never get the two of them off the *Londinium* without my help. So,' Sherlock prompted. 'May I speak with Hatty?'

'That's not my choice to make,' said W4t50n uncertainly. 'And we have a plan.'

'To smuggle the fugitive couple off the *Londinium* in one of the coffin shuttles that bring deceased AIs in for recycling. Yes, I know. Regular shuttle departures can be easily monitored, but the shuttles coming into the Clockwork Morgue aren't designed to support human life. They have AI pilots and crew for transport across the outer shells of fleet ships. Even if Ms Doran has a vacuum suit for the journey, as soon as she appears on any other ship of the fleet, her arrival will be noted. St Simon and the Doran family will find her, and know that she knows what they've done. I'd be very concerned for her liberty, if not her life, under those circumstances.'

W4t50n's mismatched eyes dilated unevenly again. 'I hadn't thought of her family.'

'Wealth marrying for reciprocal social position is an age-old story. I don't think either the D Deck St Simons or the *Liberty Belle* Dorans come out of this with pristine reputations. Frankly, they all belong in shackles on the *Botany Bay*. '

'They'll never end up there,' said W4t50n grimly. 'Families like that never do.'

'No,' agreed Sherlock, just as darkly. 'But shackles aren't the only answer. I aim to bring down that titled man and the moneyed family who conspired to abuse Ms Doran in this unspeakable manner. I have a friend in a very high place who can help. Who already helped me with the banishment of one Baron Gruner, who delighted in abusing young men and women, and scarring them to mark them as his, before discarding them. You've already met one of the women who survived him.'

'Kitty Winter.'

'The woman whom your skills helped to restore to health, yes. And I can assure you, as I assured her, that Baron Gruner has been rendered toothless, clawless, friendless, and penniless with that assistance. Gruner's assets were frozen, his crimes exposed, and he lives now on a scrap ship on the outskirts of the fleet because nobody else will take him. I'm sure he'd rather the *Botany Bay*.' Sherlock's humour was chilly, and under the frost was the heat of her anger.

W4t50n, bewildered by Sherlock's sudden ferocity in the name of justice, turned an anxious look upon her. 'But you're with the Yardarm.'

'I am a *consulting* detective,' Sherlock corrected W4t50n, offended. 'I am not retained by the police to supply their deficiencies, and most particularly not to perpetrate corruption for the wealthy. I am wholly independent. I am entirely at Ms Doran's disposal and I'm telling you, it's vital that I speak with her before she and her companion – her husband – run out of time. If they're to be free, we have to prepare the way.'

'That's not up to me,' W4t50n replied staunchly.

Sherlock could have screamed in frustration, but then a voice rose from the rear of the storehouse.

'It's all right, Watson. I'll talk to her.'

Hatty Doran appeared, accompanied by a handsome AI who had recently undergone significant repairs, with several mismatched and out of date parts filling out his neck, jaw and arm.

Hatty was dressed in drab grey trousers, shirt and jacket, decorated with shuttle crew patches. Her hair was tied up in a straggling ponytail concealed under a loose flight helmet. The skin of her temple was raised and pink around the insertion of an old-fashioned augmentation implant, ten years out of date though perfectly serviceable.

Hatty Doran's loveliness was in her frank, intelligent, green eyes which sparkled with animation now that the invasive nanites had been extracted from her system. In another time she would have been a woman of the outdoors, and even with a mostly shipboard life, she was blessed with sunny freckles and a gracefully athletic way of carrying herself. Her wide, mobile mouth was pressed into a line of dread and concern.

'You say you want to help Francis and me?' she said to Sherlock.

'I do. I will,' Sherlock assured her.

'Most people don't approve of us,' said Hatty's AI husband, Fr4nc15.

W4t50n, still cautious but hopeful, said, 'Apparently, Sherlock Holmes is not… "most people".'

Sherlock, relieved of the annoyed compulsion to refute she was anything like most people, smiled at them.

'Love is love, Francis, and as Watson pointed out, sentience includes the capacity to love. I've never been in love myself, but I'm certainly not going to make assumptions about how other people go about it. As consenting adult sentients, you choose each other. Whether or not people approve is immaterial and attempted murder of a sentient and abuse of consent are high crimes.'

Sherlock's voice was ringing with fury again. She took a deep breath and settled an avid look on Hatty. 'Watson replaced your augmentations, I see.'

'Yes. With older formats that won't support the nanites used to infect me. We can't be sure we've removed them all until I can get to more modern medical facilities that we can trust, but at least any left can't interact with the augs to affect my mind.'

'I'm sure we can see to that, as soon as I've dealt with the perpetrators.'

'Do you really think my family played a part in this?'

'I really do, I'm afraid. And Francis' attempted murder and the hijacking of your autonomy are both significant crimes. Even if hard evidence is difficult to secure, the scandal will be monumental.'

Hatty took Fr4nc15's hand. 'If it's true, then good. If it's true, they deserve it.'

Fr4nc15 raised Hatty's hand to kiss it.

'Is it true, my darling?' Hatty asked him. 'Do you remember how you were hurt?'

Fr4nc15 clearly didn't want to reply, and that told everyone enough.

'Of course. My family own the mining ships. It would be easy for one of them to have visited and arranged the accident.' Hatty's laugh of realisation was bitter. 'Which of them was it?'

'Your mother visited the mining ship on the day,' Fr4nc15 said as gently as he could. 'Your father inspected the mining site. Either could have arranged it.'

'Or both,' said Hatty bleakly. 'They always were united in business.' She leaned against Fr4nc15 for a moment, then straightened with resolve in her eyes.

'How do you mean to help us?'

'In any way I can. But first – Watson, do you still have the nanite-infected augmentations you removed from Ms Doran?'

'Yes. Most of the invasive nanites are still inside.'

'Excellent. And, if you'll excuse the indelicacy – any of Francis' broken parts? You haven't sent any away for recycling?'

'Of course not.' W4t50n was indignant. 'They may contain evidence of the crime that was committed against him.'

Sherlock beamed. 'Oh, I do like you. If you think you can tolerate me for more than ten consecutive minutes, you're going to be an excellent roommate! Yes, I know you're still thinking about it. Do you think you can look after Ms Doran and Francis until I can send you instructions? Superb. I'll be in touch, and then I'll need you to meet me at 221B Baker on V Deck tomorrow. I'd stay, but I have to call in some favours and prepare before we meet with St Simon tomorrow.'

The door to 221B slid open and W4t50n peered past the woman who opened it, seeking Sherlock Holmes. Then their eyes whirred and refocused.

'Sherlock?'

The Sherlock in the doorway was a vision, her hair twisted in an elegant coiffure in a net of fine gold wire and sapphires. Her throat was unadorned, the column of pale skin having no need of embellishment. Her eye-wateringly expensive dress flowed from shoulder to ankle in a silken wave; her low-heeled slippers were subtly embroidered with a crest. The same symbol was carved into the black stone of a simple ring she wore on her right hand.

Sherlock's smile was sly and amused. 'At your service, Watson. Are they away?'

'Yes. A Helm courier brought their papers and escorted them to the shuttle personally. You really do know someone high up.' W4t50n blinked again at the ring. 'You're from high up yourself.'

'Yes,' said Sherlock in a voice laden with regret. 'It's a curse, but it would be stupid not to use the connections for a better purpose when I can.'

'You're not disowned, then?'

'I was the one who did the disowning, really, but my brother keeps the door open. Did you bring the evidence?'

W4t50n patted a satchel at their side.

'Let's go see to this business, then.'

Lord Robert St Simon was in his office when Sherlock and W4t50n arrived. With him were the senior *Liberty Belle* Dorans, Aloysius and Louvenia. Even their workaday finery was glorious and would have outshone Sherlock's habitual dark apparel, if she'd worn it. Instead, her dark gown and its subtle luxury made their display tawdry.

'I've found your ex-fiancé, St Simon,' said Sherlock as she swept in. 'Your daughter, Mr and Mrs Doran, is boarding a shuttle to the *Gran Santiago* with her husband as we speak.'

She delighted in St Simon's obvious horror as he realised numerous things at once. The value and quality of Sherlock's attire and bearing. Her obvious connections. Hatty's marital status. The items held in W4t50n's hands.

'You're a Holmes,' said St Simon faintly. 'Of the A Deck Holmeses. The *Helm* Holmeses.'

Sherlock ignored this frankly woeful observation of the apparent, which a non-sentient could have made.

Hatty Doran's mother was less cowed by the discovery of Sherlock Holmes' social birthright.

'Why do you bring that thing here?' The disdain in Louvenia Doran's tone was deliberately audible under the superficial civility as she flicked a glance towards W4t50n.

'You can't possibly refer to my invaluable colleague, Watson?' Sherlock matched Louvenia's cold tone, cut for cut.

'You seem to be tinkering with the thing. Although I suppose it's self-repairing, to qualify as sentient. It's not very good at it.'

W4t50n squeaked slightly as they bristled, but had better manners and more pride than to justify themselves to haughty strangers. Still, they thought, *I'd like to see you sew on your own vat-grown arm and replace both eyes with only one hand.*

Sherlock's grey eyes glittered with icy anger. 'You will be *thrilled* to learn Lord Robert, Mr and Mrs Doran, that Hatty has been reunited with her husband, Francis, a senior asteroid mine supervisor, whose apparent death at a Doran Mining operation sent her into such distress four months ago. A terrible mistake was made by your own mining business's tech-medics when they pronounced him dead and attached Proof of Life testing that certified him as dead. Fortunately, his inert form was rescued by my colleague, Watson, who recognised signs of life and restored him. Just as well, or your mining interests might have been compromised by the civil and Helm lawsuits governing sentient life, addressing his injuries and near-death caused by your company's negligence.'

'Negligence?' choked out Aloysius Doran.

'Negligence or sabotage. It is one or the other, and of course the latter has much harsher penalties, especially when a business can be shown to have sabotaged its own operations for insurance or other purposes, even moreso if the sabotage caused injury or death. If it's neither of those, of course, it must be attempted murder of a sentient. So which is it?'

'An accident. A mere accident,' said Louvenia Doran faintly, pressing a hand to her red-faced husband's shoulder so that he sat down again.

'Is that what Francis' recovered memory circuits recorded, Watson?'

'It's a little hard to discern,' said W4t50n, deadpan. 'I suppose an examination by the Yardarm specialists could make out the data more clearly.'

'Just so. Naturally, they'll also be interested in Hatty's infected augmentations.'

Which W4t50n held in their other hand. 'They could certainly trace the nanites to their location of manufacture. Different labs on different ships in the fleet use subtly different metals and programming. Tracking can take a while, but I'm sure this would be prioritised, given the heinous nature of the crime.'

'No need for that surely,' said St Simon hurriedly. 'As long as dear Hatty is well.'

'And as long as she stays that way,' agreed Sherlock.

It was fascinating, W4t50n thought, how much paler already white-with-fear-and-rage people could become.

'I had dinner with my brother last night,' continued Sherlock in her best small-talk voice, like chiffon wafting over titanium. 'He wanted to know about my latest case. I told him all about it.'

W4t50n began to fear that one of the Dorans or even St Simon would soon have a heart attack. The AI's medical knowledge was surprisingly broad, but it might not be enough if one of them keeled over.

'I don't expect Hatty will be bothered in her new married life, will she?' asked Sherlock.

'No. No. I wish her only the best,' said St Simon. 'I shall send her a note.'

'I don't think you will,' said Sherlock.

'No. You're quite right. Inappropriate. Vulgar.'

W4t50n pocketed the infected aug technology and the cell of Fr4nc15's recovered memories, and watched the trio avidly.

'The Yardarm will see to you,' spat Mrs Doran suddenly, unable to contain her venom.

'Well, they know they're always welcome to call on me.' Sherlock was nonchalant. 'Lestrade and Bradstreet know where to find me, since they seek my services from time to time.'

With that, Sherlock turned on her exquisitely expensive heel, trailing a subtle and magnificent perfume, a silky train of frock that cost more than St Simon's office, and the certain knowledge that these defeated enemies couldn't act without triggering self-destruction.

W4t50n creaked and squeaked in her wake, but their self-consciousness was mitigated by the evidence of the St Simon/Doran crimes nestled in their pocket.

'Are they really getting away with this?' W4t50n asked, disappointment clear in their tone.

'Hardly.' Sherlock had unpinned her hair, which flowed around her shoulders while she folded the expensive golden net into a silk pouch to store with the slippers, ring and gown in a box. 'Their hands might be full for a little while, as the Helm puts the Yardarm to investigating the pecuniary irregularities of the St Simon family's investments, which led to the need for Lord Robert to marry a fortune. Doran Mining is also due for an audit. Mycroft – that's my brother, who is part of the Admiralty – hopes, as I do, that there won't be need to disturb Hatty and Francis at all, unless they choose to press charges.'

'Is that who you sent the evidence to?' Fr4nc15's memory cell and Hatty's infected augmentation hardware had been handed over to someone in Admiralty livery only ten minutes before.

'Yes. I'll owe him a favour for it eventually, or he might owe one to me. We haven't determined who's got the better hand, yet.'

W4t50n was quiet for a moment longer. 'Will you owe him a favour for me?'

Sherlock flung herself into a cosy chair and took up a vape pipe. 'For you? No. Why would I?'

'You know why.'

Yes, Sherlock knew why.

'You're a military AI. A soldier,' she said easily. 'And you are also more. Your skills are way beyond your previous military role.'

W4t50n's piecemeal body rattled slightly with a shudder.

'You have layered memories,' she continued. 'An AI robotics technician sits alongside the soldier. A 'droid trained in human surgery too, judging by your skilled work on both Kitty Winter and Hatty Doran. At least one other layer exists, too.'

'J04n was the surgeon,' said W4t50n, defeated. 'S4ck3r was the robotech. J4me5 was a counsellor. Orm0nd's the oldest. An archivist and writer.'

'You're a living palimpsest,' said Sherlock. 'Those memories shouldn't exist. Positronic brains are not meant to be recycled. How did it happen?'

'When I was made, someone must have used recycled memory cells instead of new ones. The layers were only revealed after my head injury in battle. It seems to have bypassed or eliminated programs that had inexpertly wiped or covered over the previously used parts of my brain.'

'And until wounded in the raid, you had no idea?'

'None. I investigated my birth once I realised what had happened to me, and to see if anyone else like me exists, but I think I may be a...a glitch. I've kept myself to myself, in the recycling room.'

'It's not your difference alone which makes you take refuge there instead of accepting your entitlement to accommodation. Is it?'

'No. I...I may violate laws on AI sentience.'

Sherlock waved her pipe dismissively. 'You're unprecedented, but that's not the same as illegal.'

The Solitary Recyclist

W4t50n resented Sherlock's unconcern. And then a thought occurred to them.

'I have to stay here, don't I? If I'm to have your protection. You're not giving me the option.'

Sherlock jerked upright in her chair, then discarded the pipe and rose to stand eye-to-eye with W4t50n.

'You owe me nothing. You may return to your solitary state, hiding in that morgue, if that's what you want. Or you can accept your right to a home and live with me here. You can still operate your unique services on ZZP Deck if you do. Or you may choose another path altogether. I am not in the habit of forcing actions on people.' A wry smile, then. 'Well, unless they are criminally deserving.'

W4t50n regarded Sherlock with puzzlement, but also hope.

'I really have a choice?'

'You do. Stay or leave, as you wish. Though I'm hoping you'll stay. I need a roommate, and I like you immensely. Also, I think you will be a real asset in my work, if you'd enjoy that. Working with me, I mean. Your choice.'

W4t50n's eyes whirred as they assessed Sherlock's words and expression. Then, slowly, they smiled. 'My J04n and J4me5 components believe you. The 0rm0nd component would like to write about you.'

'If you like. You're all one person now, Watson, and you're welcome to stay. Will you?'

'If you're willing to risk it. You already know my worst habits – I tend to literally rattle about and I'm often tinkering with parts for myself and others.'

'None of that is the slightest bother to me. We're both scientists, in that regard. If we're going to start with the deal breakers, I tend to leave my experiments about the place, my hours are very irregular, I'm inclined to play my violin or vape a pipe when I'm thinking, which is often, and I have visitors from all decks and all walks coming to me with curious problems, include the Yardarm, when they're at a loss. Which is often.'

'And you could really use my help?'

'Whenever you're not conducting your clockwork clinic, I really could.'

W4t50n held out their dark-skinned hand. Sherlock shook it warmly.

'Welcome to 221B Baker, V Deck, Watson,' she said. 'Bring up your things, and let me introduce you to Hudson. She'll be immensely relieved that I've found someone else to take up residence.'

Hud50n, thought Sherlock, wasn't the only one, but that wasn't something she was willing to admit to yet.

The Case of the Love Affair

Kenzie Lappin

When one is a roommate of Sherlock Holmes, she learns to come home to the most unexpected of situations.

Sherlock has the mind of a scientist and the disposition of a particularly tenacious detective, which means her curiosity sometimes gets the better of her and that, frighteningly, she has the intelligence to back it up.

I've returned to find my good friend's sleeve on fire, a band of brigands holding her at gunpoint, and, once, her doing something to my dog that I'd rather not talk about.

The most worrying conditions of our flat at 221B Baker Street, however, are total silence.

I came in from my errands to find this peculiar state, and considered going right back out the door.

However, no one has ever accused Doctor Watson of cowardice – an excess of the opposite, in fact.

'Holmes?' I called, stooping to pet my bull pup, Agnodice. I found Sherlock sitting in her armchair, hands steepled thoughtfully over her mouth. She was not wearing the dressing gown of which she was so fond, so I deduced she must have had company which had come and gone.

Seeing as there was no one else around, I began to shed my vestments of the day. First, the padding from under my shirt. Then, my men's waistcoat and hat. There was a feeling of relief similar to taking off a too-tight corset.

On occasion, I wonder whether Sherlock would have an easier time of it if she went the same route as I.

Sherlock does not hide her femininity, though I do think she can be tomboyish at times. She has sharp grey eyes and a hawkish nose, and she is so tall that she towers over most men, which seems to threaten them. Her being a woman makes it much more difficult to get cases, especially with Scotland Yard – who wants to be shown up by a woman, and an arrogant one at that?

On the other hand, I have been presenting as male since I snuck off to join the War. When you are as round and stockily built as I, and have taken a vow of chastity, no one questions that you must be a man, so long as you wear the right clothes and keep your hair short.

I had wanted to be a doctor, and a doctor I had been, until I took a bullet in an incriminating place and had been sent home in quiet shame.

Sherlock, of course, knew my secret, and we shared it together. At home, I dress most often as a woman; outside, I am to most everyone a man.

Holmes looked up, her eyes flashing, as I came in. 'Doctor Watson, finally, you're home.'

'I was courting,' I said. 'I see you were up to something as well.'

'We have a new case, Watson. A very interesting one.'

'A private case?' Though I know Sherlock does enjoy working with the Yard, I think she gets pleasure out of taking the small cases too. The ones that no one else will take, or believe. I think this is rooted in some of the things Sherlock, as a woman, has gone through, but it's really not my place to say.

She nodded. 'A Miss Louise Taylor came calling today. She believes her sister's fiancé is not telling the truth about who he is. That he may be after her dowry – and, indeed, that he may be intending to kidnap her.'

'An interesting case indeed. I assume you've decided to take it already.'

She smiled, that mischievous and glittering look that had, many years ago, convinced me to room with a woman who, I was warned, was possibly the most incorrigible person alive. 'Of course we're taking it. Let us away – the game is afoot!'

We met Louise Taylor at her family's estate, a short train ride outside of

London. I'm a city dweller myself, but even I sometimes find it restorative to get out of the oppressive smog and smoke of London.

Sherlock seemed to have no such thoughts. As usual, now that she was on the case, she would run after the scent until she ended, like a bloodhound with her teeth in something.

'It's nice to meet you,' I said, when I was introduced to Miss Taylor. She was a very well-dressed woman, with dark hair and worry in her eyes.

'Thank you for coming,' she said, speaking to Sherlock as well, which was sometimes a rarity. When I showed up in my brogues and hat, people tended to assume I was the one in charge.

The ones who do that either have the especial pleasure of me ignoring them until they work out the real detective of the two of us, or they become intimately acquainted with Holmes' martial skills.

'I simply didn't know who else to go to. My father thinks I've gone mad, of course, and Catherine won't hear a word about it.'

Miss Taylor led us into a nice parlour and offered us tea from an ornate set.

'Why don't you go over the story again?' Sherlock said, once we were all seated.

'Of course. Well, all is still as I told you, Miss Holmes. My sister, Catherine, has fallen in love with a man named Arthur Robinson. He is a man of great wealth and influence – or so he claims.'

I leaned forward, interested. Sherlock had not given me many details, wanting my perception of the facts to be uncoloured by her own opinions, and to see if there were any differences between Taylor's recollection of events.

'He seemed at first to be an excellent suitor,' Taylor told us. 'He was very kind, and always brought flowers. Truth be told, I have never seen my sister so besotted or so happy. He impressed me and my father – our mother having died many years ago – of his tales on distant merchant vessels and with many shiny trinkets. A lovely watch chain, fine clothes...a beautiful locket for Catherine.

'But I began to grow suspicious of him. For a man with a fine upbringing, he seemed to have little idea of the trappings of that life. Even his own jewellery he seemed to know nothing about, as if it had just showed up in his pockets one day. I thought perhaps he simply didn't care about things like that, until I journeyed to the city to visit a jeweller I particularly like.

'To my surprise, he asked me how my sister was enjoying the watch chain – he told me that Arthur had paid for the very thing with Catherine's account! And he had bought one or two other things with her money, to my dismay.'

'You told your sister about this?' I asked.

'Of course. But she assured me it was a misunderstanding and she would clear it up. That was the last I heard of it, but of course I was still suspicious. I went to my father, but he adores Arthur.' She gave us a vaguely embarrassed look. 'My father holds social class to be very important. He doesn't think any man with money could possibly do wrong. He loves the idea of Catherine marrying upward.'

'That is why you called us,' Sherlock said.

'Indeed. My father wouldn't hear of going to the police or hiring another detective. I can't suppose I blame him. I sound crazy even to myself. But I am convinced Arthur Robinson is not who he claims to be. I love my sister, and I would rather seem foolish and have her safe, than ignore it and have something happen. My father still doesn't know. Oh! If he asks, you are a friend of mine from finishing school, Miss Holmes.' She flushed. 'If that's all right with you, of course.'

My friend gave her a wry smile, though I could tell that beneath she found the concept rather funny. 'I shall endeavour to appear finished, Miss Taylor,' she said. 'Please, continue.'

'I kept a very close eye on Arthur for a time and one day I noticed him carrying a trunk to our servant's entrance – where taking it out might be very easily overlooked. I waited until he left, then snuck in and peered inside the chest.

'I found a large collection of Catherine's things! Enough clothes for a month, perhaps longer. I sprang up to show Catherine, but by the time we returned, the trunk was gone. I greatly fear this man is going to kidnap my sister after the wedding, Miss Holmes, and I fear that once anyone believes me he will be too far away to do anything about it.'

I was astonished at her tale. I felt very badly for her, having no one else to turn to. I certainly hoped my friend could uncover the brigand before any harm befell Catherine Taylor.

Sherlock had heard this tale before, but still she had been listening closely. 'There may be more going on here than meets the eye,' she mused. 'I believe I must know what was in that trunk.'

'Holmes,' I said, 'It's gone! You can't see something which isn't there.'

But Sherlock smiled, a rather sharkish smile, and gave a rather unladylike shrug. 'Who's to say? Perhaps you can tell just as much by an absence as you can by a presence.'

I wasn't quite sure that made sense, but Sherlock had already bounded to her feet, placing her teacup down on the table. 'Your sister is out, yes?'

'Why, yes.'

'Good. Show us to her room.'

Louise led us up to Catherine's bedroom, a neatly-kept room with a made bed and heavy, ornate furniture.

'You can leave us here to take a look around,' Sherlock said.

But Miss Taylor seemed confused by the turn the investigation had taken. 'I want you to investigate my sister's fiancé, not my sister,' she said. 'I don't see how this helps you.'

'You may find, Miss Taylor, that every detail to a mystery connects to another, and another. All one must do is see what those connections add up to, and to do that, you must know where to look.'

This seemed to clear things up for the poor girl not at all.

I gently herded her out of the room. 'You'll never be able to tell that we were here,' I said. 'Trust me, Sherlock knows what she's doing.'

Now she looked alarmed. 'Oh, but Mister Watson – in a lady's room–!'

'You wouldn't believe the things I've seen,' I told her, with my own private irony. 'Don't worry. Holmes keeps me honest.'

And I closed the door on her.

I think that's one of the reasons Sherlock likes best about keeping me around. I get to take care of the annoying things, like too-talkative witnesses or irritating family members, and Sherlock gets to focus on her work. Presenting as a man helps me tremendously in such situations, which is one of the reasons I still prefer to look the way I do.

'All right,' I told Sherlock, even as she went to the bed and began peering under it. 'Being mysterious and dramatic may work for your clients, but not on me. What in the world are you up to?'

'Why, I told you plainly, Watson,' Sherlock said, with a spark of mischief. She knelt on the floor by the bed, long dark hair having come a little loose, making her look younger. 'We're looking for the absence.'

I huffed. As often happens, I had no idea what my friend was talking about.

Having apparently been dissatisfied by the state of affairs under the bed, Sherlock stood and opened the wardrobe. I peered inside with her, and didn't see much. Several chemises and overdresses; a few petticoats and a large domed crinoline that must have been several years old, for it was terribly out of fashion.

Sherlock made a thoughtful noise and checked the dresser as well, then Catherine's jewellery box.

'I don't see a locket in there,' I observed, looking over Sherlock's shoulder.

'Ah, you begin to see what's missing.'

'Her clothes?' If Arthur really had been collecting belongings of Catherine's in anticipation of dragging her away from home, then certainly that was what I would expect to be missing here.

'Very good,' Holmes said. 'I have a theory, and I suspect that I am correct. And if I am, Louise Taylor does not have much to worry about.'

'But not *nothing* to worry about? Sherlock, just tell me!'

Sherlock began to pace, the way she sometimes does when she is working through a problem. 'Observe the hats,' she told me.

I went to observe the hats.

They were lined up neatly on a shelf in the wardrobe, tidily packed into hatboxes. None of the boxes were empty, but I did notice there were one or two boxes clearly missing – an imprint in the dust, or a gap in the neat shelving.

'It seems Miss Catherine is a very fashion-forward woman,' Sherlock said. 'Each of those hats corresponds to a set of clothing in the wardrobe.'

'Why, so they do,' I said.

'There are no mismatches in there. If Arthur Robinson had stolen, at random, some of Catherine's things, how would he know to take the matching clothes?'

'That is a good point,' I said, frowning deeply. 'And in the dresser–'

'Missing drawers and underthings,' Sherlock said. 'Not, and you'll excuse me saying this, Watson, something that the average man would know a lady needed on a long journey.'

'None taken,' I said. I was beginning to get what Sherlock was hinting at. She was very good at this; spotting the details that no one else saw, and noting the importance in what some might deem trivial. 'So what does this mean?'

'I can't make a conclusion without a more thorough examination of the facts,' Sherlock said. 'Where is the nearest train station?'

Miss Taylor proved to have a copy of the railroad timetables in her family's considerable library. Sherlock skimmed them quickly, her eyes hardly seeming to take in the information before she flipped to another page.

Then she paused, and gave me and Miss Taylor a triumphant look.

Louise leaned over, but seemed disappointed. 'I don't see anything.'

'Again, something which is not there,' Sherlock said, and gestured for Miss Taylor's hand. She gave it, a little hesitantly. Sherlock pressed the proffered hand to the paper, running her fingertips along it.

'Oh!' Miss Taylor said. 'I can feel the imprint of writing!'

'Someone was writing a note atop of this page,' Sherlock confirmed. 'A woman, unless I miss my guess. Copying out her preferred train times.'

'Where is your sister again?' I asked.

Miss Taylor gave an alarmed look. 'She told me she was at her needlework club.'

There was the sound of heavy steps behind us – the father, I assume. I turned to take the measure of the man.

Mr Taylor was heavily built, similar to my own stockiness, but having the advantage of height. Like his daughter, he was well-dressed, but with less of an eye for fashion, I think. He seemed displeased to find two strangers in his library.

'What's going on here, Louise?' he asked.

'This is the friend I told you about. Miss Holmes, and her companion, Mr Watson.'

'Doctor Watson,' I corrected, for I liked not the look of the man.

Sherlock was giving him an assessing eye as well. 'Thank you for having us in your home,' she said. I knew then that of course she had slipped into character – as she did when she sometimes impersonated a beggar-woman or an old maid, nearly unrecognisable unless you knew what to look for.

The man harrumphed. 'Finishing school, yes? Do I know your parents, young woman?'

'Possibly,' Sherlock said. 'This is my fiancé.' She gestured to me, and I fought not to gape.

'Ah,' Mr Taylor said, with a touch more respect. 'I was worried a woman was going about unchaperoned. A pleasure to meet you, Doctor.'

I knew Sherlock had an angle, so I stuck to giving him a polite yet aloof nod, something I had perfected as a man.

The Case of the Love Affair

'It is a love match,' Sherlock added.

Mr Taylor looked a little less approving now. 'Against the wishes of your parents, then?'

'Oh, yes. Doctor Watson is quite poor.'

I might have been offended, but I could see that Sherlock, ever the dog on the scent, had gotten her teeth into something now.

'I see.' His voice was cool now. 'Louise, finish your business with your friend soon, please. We have company coming over for dinner.'

With that, he left the room, without so much as a by-your-leave.

'I'm very sorry about that,' Louise said, a little flustered. 'I did tell you he wouldn't approve of my searching out the truth about Catherine. I hope you aren't offended.'

'On the contrary,' Sherlock said. 'I was hoping to run into him. Indeed, many of my suspicions have been confirmed, and I believe I have the lay of the story now.'

'Are we going to the train station?' I asked.

She gave me a pleased look. 'Right you are.' She closed the book with the rail tables and stood. 'And now we know exactly what time to be there.'

'You mean he's taking my sister *today?*'

'Oh no,' Sherlock said. 'I can assure you that your sister is in no danger. In fact, I think congratulations might be in order.'

That clearly gave Miss Taylor some pause, but I was beginning to see what Sherlock was driving at. Sometimes you don't get happy endings in our line of work, but sometimes, if you know how to look, you do.

Miss Taylor had a carriage which she gladly lent to our use, climbing inside along with us. We dashed to the train station, aware that we didn't have long before the train departed.

Upon reaching the platform, we saw many people on their way to and from their business, some waiting for the train and some reclining on benches.

Miss Taylor gasped, pointing. 'There!'

Catherine Taylor was wearing a fine travelling gown, with a lovely locket set around her neck. Her young man was similarly attired, and I could see the flash of his watch chain. Between them, there was a suitcase and a trunk which I suspected I knew the origins of.

Louise practically flew to her sister's side.

Catherine's eyes widened. 'Lou? How did you find us?'

Arthur Robinson did not have the disposition of a man on a furtive errand. Indeed, I could see a sparkle of some kind of excitement in his eye, and he gave Catherine a generous distance of privacy with which to speak to her sister. He had a gentle look which you do not see in many men, and I found myself inclined to trust him more than our client's father.

'I hired a detective,' Louise said. 'The great Sherlock Holmes, from London. I was so worried for you, Cat. Tell me – what are you doing?'

'I never meant to make you worry,' Catherine told her. 'I am sorry about that. We were going to send you a letter once we got there.'

'But where?' Louise cried. 'Oh, please, tell me what this is all about.'

Catherine took her sister's hands. Arthur drew close, laying a comforting hand on Catherine's shoulder. 'Arthur and I were going to elope,' she said. 'We didn't want Father to find out, not until it was too late.'

'But why?' Louise said. 'He already approved of the match.'

'Perhaps because he really *isn't* who he purported to be,' I said, realising what Sherlock must have known for some time now.

'That is right,' Arthur said, speaking for the first time, taking off his hat to duck his head down low. 'I am not moneyed, nor influential. My family came to London to find work, and work is all we have ever done. I never knew I could feel love such as I do until I met my Catherine.'

'We needed the dowry, you see,' Catherine said. 'Father never would have given it to us. So, together, we devised a scheme. We would make Arthur seem the kind of man Father would give his blessing to. We bought him expensive clothing, made up stories of his past. Then, in secret, we packed my things. We're going to the countryside. We're going to marry there then go off on honeymoon somewhere beautiful and secluded. By the time we return home and Father figures out what we were really up to, it'll be too late.'

'Why didn't you just tell me?' asked Louise plaintively.

'We didn't wish to make you choose,' Arthur said. 'Catherine loves you and your father very much. She never wanted to cause you a dilemma. All we ever wanted was to get married.'

'All *I* ever wanted was for you to be happy,' Louise said. 'I would have supported you no matter what you wanted. All I feared was that Arthur had ill intent towards you.' She turned to Holmes. 'How in the world did you know? You told me she wasn't in danger.'

'In the end, the clues were simple,' Sherlock said, stepping forward. We all watched, enraptured, even now we knew the story's end. Holmes simply has that kind of commanding presence.

'I first realised when it became clear that Miss Catherine had packed her own bags. All her favourite clothes, and, indeed, her best-loved jewels. Then, of course, the fact that Mr Robinson went to Catherine's own jeweller to buy her the gifts. If he was trying to keep it a secret from his fiancée, why not go to a more out of the way establishment? So it followed that she must have chosen the presents herself.'

This all made sense and yet, though I had seen the clues, I had not really understood them.

'Then there was my meeting with Mr Taylor,' Sherlock said. 'Where I discovered he was the type of man to judge a marriage based on social standing – of course I apologise for the subterfuge, Watson.'

'It's not the strangest thing I've done for a case,' I told her.

'Regardless,' my friend said, 'I could tell that the match between two social classes bothered him quite completely. No doubt it would be the same for his own daughter. If Mr Robinson was lying about himself, and his fiancée knew of it – well, there would only be one reason.'

'Remarkable!' said Catherine.

'The train table was easy enough to deduce,' Sherlock said. 'You would go for the easiest and quickest route out of town. In the end, it was simple.'

'Hardly,' I said, just as impressed as the others.

'Are you going to call the law?' Arthur asked nervously, pulling his young fiancée close. 'Impersonation is a crime, after all.'

'Why would I do that?' Sherlock asked, seemingly puzzled. 'I was hired to find out if Catherine was in any danger, and, upon discovering she is not, my work is finished.'

'Miss Louise is the client, not the Yard,' I explained. 'Sherlock does not see much difference.'

All three gave me and my friend a joyful look.

'We can't repay you enough, Miss Holmes,' Louise said. 'I could never have forgiven myself for missing my sister's wedding. I think perhaps I will meet them in the countryside for the ceremony – if they would not protest, of course.' She gave her sister a sly look, and Catherine blushed.

'You would be most welcome,' Arthur said. 'It is a happy occasion, after all.'

'Indeed,' Sherlock said. She is not an outwardly effusive person, but I could tell she was just as pleased as I was about this unexpectedly romantic ending.

'We wish you good luck,' I said, extending my hand to Arthur.

He took it with a sort of dazed, delighted look to his face. Sherlock offered him her hand as well, and I could see the confusion and hesitation in his eyes before he gave in and shook. That bubbling glee was still overtaking his senses. Sherlock turned and shook the hands of Catherine and Louise, who smiled.

Louise kissed her on the cheek.

'Thank you indeed,' Catherine said. 'Oh! Our train is here.'

'Better not miss it,' Sherlock said.

We watched the trio rush to buy a third ticket, then get onto the train as if off on a grand adventure. They waved out the window as they went.

'You are more soft-hearted than you look,' I told Sherlock, once they were gone.

Holmes put her nose up in the air, with an expression of such disinterest that a lesser woman might have been fooled. 'I have no idea what you're talking about.'

'Certainly,' I said. I could deduce too.

Some time later, we received a letter at 221B Baker Street, fat with a photograph, carefully placed inside.

It was Catherine and Arthur Robinson's wedding photo, where the two of them beamed joyfully out at the camera. They made a very handsome couple.

ADJECTIVES ARE FOREVER

Verity Burns

'The word you're looking for is "transitioned",' Sherlock snapped at the new crime scene tech, who was clearly as opinionated as he was ignorant.

'Huh?' challenged the moron. Moronically.

'"Transgender" is an adjective,' John chipped in. 'Like "gay" or "black". You wouldn't describe Elton John as "gayed", would you? Or Idris Elba as "blacked"?'

'He might,' muttered Sherlock, squinting at the piece of debris she'd retrieved from the victim's pocket.

'If someone moves from living as one gender to living as another, they are said to have "transitioned",' John persevered, with the air of one who is more than happy to escalate should a verbal defence of his flatmate prove ineffective. '"Transgendered" is not a word. Any more than "gayed" is. Got it?'

The moron opened his mouth.

John looked at him.

The mouth closed.

'Good,' said John.

'How is it so simple for you, to accept me as a girl?' Sherlock demanded moodily, as the cab took them home. 'I'm not exactly a model of femininity.'

John shrugged. 'Well, my default is to respect people, so that's a good start,' he dissembled, turning to the window.

But the moment was there in front of him… Did he dare?

He swallowed, heart beating in his throat, but courage had never been John Watson's weakness.

'And I've never been attracted to boys.'

The Clothes Maketh the Man?

Sarah Tollok

Ever since an ambush during the final withdrawal from Afghanistan had left him with a partially paralysed hand and noise-induced PTSD flashbacks, Captain John Watson of the US Army Medical Corps struggled to forge a new path for himself.

He took on travelling physician assignments across the country. When an ER nurse told John about how the LGBTQ+ resource centre she volunteered at had just lost the doctor who used to do weekly trans medical advocacy clinics, he found himself in San Francisco. He didn't know much about trans-specific health issues when he first started, but he quickly found out that what often brought folks into the clinic wasn't even related to their transition status, but was rather general medical questions and issues. Many had poor experiences with mainstream medicine, so the clinic seemed safer and more welcoming.

Studying up on gender spectrum topics opened John's eyes to a lot of the nuances he wasn't aware of before. Some struck resonant chords deep within him, but he didn't really know what to do with all that. He was still getting used to working around his injured hand, which therapy seemed to have plateaued with, losing his military career, and managing his PTSD, all while picking up and moving to another ER assignment every few months. And he was pushing forty. For his entire life, he was always just John Watson. Even if sometimes his identity felt like an ill-fitting suit, it was one that he knew every stitch and seam of. It was familiar. So he was only applying his newfound knowledge to his clinic patients, not himself.

The clinic had just wrapped up for the day. John was gathering his notes for research next week, and thinking about hopping on one of the Muni streetcars to explore more of San Francisco, maybe jump off if he spied a little bookstore or cafe along the way. Jodie, the centre's director, was locking the front door. Just as she extended her hand towards the lock, the door burst open, sending her reeling back and tripping over her own feet. Luckily, the woman who entered had excellent reflexes. Despite having a large duffle bag slung over her shoulder, she caught Jodie's hand, heaved her upright, and quickly set her onto her feet again. The hand grab then morphed into a firm handshake.

'Sherlock Holmes, she/her, and you're Jodie Lucas, director. You changed your hair since the picture on the website. I like it, the pink suits you.'

Ms Holmes then proceeded to stomp a quick loop around the small office space and casual seating area, her rose-embroidered Doc Martens clomping on the cheap carpeting. She peeked in desk drawers, looked behind the framed pictures on the wall, and used a wooden stirrer from the coffee service to poke through the garbage can.

Before Jodie, John or either of the two other volunteers could ask how they could help this Sherlock Holmes, she turned to all of them, dropped the duffle bag to the floor, clapped her hands once and announced, 'Right, so here's the deal. I need all of you to quickly use the tarps in this bag to cover the computers and anything else that you don't want to take on water damage when the sprinklers go off. Then you need to grab anything else that's important and head out the back door to the alley.'

The first to come to his senses, John asked, 'Okay, and why is that exactly?'

Sherlock looked John's way with the start of an exasperated expression, but when her eyes settled on him, he suddenly found himself being examined so fiercely he had to fight the urge to stand at attention, like when generals came to visit the base. Sherlock squinted ever so slightly as she looked at John's name tag, an 'Ally' ribbon hanging from the bottom.

'Dr Watson. Even better, a former army doctor. Yes, I can work with this. You'll be today's hero.'

If there was anything John couldn't stand more than sudden surprises, it was being called a hero.

'Not sure how you know all this about me, but let's start with this: who are you, Ms Holmes, to come in here telling us we need to throw tarps around? What the hell are you playing at?'

'Sherlock Holmes, consulting detective. This centre was identified by a right-wing militia to be bombed. I'm here to make sure no one gets hurt and that there is minimal damage.'

'Oh my god!' Jodie yelped, 'Shouldn't we call the police? Who's the bomber?'

Sherlock walked over to Jodie, put a gentle hand on the taller woman's elbow as she looked up into her eyes.

'It's all going to be fine,' she said with a glimmering smile, 'I'm the bomber.'

Before John could do any tackling, Sherlock held one insistent, elegant finger aloft in his direction without turning her head. To John's great surprise, this stopped him in his tracks.

'To clarify, I have been using multiple fake identities for several months on numerous white nationalist forums. I was very thorough and very convincing. So convincing in fact, I was recruited for bit of bombing. Now, you'd much rather have me take on that task than anyone else because I am not going to *actually* bomb your centre. I'm just going to do some light damage while making it look like I truly bombed it. By making it look like I carried out the plan, I will be promoted to bigger targets and, in that process, given access to the higher ups in the organisation. Once I have their identities and evidence of their terrorist activities, I will take an air-tight case to the FBI and the press.

'Now, since we are on a tight timeline,' Sherlock bent to unzip her bag, pulled out a plastic tarp and snapped it open with a crack that reminded John of towel-snapping shenanigans in basic training, 'let's get to protecting your valuables. Dr Watson, you're with me.'

Jodie and the two other office volunteers, in an adrenaline haze, started unfurling tarps.

Sherlock took her backpack off and started to unpack new items with much greater care.

John recognised some of them. 'Flash bangs, smoke bombs, military grade, where did you get those?'

'The internet, darling. Your little nephew could do the same with a valid credit card number. But this,' Sherlock lifted something much more homemade and sinister looking from the bag, 'this I made myself, using the plans forwarded to me by my nasty new friends who think that they recruited me. Now, I did significantly decrease the charge and I applied the debris load to only one direction. It will blow out the windows, but send no nasty bits back into the centre itself. The only issue inside should be the sprinklers going off, hence the tarps.'

'I have so many questions,' John sighed.

'Well, in approximately five minutes an acquaintance of mine will pretend to stall his truck at the intersection, blocking traffic down this one way street and making sure no cars are driving by. At that same time, my new friend Billy who lives in the alley…do you know Billy? Lovely chap. Billy will make sure to act good and crazy in the direction of anyone coming down the sidewalk. When the way is clear, I blow up, or should I say, blow out, the front of the centre. So ask away, but only for the next 5 minutes.'

'All right. Why are you doing this? Did someone hire you to play vigilante protector of LGBTQ sites? And how are we going to explain all of this to the police? Don't you think they'll notice that this was only a staged bombing?'

John took a much-needed breath, tried to rein in his exasperation, but lost the battle. 'And you said I was going to be the hero, what does that mean? How did you know I was in the service, and how the *fuck* did you know I have a nephew?'

Sherlock didn't miss a beat as she set up the explosive devices around the front of the centre. 'I happened upon the groups when I was doing a bit of cyber espionage to weed out white nationalist sympathisers and other unsavoury types who had applied to high level security jobs in my brother's consulting firm. When he hires people to do questionable things, he likes to know they won't allow things to get messy because of biases and grudges they bring aboard with them. People motivated by hate are impulsive and sloppy. People motivated by money follow orders and keep their eyes on the prize.

'Anyway,' she paused briefly to run her fingers through her deep brown chin-length hair, getting stray strands away from her eyes, 'that took me barely any time at all and this was far more interesting. So, in short, I'm doing this because I can.

'As for the police, I have a colleague I have hand fed many a solved case over the years. I will text him moments before the bomb goes off with the pertinent details. He'll take things from there. You will be today's hero by being a very believable reason why there were no injuries. You noticed the bomb left in a backpack just before it went off and got everyone to safety out the back. Even the stupid fascists can't begrudge that a combat veteran would be capable of that. You have a US Army Medical Corps caduceus tattoo peeking out from under your rolled sleeve. By the very fresh colours and by the names that appear on the ribbons surrounding it, you were a part of the unit that was ambushed during the withdrawal from Afghanistan. I'd say I'm sorry for your loss, but I'm sure you've had your fill of that. As for your nephew, you have a key chain made of macaroni hanging from your pocket, with uncle spelled wrong in lettered beads. I took a guess at the child's gender.'

John laughed. Then he laughed at the fact that he was laughing in the middle of a staged bombing. He composed himself when he realised his laughter was teetering on turning into tears, because wasn't it incredibly sad that the first time he genuinely laughed in months was due to ridiculous circumstances involving a mad woman and a homemade explosive device?

Sherlock received a text. She then sent a flurry of replies and hustled John and the others out the back. As everyone waited in the trash-strewn alleyway, John walked a few steps from Jodie and the others, turned away from them and covered his ears, knowing how the explosion would likely send him places in his head that he would have to fight his way back from. He doubted that knowing it was coming was going to make it any easier. If anything, the waiting was ramping up his anxiety even worse. He peeked out through squinted eyes and saw Sherlock standing in front of him, watching him intently. She studied his face as if he was the most interesting thing she had ever seen. From the little he knew about the woman so far, that had to be fairly impossible. She motioned for him to take his hands from his ears.

'Doctor Watson, were you a doctor before or after you signed up?'

'I signed up for the Health Professions Scholarship Program just before I started med school because I was struggling to pay for things on my own. But I found I liked the military, both the structure and the excitement. I stayed beyond the required four years, rose up the ranks to Captain, and I was assigned to a combat ready unit.'

'So, it's Captain Watson, then?'

'Not that I ever threw my rank around very much, but yes, Captain.'

'So when the reporters come afterwards and want at least a quick sound bite from our hero of the day, would you rather they put Dr, Captain, or just Mr Watson on the screen under your crooked but charming smile?'

John fumbled to find his answer. He juggled the terms and weighed each one against himself. Each carried their own clunky baggage.

'Hmm, yes. Right,' Sherlock said, even though John hadn't responded yet.

Then in one deft movement she whipped off her blazer, which was quite the feat for something so well tailored, wrapped it around John's head and pressed down on his ears. The explosion came but it was just a distant, muffled thud and crash. There was no smell of smoke, no screaming. There was some very expensive smelling cologne, something woody and mossy and, after his eyes were able to focus on the only detail in front of him, he read the Yves Saint Laurent label.

When Sherlock unwrapped John's head, there was no death and chaos happening around him. The alley was relatively quiet besides a single car alarm going off. Jodie had already gathered herself and was unlocking the clinic's back door to enter and disengage the sprinklers from the main shut-off valve, trying to minimise the water damage.

It was so utterly different from Afghanistan that John was able to get up and get moving without the grounding techniques he usually had to utilise when his trauma-induced panic set in. As he went to head in and get ready for emergency services to show up, John handed Sherlock her blazer back, which she shrugged on over her ragged black Guns N' Roses concert T-shirt.

He stopped her before they stepped back in, just a touch on her sleeve.

'Thank you,' he said softly, 'for the,' he motioned to the covering of his ears.

'Of course. Now, dear Watson, it's showtime!'

As they removed the tarps and stuffed them into a storage closet, Sherlock fed John lines to tell the press.

Two news vans and several freelance reporters got there right on the heels of the police and firefighters. The reporters liked that John was a veteran. They wanted to make that the story's hook, he could tell. He dodged questions about his deployment history, but a little bit of internet digging could probably find his name somewhere in the original news stories about the ambush he survived.

Sherlock stood by the sidelines, nodding along and even mouthing the words they had practised as John spoke with the press. She strayed away now and then to whisper with the police detective she had called in to keep things quiet. John also saw her stealing glances at her phone, likely scrolling through social media posts about the explosion and checking the message boards of the white nationalists that had "recruited" her. But she always kept one eye on John.

John was repeating his carefully practised story for the third time when Sherlock abruptly stopped her casual pacing and her whole demeanour changed. She scowled at her phone with scrunched brows and squinted eyes, which brought attention to her crow's feet. She then quickly ducked behind the crime scene tape, leaving John alone with the same questions over and over again as even more news outlets arrived.

Just when he thought he couldn't take the lights and the microphones in his face for another second, Sherlock swept back in, wrapped herself onto John's arm, batted her lashes and gushed praises for his saving her. Had she put on lipstick to be more camera ready? Either way, it worked. The cameras focused in on the million dollar smile she was flashing.

'Oh Captain Watson, I don't know what we would have done if you weren't there! You absolutely must be the guest of honour at tonight's impromptu fundraiser for the centre!'

She turned directly to the cameras. 'Please let all your viewers know that in addition to an online fundraiser, there will be a good-will collection at the door of the Lovely Love Club on 16th Street. The Woman and her Suitors will be returning to the stage for one night only for this charity event. All the cool queers will the there!'

To the protests of the reporters, Sherlock swung John around like they were square dancing and whisked him back into the centre with her. As soon as they were away from the cameras, she dropped the fake smile but was slower to let go of John's arm.

'Is there actually a fundraiser?' John asked.

'Yes. Doors open at 8, the show starts at 9.'

'Wow, someone put that together rather quickly. It was nice of them to do that for the centre, even if we really only need new windows and a good cleaning. If they raise enough, maybe we can upgrade the computers from those ancient desktops.'

Sherlock smiled at John, not the one she flashed at the cameras, but something softer and more genuine.

'What?'

'You said "we" about this place for the first time.'

John shrugged, felt himself blushing.

Sherlock continued, 'I had to call in a rather large favour, but once I secured the main attraction the whole event fell into place rather quickly. The Woman and Her Suitors were always in high demand but haven't performed together in years. Luckily, the Woman was free.'

'And her suitors?'

Sherlock smirked, straightened her jacket, then bowed deeply with a dramatic hand flourish. 'That would be me. I am the suitors. At your service, Dr Watson.'

'You stage bombings, hunt down domestic terrorists, plan fundraisers, and you're in a band?'

'A band? Goodness no. I play violin and can manage a bit of piano, but The Woman and her Suitors is a drag act. I am, on occasion, a drag king, or at least I used to be. As I said, we haven't performed in years. But it's for a good cause, so needs must.'

John flopped heavily into one of the damp chairs. Just a few hours ago, he sat there as he met with clinic visitors. Since then, the day had taken quite the turn. He scrubbed his fingers through his short-cropped hair, shaking loose bits of ceiling dust from the aftermath of the explosion. The crash after the excitement was finally hitting him.

'No offence to the art form of drag,' he said, 'I'm sure your act is amazing, but I've had a rather eventful day and I think I'll just go home to my tiny apartment, have a cold beer, and get a good night's rest. Thanks for the invite though, and everything.'

Sherlock found a rolling stool underneath one of the nearby desks. She hopped on and wheeled over to John. 'Not taking no for an answer, Watson. Haven't you heard, you're the guest of honour? He'll be waiting there for you. C'mon, I'll even help you pick out something nice to wear.'

Sherlock winked at him as she started to twirl around on the stool.

Was she flirting with him? Did John want her to flirt with him? He was about to politely decline the invite again when he ran what Sherlock just said back in his mind.

'You said "he'll be waiting there for me". Who's "he"?'

'Bill Thompson, that's who.' Sherlock continued her revolutions. 'He's the red-cap-wearing man who wants to kill the "fag-loving disgrace of a veteran who spoiled a pervert blood bath". He hit the message boards within minutes of the bombing hitting the news. He's been on my radar for some time. I thought he was all talk, but he's a frustrated military reject who comes from a long line of soldiers, so you saving the day triggered him into action. So I told him where he could find you. Forced to act this fast, he'll be fired up, messy as hell, and easier to spot. He's been rolling around in the mud with other white nationalists for a while, so I'm hoping he'll give some of them up when he's arrested and isolated.'

John felt dizzy watching Sherlock. He sat forward and caught her mid spin. 'And you want me to dress up to get shot at?'

'Yes, I have a lovely selection of Kevlar back at my place. I have to pick up my kit for tonight anyway; shall we?'

John must not have looked convinced, so Sherlock rolled her eyes and informed him, 'Oh, and undercover police will be posted both in and outside the club, each with red-cap's latest Facebook profile picture. They should be able to nab him without any shots fired. With the message board screen shots, his presence, and a weapon, that will be plenty to make an arrest. There's a fantastic little Jamaican restaurant just a block from my flat. We can grab some plantains and hand pies on the way. I'm starving!'

She hopped up and, with only a little sway to her step from her stool spinning, headed out the door. She didn't even look back to see if John was following. To his own surprise, he was.

So an hour later there was John, sweating in a bullet proof vest under a designer royal blue dress shirt that probably cost as much as a soldier's monthly salary, trying to balance a takeout container with his wounded hand while shovelling perfectly fried plantains into his mouth with the other. Once the adrenaline settled, he found he was also, in fact, absolutely starving.

He would've sat down, but Sherlock's place didn't seem to have any open surfaces. Her bookshelves were weighed down with science textbooks of all disciplines. She also had a sizeable manga collection, loads of French novels, and a stack of gun enthusiast magazines. What was maybe a coffee table had at least a dozen types of rope on it, all tied with different knots. There were several fencing foils leaning in the one corner of the room, both new and ancient, one of which had a suspiciously dirty blade. Framed crookedly on the wall, as one would their diploma, was a letter from the president of the Oxford University informing Ms Sherlock Holmes that she was summarily expelled from the institution and banned from the campus.

The Clothes Maketh the Man?

'Did you save me one of the vegetable pies?' she asked as she re-entered the parlour, pulling a large piece of luggage on wheels.

Sherlock's hair was slicked back from the shower, the sides and back freshly trimmed close to her scalp, the lines so crisp and smooth it looked like she had been to a professional barber in the fifteen minutes she had disappeared into her bedroom. She wore a fitted little black dress that appeared to be sewn onto her every curve, and earrings that were actual origami cranes. She completed her look by pulling on some old, spray-painted Chucks. Sherlock grabbed the last hand pie and finished the entire thing in four bites, crumbs tumbling down the front of her dress without a care.

John was afraid he watched the path of those crumbs for a beat or two too long, so he cleared his throat and asked, 'What's all in the suitcase then?'

'The artificial trappings of the construct we call "manliness".'

Sherlock flopped down sideways across a slurry of police reports on a well-worn armchair. Although she appeared relaxed, her eyes felt like lasers to John.

'But you know all about that, don't you, Johnny boy?'

'Don't call me Johnny boy!' he roared.

John knew immediately that it was much louder than necessary. His raised voice seemed to echo in the cosy living room. Sherlock didn't stir a muscle. She waited.

'I'm sorry,' John said in a quiet, apologetic tone, 'I...the only one who ever called me that was my father, and he was a bastard of a man. He disowned my older brother when he found out he was gay. Then he leaned on me even harder to be a macho jerk with no feelings and no room to fucking breathe. I left home as soon as I could to get away from him.'

She gave his explanation a quick nod of understanding, then shared, 'My father wanted my brother to be exactly what he became, brilliant and powerful. He saw that I was also brilliant, but I was supposed to wear my intelligence and wit like a fine piece of jewellery, something to be displayed but never useful, because I'm a woman. I was a novelty to him. So I shaved my head and caused a wee bit of a ruckus here and there.'

'Like at Oxford?' John asked with a grin.

'Oh, that was a fun time,' she replied with wistful pride, 'I've heard there are still scars on the walls in the old chemistry labs.'

'Well done!'

'I thought so,' she said, but her smile faded.

'Then I tried a lot of things, many of which weren't very good for me. I had to fight for everything I am now. I am my own woman. I'm in business for myself. I take cases that I want, tell the ones I don't want to fuck off.'

'And your performing, where did that fit in?'

'Well, I met Ira Adler, The Woman, when I was partying. She was doing a show and she was brilliant, but the club's pianist had a few too many and kept messing up the music. Ira was getting flustered. Some drunk straights were starting to heckle her. I shoved the piano player off his stool, grabbed his horrible fedora as he tumbled off the stage riser, picked up the tune, and we started to banter. It was magic.'

Sherlock took off one of her origami earrings, fiddled with it as she spoke, making the crane's wings flap.

'I could be biting and crude and make a mockery of every man who ever underestimated me or who never bothered to look past my tits and the crowd loved it. We developed a whole act around it. I stopped partying with substances so much. Performing was more of a thrill than any drug. I realised, by playing a man, I could thumb my nose at the whole farce of gender expectations and make others see it too. Through my time on the stage, I realised I didn't owe anyone a performance in my real life. I could be butch, femme, or anywhere in between. I could be a queer demisexual woman no matter who I decided to have sex with or not have sex with. Under all the costuming, I became more me.'

For the second time that day, John found himself getting inexplicably choked up. Or wait, themself? John sat down on the floor with a thump, slid into a slow breathing technique to counter the odd panic/excitement rising in their chest. It was a coming apart at the seams, but from growth rather than an unravelling.

Sherlock leaned forward in her chair, looking like she was going to take their hands in hers, but she stopped short, clasped her own hands together instead and said, just above a whisper, 'You've worn a lot of uniforms and titles, John Watson. Soldier. Captain. Doctor. Like that Kevlar vest I gave you, they created a certain amount of protection, didn't they? The titles saved you from being called "Mr" They saved you from being the good ol' Johnny boy that you never wanted to be.'

John bit their lip hard and blinked fast, willing the tears to not fall.

'How did you know? I barely knew. I thought I hid it. Hell, I even hid it from myself.'

'I've been where you are now. When you've walked around wearing a cumbersome costume that never quite fit, you get really good at spotting other people slouching and itching under the same kind of burden.'

With a pained expression, John explained, 'I've never been a showy person. I like my comfy shirts and my jeans. I even like my army boots. I'm not one for jewellery and I don't think I own any socks that aren't black, brown, or white. I don't fit with what people expect of queer, but I also don't think I've ever fit as a man either. I just don't…'

'Listen John Watson, you don't owe anyone a show of masculinity, femininity, or androgyny no matter where along the gender spectrum you find yourself. You can change your pronouns or not change them. You can still wear the clothes you like and even still keep "John" if you'd like. You and your boring sock collection can be as visible or as private as you want to be about your gender. But be true to yourself. The rest will work itself out over time as long as *you* know who you are.'

John allowed themself to cry. They wept for their whole identity settling into a new kind of peace that they never allowed themself to feel before. Sherlock finally reached across that little distance between them to hold John's hands in hers. John squeezed as hard as they dared to without hurting her, and she squeezed right back. It was wonderful, being seen.

'You must think I'm a coward. A grown up, waiting this long to really explore or acknowledge something like this.'

'John Watson, you're one of the bravest people I've met. I'm glad I had to blow up your building today. Now,' she gave their hands one last squeeze, stood up, brushed the crumbs off her dress, 'let's go get you shot at.'

When they arrived at the club, Sherlock led John by the hand, parting the crowd with her aluminium luggage on wheels and creating space between John and anyone who tried to get a bit too cosy with the hero of the day. Once they reached the cramped backstage dressing room, John almost ran headlong into the generous, sequin-covered bust of a drag queen. With her stiletto platform heels on she was easily over six and a half feet tall. John had to look almost straight up to finally meet her eyes.

'Close your mouth John, lest you drool on her shoes. Size 14s need to be special ordered. Ira, this is John Watson. John, this is The Woman, otherwise known as Ira Adler.'

'Enchanté,' replied a deep baritone.

The Woman held her hand out to John, like the pope offering his ring for kissing. Bewildered, John took it.

'Sherlock, he's adorable,' Ira said as she turned back to the mirror to hike up her chest and touch up her lipstick.

Sherlock looked at John, eyebrows raised.

John cleared their throat, tried to sound casual, 'It's they/them actually.'

There were no thunderclaps, no fanfare, but John was surprised by the relief that flowed over them. It was like taking off a too-hot jacket on a warm day and feeling the breeze against their skin for the first time.

'My apologies,' Ira quickly corrected. 'Sherlock, *they're* adorable. And why aren't you dressed darling? You always wait until the last minute.'

'I do most of my costuming on stage, Ira. What's there to get ready? John, unzip me please?'

John did as they were told. Their hand slipped off the zipper twice, and it was their unwounded hand, so they could hardly blame their war injury. They then turned away as Sherlock unceremoniously pulled the dress over her head.

'I think I'll just go out and find a seat,' John announced.

'You have a spot reserved, front and centre,' Sherlock said, as John tried not to think about her state of undress. 'There should be a card on the table. San Francisco's finest will be scattered throughout the room, but I trust your instincts far more than any of them, so keep your eyes peeled for anyone suspicious. You still have the photo I gave you of your would-be murderer?'

'Yes,' John said while still facing the dressing room door, 'I literally have it up my sleeve so I can keep checking it. Break a leg, or whatever it is you say in drag!'

As John shut the door behind them, they heard Ira snort a laugh. 'Absolutely adorable.'

John sat on the edge of their seat, awaiting the start of the show. They ordered a soda with lime and tried to look relaxed, but it was easier said than done. Between the crowd, the stage lights, the Kevlar vest and the fact that someone was coming there to try to kill them, John was sweating bullets.

Looking around the room, they were able to clock the police despite their plain clothes. Except for the one female officer with the short cropped hair and the Angela Davis t-shirt, who John only recognised due to the bulge of her holster under her denim jacket, they all looked a bit shell-shocked surrounded by the gender nonconformity. It would have been comical if they weren't there to make sure John didn't get shot.

When the lights came on though, John almost forgot about the dangers of the evening. The Woman commanded the stage completely as soon as she set foot on it. She used an old princess phone prop to have a mock call with the audience to thank them for attending and supporting such a great cause.

'But I must go, sweetie, my husband is almost home. You know how he is when he gets home from a hard day's work.'

With applause and hoots of encouragement from the audience, the Woman dragged a man from the audience up onto the stage. He quickly went all red-faced but was cooperative and played along. He dutifully read his lines from the cue cards the Woman took from her garter.

'I've missed you dear! Looking forward to having you all to myself tonight!' he said with stunted unpreparedness.

'Yes, fantastic,' she deadpanned, while she threw an eye roll to the audience.

Then there was a knock at the stage door. As soon as the Woman opened it, disco music started to play. It was Sherlock, dressed in a tight pants and a shirt straight out of *Saturday Night Fever*, unbuttoned to the bottom of her sternum. She wore a skin-coloured binder tank top with a patch of chest hair on it. With some artfully applied contour makeup, her face took on a more masculine shape.

Sherlock and the Woman set up the scene. Sherlock was the young suitor whom the gorgeous, bored housewife was having an affair with. The suitor boldly walked into the living room and introduced himself to the husband as a door-to-door insurance salesman, made thinly veiled saucy comments about the wife, all set to a greatest hits mix of 70s disco. While the unsuspecting husband read the paper as the wife had suggested, she and the suitor had a tryst behind a backlit Asian screen in the corner of the room.

The suitor then exited the domestic tableau, but the audience could see him grab a suitcase and do a quick change into another persona. With the help of a knit cardigan, thick bifocal glasses and beat up old hat, Sherlock completed the transformation by totally altering the character's posture and voice. This one was an old man looking for his lost cat.

The references to his 'poor lost pussy' and pantomiming with his cane ensued. As the show continued, Sherlock became a nerdy college student doing a survey for a research project, then a sleazy politician looking for votes, and finally a buffoon of a detective, looking for leads about a series of break-ins in the neighbourhood. John wasn't sure why the weird deerstalker hat worked on the detective, but it just did. Every character came with their own unique soundtrack of well-known hits that kept the audience all the more engaged.

Mid joke, Sherlock suddenly broke character and stared wide-eyed in John's direction. No, not at John, just past them.

John instinctively hit the floor, yelling, 'Gun! Gun!'

Sherlock grabbed the small end table from beside the thoroughly confused "husband" onstage, whipped it with all her strength in John's direction. There was a shot, but it hit one of the stage lights above, sending glass raining down onto the panicked crowd below. The cop in the jean jacket leapt over cowering club-goers and tackled the shooter to the floor. He tried to reach for his dropped gun and just about got to it when Ira jumped down from the stage and impaled the man's hand under her heel.

'Stay down, stupid!' she yelled. Her voice was so loud and thoroughly commanding that half the fleeing audience hit the floor in compliance.

As the shooter was being cuffed, Sherlock ran to John and examined them. 'Are you all right? Were you hit?'

John steadied her hands in theirs, surprised at how they were shaking, and assured her they were unscathed.

Satisfied, Sherlock turned her attention to the police. She was *livid*.

'Dressing as a waiter is the oldest trick in the book! Just because he was shirtless like the other barmen, you let him by? Were you too shy to give him a good look over? He tied a bandana over his White Power tattoo where you were all briefed to look! And don't get me started about how no self-respecting waiter at a gay club would walk around with such an ungroomed treasure trail!'

Ira held onto John's shoulder to take her shoes off and survey the damage. 'Damn. Going to have to send this to my shoe guy to get the blood off of it. Oh well. You were worth it, sweetie.'

'Thanks for that, really. And where did you learn to bark orders like that? You reminded me of my drill sergeants.'

Ira gave them a slow wink, pulled aside her stack of rhinestone bracelets to reveal a dainty US Marine Corps Special Ops tattoo on her inner wrist, 'Oorah, baby.'

Ira bent to plant a kiss on John's cheek, then turned and sauntered over to the bar.

John helped to triage members of the crowd who sustained minor injuries in the chaos. Once they were all interviewed and dispersed, John was confronted with a still disgruntled Sherlock. She scowled at the big red lipstick mark on their cheek. She reached into the pocket of her trousers, retrieved a white handkerchief. Just like John's grandmother used to do, she licked the cloth to rub the lipstick from John's cheek. They put up with the rigorous scrubbing, then picked up a damp cocktail napkin and wiped the drawn-on pencil thin moustache from Sherlock's upper lip, a detail from her last on-stage transformation before the shooter brought the show to a halt.

'Thank you,' John said.

'For what, throwing a table at an assassin when the police all missed seeing what was right in front of them?'

'Well, yes, I suppose that too. But I meant everything. This has been the best day I've had in a long time, which is really odd since it started with you blowing up the centre and ended up with me almost getting shot. But it was all fantastic. And I'm finally accepting me for me. Thank you for that the most.'

'So I ordered you around, blew up a building, wrapped you in Kevlar, challenged your gender identity, then took you to a drag show to get you shot at and you thought it was a great day?'

'Pretty much, yes.'

'You know I still have to take out the rest of the organisation that wanted me to bomb the centre. Could be a bit of legwork, possibly some violence. Interested?'

'I'm all yours.'

Sherlock stuck her arm out for John to take, which they readily did. 'I think I'll keep you, Watson.'

'Please do,' they replied.

The Mystery of the Vanishing Echoes
(A sauútiverse story)

Eugen Bacon

It happened on a dawn I was minding my business, pruning my cassava patch, and Wa'watison was silently galloping around on a stick, being a child and refusing to make himself useful.

'What about the kudu fertiliser I asked you to get already?'

My words did not diminish the galloping, and I could swear by Our Mother that he put his trotting to slow motion in that strange way of his, calming time, which equally slowed down the pace of my cropping and lopping with sheers at the giant weeds that were strangling my cassava leaves.

Just then, the walls of my humble cottage in Kitale wobbled and the touchscreen activated. To my chagrin, Wa'wati recovered his usefulness and nearly tripped on his stick and bare toes in haste to reach the screen and touch it first.

'No, Wa'wati!' I called, but did he listen?

Children are to be seen, not heard, so I had nothing to worry about because the boy had no tongue. But, blessed Mother, it was the leaders of the federation of councils at the Boāmmariri where they met every five juzu. No one else summoned me across concealed technology for cases to sleuth.

The federation had every reason to trust me, as I'd already solved for them the mystery of the sleeping flute in Órino-Rin, which unravelled a burglar with hypnotising music that entranced citizens. The mystery of the long night in Zezépfeni was simply a trickster's illusion because nights there are short and never dark, and my solving it was a matter of finding the right clues, not a stroke of luck. There was the mystery of the technology bug in Pinaa, and I found myself on a moon with machines that signed and spat out mathematics – indeed, that AI hack was an intricate one to solve.

I pondered what might be the problem this time, and I gazed into the hologram. There they were, five – no six – leaders in what looked like a multi-windowed tower. From my view, it resembled a mausoleum of many-eyed gods. It blinked with height and prosperity hosting its delegation filled with self-importance. However, the delegate from my home planet, Wiimb-ó, was so nondescript I could not have picked him from a line-up of one – which was the newest low, especially for a sleuth of my renown.

The system identified him as Mkh'alingh'a.

'You're new to the council,' I said to him.

'That is not public knowledge,' said the main spokesperson, the tall robed one from Zezépfeni.

'It doesn't take much reasoning to deduce someone uncertain of their bearing, who'll obscure themselves to stay unnoticed,' I said. 'I can see no reason other than newness for Mkh'alingh'a to shroud himself in a leadership group.'

Hogheh – the system vibrated his name – frowned.

I wondered if it was the asteroid belt or a meteor strike that had unbalanced his head and given him that nose of snobbery. I also wondered why there were six, not five, leaders representing the planets.

The leaders looked warily at Wa'wati, and it was clear they would not commence any deliberations within the child's hearing or sight, so I said, 'Shoo!'

My dear adopted child fled, but full of mischief, and I knew he would overhear everything. He had a way of thinning and wisping out of view as if he didn't exist, but it was only a trickery, some mind play, because I could see him when he did this, but others didn't seem to notice him. I'd always wondered wistfully – wouldn't you? – if perhaps he'd arrived from another planet. Wouldn't that be something? Someone had lost him in a forest, and I'd found him.

Now at ease, the council's greeting resounded from person to person on hologram. *Greetings, greetings...* I was impressed by my reception in echo language by one delegate:

Wey-ma. Wey ma. U.

The hologram's whisper identified the sweet-voiced one of the special greeting, she was Rehema're from the planet Ekwukwe.

Hogheh from Zezépfeni addressed me again, without preamble. 'You must tackle some detective work.'

His posture was as if he was in bone pain. He barked his words with too much arrogance in them, and his skin looked bad. He wiped his face. The time I'd travelled to Zezépfeni to solve that mystery of the long night, I hadn't been too impressed by the food and suffered constipation for several bés, as they called their days there. Thank Our Mother, the creator, it didn't take a whole juzu to recover. From the man's countenance on holo, I could only suppose that he was constipated or holding back a silent but deadly fart.

Our dislike of each other appeared mutual and immediate. I was always allergic to arrogance and was never one to bow and scrape to it. I couldn't care to consider what it was about me, other than my being female and renowned, that he was averse to.

'Is it pro bono?' I asked with the right innocence to irk him. 'Because I won't take it if it is. A woman's got to eat, and I've got a mute child who's eating out my house.'

'We don't make paupers of folk!' he barked, losing his composure at my bait. 'We will pay you handsomely!'

I noticed how two of the leaders – one of them Rehema're, and the system identified the second as her brother, Sina'aa of Ekwukwe – eyed the man with disapproval at his discourtesy. It explained why there were six leaders at the federation, and I deduced that whatever needed solving was happening in Ekwukwe.

'Ghehho,' I said to further annoy him, despite clearly remembering his name. 'That is good, then. I will take the job.'

'Without knowing what it is?' asked Sina'aa.

I was astonished that he didn't speak in echo language like his sister

Rehema're. He was bald, lean but strong, and was dressed in an off-shoulder cloak covering his back to just above his knees. He spoke with depth and quietness, as if he wanted to protect his voice, as if he feared that he might lose it, were he to project out loud.

The system whispered a swift summary of his story: Sina'aa the beast hunter, master of the V'hushalele – the spear of spears. Some called him the V'hushalele god. But he was born nothing special, so they thought, echoless, and his parents, Fatu'fa and Juta'uu, had the decency to give him a name, Sina, before they abandoned him in a forest as an outcast. His aunt Zawa'Zawa rescued him, and Sina'aa found his new name.

'Are you convincing me not to take the job?' I asked.

The other from Ekwukwe – Rehema're, a diminutive figure who wore tight ebony curls, ash-coloured along the temples, golden eyes and a batik, stirred and spoke again in an echo tongue.

Wey-ma. Wey ma. U.

Her words came out sweetly and in song. The sound entranced me, and I wanted to listen to her for eons. She had only to glance at me in a certain way and I would have married her in a blink.

The system translated her echo language.

'Something is happening to people's echo magic in Ekwukwe. We're unsure what it is, but we've built a boma to protect the echoless refugees who can never survive the beasts of Ekwukwe without echo magic.'

The touchscreen vibrated a quick rundown of the night creatures of Ekwukwe, and I had no deep inclination to encounter the notorious impudu-pudu, the lightning bird, the inka-inka, wet and slippery, all fins and flippers, raging for your body water, or the tikolokolo, the spirit gremlin. I had no echo and one thing was certain: unless you were Sina'aa, the beast hunter, you didn't want to be echoless, without magic, in a place like Ekwukwe.

Wey-ma. Wey ma. U. The system translated: 'Great sleuth, Shaalok Ho-ohmsi, do you understand why this situation is of great concern to the council?'

'You're unsure as to the cause and extent. It could be a pandemic capable of wiping out the entire planetary system,' I said.

'Precisely,' said Sina'aa. 'Furthermore–'

'It is costing you to house the refugees who have lost their echo,' I said. 'Not only are you protecting them from the wilderness beasts of Ekwukwe, you're also quarantining them from potentially spreading that which afflicts them to the rest of Ekwukwe and the other planets.'

'Why, of course,' said Sina'aa. 'It was a solar flare that almost destroyed our great races hundreds of thousands of juzu ago, but we survived. Climate changes continue to harm the planets, meteors bounding at Zezépfeni, outlandish creatures leaping or crawling into Ekwukwe, sonic storms roaring at Órino-Rin, and what else. We can't afford a biological catastrophe that might sweep us entirely out. Will you help us to find what's behind this malady that vanishes echoes?'

'That is a rhetorical question,' I said. 'You knew I'd help for naught before you summoned me. But you know my other terms – you'll need to arrange my transport to Ekwukwe. Because, Wiimb-ó, the technology–' I shrugged.

Wey-ma. Wey ma. U.

'Are those all your demands?' the system translated.

'Wa'wati, well–' I began.

'The child has no-one else,' said Sina'aa, with an insight into orphans that astonished me.

'That's right. He'll have to accompany me.'

'But, but–' spluttered Ghehho, who I preferred to keep in the unbecoming name.

'It shall be done,' said Sina'aa, in that dear and cherished voice of his, a precious thing in the world of echoes. 'Preferably before nightfall in Ekwukwe,' he said, as if to challenge me in a measure of my capability, or perhaps in understanding of the perils of Ekwukwe's dusk.

I had enough belief in my head – didn't they say high achievers summoned excessive confidence, and self-belief to do the extraordinary? What was the term – to believe the impossible?

'Before nightfall,' I agreed. 'Final thing, a request.'

'Another one?' barked Ghehho. 'Is it a request or a demand?'

'I can assure you it's a request. Send me on holo the profiles of all the victims,' I said.

Ghehho hesitated.

'Sure thing,' said Sina'aa.

Agreeing to their timeline was about convincing them, and me. But even I doubted that such a mystery, one of vanishing echoes, could be solved before the night fell.

An acorn – please don't laugh – delivered us to Ekwukwe. The technology of the planets is astounding. This is how it happened: we stepped into a baobab tree – yes – and, somehow, the tree wobbled, and we shot out of its buttocks. Not all trees were techno-capable, just hidden ones like this, whose secrets the leaders of the council had invited me to learn. And, of course, it wasn't a natural phenomenon: simply a technological illusion. We found ourselves squeezed inside an acorn that was bigger on the inside than it was on the outside. It shot skyward, vibrated for what could only be eons. It was a forever time, but was most likely a quarter a bés, by which time I was as hungry as if that millet porridge for breakfast was air. And Wa'wati looked just about ready to eat his fingers, or me.

I used the travel time to study the holographic information on each victim whose echo magic had vanished. Ada'adaa, it means born of beauty, the system vibrated. She was the first victim. Eko'onaekon, it means filled with strength. He was the second victim. Ma'as-sama, it means the noble one. He was the third victim. Pázila-pázi, it means born in birdsong... and so forth. I noticed that the malady was not discriminatory on gender or age. Ma'as-sama was a child about the same age as Wa'wati.

But I observed something peculiar, and made a note of it. Just then, the acorn exploded on impact with Ekwukwe, and we stepped out on the planet, shaken but unharmed, in a place called T'Songesonge.

I looked at the two suns and blinked as their pale blue glows neared each other, and they fused in a brand new dawn. That was astounding in itself, but what was even more startling was that Wa'wati coughed and said, 'My word.'

It came out in the croak of a forgotten voice, and I gazed at him as if he were a ghost.

Let me put this in perspective. I collected this boy from a forest, with its bushbuck and crowned eagles, and he never made a sound. That night I was out hunting – who doesn't? – I was expecting to catch a kudu, not an abandoned baby kicking the plumpest legs on a sisal mat. Even as I scooped him in my arms and wondered how this child of a black god had arrived at a forest full of stars, and survived the cobras, adders and spotted hyenas, I marvelled at how long on his blanket he had played in silence with three-horned chameleons and leopard tortoises of the forest before I found him. His eyes caught light when I scooped him up, they shifted like a jewel, and I saw him in my destiny. It was as if he were waiting, as if he knew I would come for him.

His fat hands tugged at my amulet, one of many, this one close to my heart. He pulled it to his mouth like a dummy, secured its positioning with a thumb as he sucked both, coiled on my chest and fell asleep.

There were those who called him a changeling, but I didn't care about all that nonsense, much as I didn't care that he had no tongue, and no sound came from his lips. What troubled me was the silent crying when he woke up with a start. But he viciously fought me against the bowl of milk and the millet porridge in which I'd cracked an egg yolk. He spat a whole blob with such accuracy into my retina, and it hurt a long time, and I despaired of him.

To distract myself from the anguish of that silent cry – I did try my tit to his mouth, and he gave it a useless tug – I returned to my chores and wrung a pheasant's neck. I dipped the bird in boiling water and defeathered it, then rubbed it with pink salt and cloves. I chopped some onions, tossed in some chillies and red beans into a claypot, and I slow roasted the pheasant. But I was so distracted I nearly charred the lot.

It was then that I noticed the boy's mouth was no longer yawning in a silent wail. On a hunch, I dipped a finger on an oily wing tip, and pushed it in the child's mouth. His mouth shaped a form that could only be a coo or a gurgle, as he gripped my hand and sucked so hard that I feared for a moment that my finger was lost. But he let go and looked at me expectantly, so I broke a drumstick and blew on it as he kicked his chubby legs in expectation until its heat was gone. I stretched it to the tot with an idea for him to suck as he'd done my poor finger. He wrestled the pheasant leg out of my hands with supernatural strength no bub should have, gobbled the whole lot, spat out white bone and sank into the silent sleep of the gods.

And now, this hitherto silent child, had said, 'My word.'

Together, we looked around, marvelling at the wilderness of this world, evolved yet alien.

Echoes of it bounced everywhere, from the hillocks and mountainside to the underground houses that were lavish caverns, mineral stoned. I wondered at such beauty, such barrenness, and looked at Wa'wati, who wore a countenance of utmost peace. I'd never seen him more at home anywhere than on this world buzzing with sound magic.

Our Mother! He seemed to have a glow about him.

Just then, a nearby oak tree wobbled, and Sina'aa appeared in hologram.

I reached towards the techno ripples, but Wa'wati eagerly touched them first.

If Sina'aa minded, he didn't show it. 'I see you landed safely,' he said in that deepest and calmest voice that felt like water and wind all at once.

'Yes, but the child—?' I started. 'He is from Ekwukwe.'

Sina'aa smiled sheepishly and looked a bit humble. 'How do you know this?'

'The natural way that his body and mind accept this world is telling.'

'Wa'watison is an orphan from Ekwukwe.' There was something in his voice, almost an affection.

'And you're behind it,' I said.

He looked startled. 'And how do you know *this*?'

'I always knew the boy was alien to Wiimb-ó, and that someone was behind it. The affection in your voice suggests you had a big role in the boy's placement.'

'Please don't speak about me in third person,' spoke my beloved boy with absolute clarity, his language fluid as ever in this world.

Wey-ma. Wey ma. U.

Rehema're appeared with the sweetness of her voice on holo, and my heart staggered.

The system translated: 'We thought he'd be safer with you in Wiimb-ó.'

'Please explain.'

'Rehema're and I have been rescuing outcast children from the forest,' said Sina'aa. 'Despite all our efforts in educating folk, they are unable to stop being superstitious about children who are born—' He looked sad as he sought the right word. 'Different.'

I caught at a glimpse, the barest touch of Rehema're's fingertip with her half-brother's.

I felt a longing for such connection, but inwardly shook my head against such wistfulness. 'I have studied the holographic profiles that you sent on the victims,' I said. 'It turns out they all have some affiliation with T'Songesonge market. Some are stall owners, some are customers, and some are related to folk who visit the market regularly.'

'Oh?' said Sina'aa. 'I didn't register this coincidence, but now that you say it—'

'I suggest that we start at the marketplace.'

'I'm hungry,' said Wa'wati in the clearest voice.

I sighed.

'Take this route to the marketplace where you can look about, and get some food for the boy,' said Sina'aa. He charted a map on the screen. He eyed the amulet on my neck. 'That should do for a good barter.'

'What?'

'We're on our way from the Boāmmariri, shouldn't be long. We'll meet you at the marketplace, which is also the closest way to branch off to the forest, then to the camps where the refugees are held.'

Truth is, I was torn between wanting to first visit the echoless refugees to start finding clues, because that is what you do: you start at the scene of a crime, and then go to the marketplace that appeared to link all victims. But Wa'wati's stomach spoke too loudly, as did his annoying hum. 'I. Am. Hungry. I. Am. Hun-gry.'

For his sake and mine – as the echoes of this world, their pinging and bouncing, hollow reverberations every which way, overwhelmed me – I hoped the marketplace had his favourite food of fowl; any kind would do because the boy gobbled anything.

But maps are *revolting*, and no sleuth of honour should ever have to use them! It didn't take us long to realise that we were hopelessly lost, and Wa'wati was eyeing me with exceeding greed that approached cannibalism. I walked swiftly, keeping ahead of him. I did contemplate whether it might be a better option to prod him in front of me, lest he ate me from behind.

Night was approaching, and this was equally worrisome. If Ekwukweans were frightened of their own beasts… Just then, I noticed unusual charring on the ground. The ground here was unlike anything I'd noticed in Ekwukwe before, and it was person-width. The scorching seemed to intensify in depth and circumference toward a certain direction, and my curiosity was well piqued. I touched the soil and scooped some into my hand. It smelt burnt and acrid.

'Here.' I palmed some to Wa'wati.

'Awwww!' He threw the soil from his hand and, to my curiosity, there was a burn mark left on his palm. I looked at my own palm, and there was nothing.

In my eagerness, and with Wa'wati's new wariness of painful things I might put to his touch, I abandoned my apprehension of winding up in the boy's intestine and out his colon.

'Follow me!' I cried.

Wa'wati followed cautiously, and I noticed how some intrinsic self-protection leapt him over any patch of burnt ground as if it were a puddle.

This is how we arrived at the market. I ought to have been pleased, but there were echoes everywhere, and they were doing my head in. The ground at the entrance was much charred, and the scorching worsened the deeper you walked into the market, especially toward the far-most stalls.

'See this?' I said rhetorically to my ward – surely he'd seen it.

But Wa'wati was conversing with everybody as if he knew them. When he finally gave me his attention, he said, 'I'm hungry.'

In resignation, I handed him my amulet and had no clue where to start. Everything had a stupid name that Wa'wati faithfully translated, and I wished he wouldn't. He handed me a piece of charcoal roasted klalabash – Our Mother! Why not simply call it a calabash? He handed me a drink from a…palm-palm? The ridiculousness of this hollow planet with its echoes and echo names was beyond belief. We passed a stall that was selling dried "t'apiapia", which was, of course, tilapia. What, I wondered, would they call plain old cassava – cass'avava?

Wa'wati's stomach guided us to a stall that had a twice cooked suckling piglet on the spit, and they were calling it a nguwe'we. They served it with blood sausages, garnished in a ginger sauce and what looked like kale.

If this was the intended meeting place, Sina'aa and Rehema're were nowhere in sight.

But there was a snake charmer, who enchanted us with a mamba'ba, the giant snake. At the heart of the market, a musical trio played the k'hora'aa, the luhte'te and a ngonini. If it weren't for sound magic and the sweetest melody of the music, I would have guffawed in scorn at the absurdity of those names! Now Wa'wati, who had hitherto neither spoken nor danced, grabbed my elbow and pounced with me in a step and delirious glee that I, too, was beginning to feel. My scientific mind could only firmly attribute my condition as a yielding to the klalabash of mbe'bebe – banana wine – I had generously imbibed.

Just then, at the pinnacle of the purest melody, as a kudu-kudu – another ridiculous name – roasted in smoke and herbs, Wa'wati clutched his head and gave a terrible cry.

I fell unto him, my child who had no language before he arrived in

Ekwukwe, and did what a mother can only do, foolishly ask: 'What is it, son? What!'

He was sweating, which reminded me of when he was as a baby and just about to have a poopy. His skin would get all drenched that way, as though he was resisting a spell, and he would stay in that misery until he had pushed out the worst-smelling, blackest liquid turd that would spoil my appetite for bés. Once he'd squeezed out the foulest thing, his fat legs would kick and stretch until his tiny toes reached to tickle my face, and he'd give the most blissful toothless grin that stole my heart.

Yet here he was again, curled in agony and sweating, and this time, Our Mother, it was worse.

And then he did his thing, slowed down time, and he was howling in slow motion, but less fiercely. It was as if he was spreading out the pain to hurt less.

'It's like,' he finally moaned, still curled in foetal pose, his voice strained, 'like someone is pulling me inside out.'

I looked about for anyone suspicious-looking, and my gaze fell upon the palest man with a pock-marked face staring with abnormal intensity in our direction. He wore a loincloth in ochre hues. His eyes shimmered like a blaze. When he realised I'd seen him, he slipped away into the crowd. I could not help but observe that it was in the direction of the deepest charring on the ground – a clue I should have pursued earlier were it not for Wa'wati's stupid appetite.

'Him!' I cried. 'Stop that man!'

Now, a sleuth hunts for clues, and they were scattered everywhere. I studied the area surrounding a stall with much-charred ground about close to where I estimated the witch man had stood. There was shrubbery in some form of desert plant near it, a succulent thing with thorns, but it too exhibited burn marks. I found a tear of bright red clothing on a protruding blackened tip. I fingered it. The ragged shape of the rip suggested rush, and a piece of fabric unwittingly caught. I smelled the cloth, and it had some strong alkaline scent I could not fathom.

'Touch it,' I said to Wa'wati, who innocently did.

'Awwww!' he cried, and immediately snatched his palm away as if the fabric burnt. I wondered why the clothing had no such effect on me.

I looked about the area, and saw an adjacent stall with shrivelled vegetables, charred. Alongside the trail, I found the kudu-kudu that was becoming a blackened skeleton by itself in too short a time. And the distraught snake charmer showed me the dead mamba'ba that was already in a state of advanced putrefaction.

The marketplace was full of echoes and all sorts of commotion, and I was suffering a furious migraine. Still, I endured and followed the trail to the furthest stall at the edge of the market, and it exhibited the same signs of a strange burn. There, I found pellets and sniffed them. They were the droppings of a p'hobawawa, the one-eyed bat. Such a bat, a beast of the night, was generally associated with a witchdoctor, and served as a witchdoctor's familiar.

I looked inside the stall, but it was empty. But the pellets led to a rubbish pit...

And the palest man with the glowing eyes leapt from it with a roar of echo, that appeared to be more magic than language from the vehemence in his eyes, and from the vigorous motions of his hands as if he was flinging them:

Omni-omni-ng'ede-ng'ede!

He hurled at me what appeared to be an echo magic spell, and I braced myself to shatter, vanish, collapse into a rodent or burst into flame. I looked at myself, astonished, as was he, at the lack of effect. He looked at his hands, and then at me, perplexed. He repeated the spell, again throwing his hands. *Omni-omni-ng'ede-ng'ede!*

OMNI-OMNI-NG'EDE-NG'EDE! he chanted, but still nothing happened.

'I'm not from here, you dumb twat,' I laughed harshly. 'It appears that echo magic does not work on me.'

But my Wa'wati, oh, my boy! He was once more on the ground, tears squeezing from his eyes, sweat pouring from every pore, and his fingers were gnarled. Then he took on a grimace in slow motion – he was again pushing out time, resisting the force of something potent that was killing him.

So I did what else a mother can do. I leapt at the pale man with the glow and bit his nose. *OMNI-OMNI...* He squealed mid-spell and we crashed to the ground. I scratched his face, bit him again and, oh, he tasted unpleasant – the alkaline smell I had observed on the cloth now transformed into a rank, acrid taste of skin. I yanked at his dreadlocked hair. He was dressed in a loincloth, so our tussle was thoroughly undignified, but I sat astride his chest and dug my thumbs into his eyes.

By now a crowd had gathered at the commotion and was chanting some repetitive hum that appeared intended to have a magical effect.

Yasiyasi – ratata!

And then my Wa'wati was on his knees, then his feet, and was joining in the hum, this time in his own wordage. He was picking up the magical echo and casting some sort of deterrent spell. I noticed the unusual sweeping of his hands, the stirring and swirling motion I'd never seen him use before. A certain tempo, rhythmic, accompanied his words:

IamhungryIamhungryIamhungryIamhungryryryry.

The words came out conjoined, but in slow motion echo.

With each chant from the throng, the witch man weakened. Now he was shrivelling, his skin desiccating like the bark of a sick baobab tree in the stomach of summer.

Yasiyasi – ratata!

IamhungryIamhungryIamhungryIamhungryryryry.

But he was a stronger witch man than anyone could have suspected and he was starting to glow again. With each radiance, a person in the crowd shrieked out loud and fell foaming to the ground. With each collapse, the witch man shined brighter, and double the number of villagers plummeted in froth and tremors. I knew what was happening.

He was stealing their echoes to rejuvenate himself.

And then diminutive Rehema're with her flaring golden eyes was there. She bent and swirled her echo magic with her hands, floating, reflecting and transitioning it with a melodious chant, this time her words magical, not everyday language. The flow of her intonation was different, and she bent and swayed her hands in a manner I hadn't witnessed before. It was as if she was making invisible water, forming and deforming its waves, directing and spiralling its wash.

Wey ma, wey ma. Uuuuuuu.

My heart again staggered. If this was infatuation, dear heart, it was a cruel thing! Here I was on the jaws of death, likely trampled upon in a stampede rather than obliterated by a spell. Imagine the headlines: GREAT SLEUTH STOMPED TO HISTORY. Yet I was entranced with a woman to whom I was most likely a hard pass, because interplanetary liaisons were as rare as they were problematic.

Wey ma, wey ma. Uuuuuuu.

But it was Sina'aa's V'hushalele that did it. I saw his graceful leap, the twist of his hips, a loosening of shoulders, then the release. The

V'hushalele whistled in a straight path right into the heart of the witch man, who exploded into echoes that fell onto the ground in a dust of volcano, or simple ash. Sina'aa stretched his hand, and the V'hushalele cruised back, harmless, into his palm.

'His name was Mga'agaa,' Sina'aa later said in that deep and beautiful voice of his.

'Well,' I tried to make light of it, 'if someone had named me Mga'agaa, then perhaps implosion is not the worst thing that could happen.'

'Would you be livid enough to steal other people's sound magic, even if that meant condemning them to certain death in the maws of some fanged, saliva-dripping omen?'

'Why, no!'

I was glad we didn't have to stay until nightfall to solve the mystery – Ekwukwe was renowned for the blackest dusk.

But I had some good takeaways from the excursion. I'd like to say the highlight of my visit was Rehema're's echo magic, or Sina'aa's adeptness with the V'hushalele, not to mention the explosion of a powerful witch man in the heart of a marketplace, but no. Have you experienced freeing refugees, giving them back their lives?

They blinked at the sun from the doors of their camp huts, walked out of the gates, their gaits straightening with each step, and I witnessed with my own eyes – I swear upon Our Mother – their echoes returning. Each echo was like an aura, shimmering in halo, the strength of its return bourgeoned, as if they each now also had a piece of the witch man's echo.

It was a mission accomplished. I'd had the privilege of standing across Sina'aa, the regal one who was once an echoless outcast, and his sage sister Rehema're, who was now speaking in her most beautiful and familiar intonation: *Wey-ma. Wey ma. U.*

'It was nothing,' I said, understanding her gratitude. 'You might think I'm the greatest sleuth alive, but today the accolade is not mine.'

Because was it not Wa'wati whose sensitivity to the echo magic, and his resistance to it, that had led us to solve this mystery? I looked at Wa'wati–

And, to my chagrin, the boy had discovered a *stick* and was galloping about and being an *ass*, the bray of his laughter flowing around me in slow motion. It was ludicrous trying to convince the leaders of the Boāmmariri that it was he, not me, who had unravelled the mystery of the vanishing echoes.

So, instead, I said to the constipated one of Zezépfeni, 'Hogheh, I have delivered. Once again.'

He wiped his face with unhappiness, bowed, and yielded to my status. 'Yes, Great Sleuth Shaalok Ho-ohmsi,' he said with the most pained countenance. A part of me wanted to imagine it was the moment that he fouled himself. My screen showed nothing, but the federation is quite capable of having the technology to mask biological dysfunction in a hologram.

It was then that I astonished him, and myself, with an observation. 'See the Uroh-ogi about kidney stones. Do not wait until you see blood in your urine.'

'Wh-what?' he stammered.

'Your bad mood, the bone pain – your posture. Sweating and the constipation. Am I right?'

'I've been putting it off to visit the healer…'

'Don't put it off any more, my friend,' I said.

To this day, nobody knows how Mga'agaa acquired the potency of magic that could steal echoes from others, empowering himself while weakening them.

I proposed a possibility: 'What if Mga'agaa was one of those anomalous child outcasts of Ekwukwe, abandoned to the forest, and somehow survived, now returned with a vengeance to settle?'

'It is possible,' agreed Sina'aa. 'People fear what they do not know and, in so doing, they don't realise how closely they might inadvertently create the very monsters they dread.'

With the incineration of Mga'agaa, no more echoes vanished in Ekwukwe, and the rest of the planets stayed unharmed.

So that's that. I am Shaalok Ho-ohmsi, and this is how we solved the mystery of the vanishing echoes. For a mystery with such a complex name, it was the simplest to solve.

We suffered the indignity of the acorn, and stepped out of an old baobab at the elbow of Wiimb-ó. We're now back in our cottage in Kitale – actually, it's a renovated mansion. The Boāmmariri paid us handsomely and I stretched the cottage into a four-roomer with a pheasant farm extension. We had much of the payment left over, and managed to create a turquoise lake further out from my cassava patch, so the waters couldn't flood it. There Wa'watison – when he's not helping, which is often – leaps bottom first, knees folded into the water's splash.

But, alas, Wa'watison is back to silence, his tongue once more lost.

I have prayed to Our Mother: nothing is happening.

I'd like to think he's pretending and expect him at any time to pounce upon me as I prune my cassavas, pulling at weeds and tossing them away to dry up, tinder for the storytelling flame just before his bedtime.

Perhaps, he will yell, 'My word!' as he startles me, and scatters kudu fertiliser into my eyes, for the simplest impertinence of seeing me cross.

And I will holler at him, 'No, Wa'wati,' but with every impossible restraint I can hold back in my heart a mother's deepest pride.

The Game is a Foot

Atlin Merrick

SHERLOCK HOLMES ELBOW-CRAWLED THROUGH THE GLOOM.

She'd been searching for hours, moving with the silence of secrets, a creature of liminal spaces, elusive, invisible.

Also, the aeroplane was dark with artificial dusk, and no one expected to see a four-year-old slithering beneath their seat, so there *was* that.

While every adult fitfully slept on the half-full jumbo jet, Sherlock's dark eyes remained sharply focused, searching relentlessly for she knew not what. The child might be only little, you see, but she suffered from a boredom double her diminutive size and had long since grown adept at battling ennui with action.

And so, while Flight 38 from India flew through the long night, most passengers were so exhausted by the fourteen-hour journey to England that they slept in complete innocence of the child from 31F relentlessly slithering between their legs, carry-ons, and socked feet searching for…

Some might say adventure, but if pressed, Sherlock Holmes would say *clues*. Clues concerning what? She'd know when she found them, and find them she would, just as she'd found Mummy's anti-nausea tablets and Auntie's boarding pass right before their flight.

(Sherlock did not know, will never know, that both items were purposely misplaced by each woman so the little girl could locate them. *See also:* the whole boredom-ennui thing.)

As it stood, right now the clear facts were these: the world was a dreamy, almost-dark meant to imitate the night through which they flew; so far every single adult had greeted Sherlock's slithery passing with snores; and if she remained briskly aware of her silent surroundings, the child was 78% confident no one would scream at the soft brush of something against their ankles, therefore her am'ma and pinni would remain asleep and blissfully unaware they'd failed to keep her small body corralled between them in seats D through G.

Again.

While all these facts held true – and she was aware anything might shift in any direction at any moment (a thrilling thought) – Sherlock Holmes continued to wriggle like a brown-skinned snake, hunt, hunt, hunting for something that looked like adventu– uh, *clues.*

She did not count in this grouping a startling number of unopened packets of curried nuts she's found and shoved down her pyjama top, nor the frankly shocking number of half-sandwiches discarded on the floor. These she fussily finger-flicked into the gloaming behind her.

No, Sherlock wanted the bounty of a lost mobile phone, a passport, something *important.* Yet for the last hour she'd found only food scraps and heard only snores.

That – as well as Sherlock Holmes' entire short life and all the many years ahead of her – was mere minutes from changing.

This was because another child wandered in the gloom, he from another world entirely – 82D. It was from this land John Watson snuck away soundless, moving quiet as a criminal from seat to seat, carefully invading the personal space of dozens upon dozens of his fellow passengers.

Four-year-old Watson was a *make-things-right* sort of child, you see. He pushes long ears from his stuffed rabbit's eyes so her gaze is unhindered, he solemnly rights the neighbour's empty bin on rubbish day. And though he was still small, John Watson was already an energy-conscious little pedant, who believed firmly in saving electricity. So, short hair still rucked up on one side from a refreshing nap, John moved stealthily through the Air India Boeing 747 from Hyderabad, bound for London, turning off the movie screens of every single passenger sleeping through the end of a Tollywood blockbuster or last year's hit binge-watch.

In the forty minutes since he'd begun, John had come across not one reading adult, not a single stirring infant. Even the crew seemed to be somewhere not here, and so, with the serenity of justice accompanying him as he crawled over napping nannas, dozing dads, and kipping kids, John made the world a better place one saved electron at a time.

Until he got the crap scared *right* out of him.

To be fair, Sherlock was just a touch over-excited to see another kid *doing stuff.* At home she tends to be regrettably alone in her explorations – her brother is too old, other children too childish – but this boy looked just right and whatever he was up to, it looked interesting and possibly forbidden. So when Sherlock saw the little boy spider-walking across three sleeping kids, she reflexively reached out to grab his skinny white ankle before she'd thought through the ramifications.

Know this: when John Watson has the wits scared straight out of him, he manifests his alarm *quietly.* As in this case, where he levitated to the back of an empty airline seat and peered wide-eyed down into the shadows, to find two brown eyes peering up.

Here's the thing, the absolute thing about what happened next: it made all the difference in their world and their futures. Because Sherlock Holmes looked at that other child looking at her and, with a grin big as a jumbo jet, she put her finger to her lips.

Nothing, not anything *ever* was better than the thrill of a secret, so John Watson – heart still thrumming merrily in already-forgotten fear – monkey-clambered over seat backs, landed quiet as a panther in the airplane aisle, then elbow-crawled under a bunch of airline seats – the space was small but he was smaller – until he was next to his thrilling new friend.

'Thorry,' Sherlock said first, before wiggling her tongue around to make it sit in her mouth better. 'I'm Sherlock and I'm looking for clues, what are you doing?'

Now here was the thing: John Watson is four years old, so he doesn't exactly have a lot of space to remember things yet. While ordinarily John might have answered honestly – 'I was turning off TVs because everyone should save energy and not leave things running if they're not using them' – the word *clue* made him forget that and remember something else entirely. 'I'm John. And I found someone's present.'

It had taken the littlest Watson a good five minutes to successfully sneak away from his sleeping family and that couple across the aisle who deputised themselves as part of the Watson child-rearing village, so once John escaped, he had little intention of speedily going back, hence the video screens and absolutely forgetting that while in the loo he'd found and pocketed–

'This.'

John held up a small box only a bit bigger than his palm and said absolutely nothing, already somehow knowing his new friend required the spectacle of a good unveiling and the drama of the unspoken.

Sherlock's dark eyes grew big, first at the box, then at John himself.

A clue her brain sang. 'A *wedding* ring!' she whispered.

If asked how she knew that, Sherlock wouldn't have been able to say, but all the clues were there to a certain set of eyes. The box's size and shape said "ring" of course, while wedding was easily inferred from the box's pricey, custom-made, geodesic shape, its green silk sides, and an inset of abalone so beautiful it looked like an aurora as it caught the twinkling floor lights. Why spend so lavishly on a mere box unless it represented something grand?

'Should we open it?' John's whisper was one part scandalised at the thought, two parts hopeful, with a rogue fourth part probably willing to go to prison if Sherlock's reply was thrilling enough.

She didn't answer though, just reached out a little hand and *squeeeaked* the hinge open.

Now the world beneath low-lying airline seats is not a well-illuminated one, but even so, both children could see that the ring inside was big, and it was rare. It too was inset with a swirl of light-capturing green and blue, while the bulk of its body seemed black. It was the most beautiful thing Sherlock had ever–

'I was gonna give it to someone.' John pointed in the general direction of the cockpit. 'To give back.'

–oh hell *no.*

Sherlock Holmes doesn't swear and didn't then, but her little brain was already eight steps along on an *adventure* – um, into the deduction of the clues represented by this treasure – and so before her new friend could be an upright citizen or, worse yet, grow bored with her, Sherlock skipped pell-mell toward *action* and said with certainty, 'But we can do it! We can give it back to the correct person! It's a big ring! So let's go look for big people!'

In the future, John Watson will come to adapt his level of law-keeping to that which works best for his closest friend. And it was here, at 42,000 feet in the air and with a brisk nod, that John started as he meant to go on for the next eighty years.

Things did not go as planned.

As they themselves were only little, it turned out that Sherlock's and John's assessment of large was somewhat skewed. It also didn't help that in the half-full plane of adults, most were slumped, sloped, curled, or crumpled into sleepy little balls, so "big" was a bit hard to discern.

At least they could be pretty sure the ring belonged to a man, simply because even tiny children have already been faced with Tube adverts and TV commercials showing that what was for males was not supposed to look like things for females. While the dubious logic escaped them, each still suspected that the jewellery was meant for a certain sort of hand.

That's not to say they didn't hold it up close to the lady who snored as big as she was tall, or the one who talked in her sleep, but when they finally managed to glimpse these many hands in the half-light, each was too small for the ring.

And so it went, from Air India seats 82 to 31, before a true test came to them.

First class.

Both children knew that those twelve seats ahead of them were the land of special people. A quiet country behind a sheer curtain, there were fluffy chairs and big TVs and an ever-present air of "can't, mustn't, and don't" about it. They knew it was barred to little kids and so of course, standing in the dimness beside an exit door and directly in front of a flight attendant dozing in his chair, the children checked in with one another. This involved a silent gaze, seconds long and then, as if these next steps were familiar, old-hat, the usual way of things, they clasped each other's hands and *skulked*.

To the right, where the first shadows lurked, then *freeze!* while the flight attendant sighed heavily. Left next, right, and left again until they were behind the first seat in the last row. Peering carefully around it, they found a brown poodle snugged up in a blanket, snoozing. A big, round, pretty man dozed next to the dog, one hand resting on the pup and another on his belly. They saw with interest that each finger on both of the man's hands was beringed, that he likewise wore several necklaces and ear studs. For a moment John wondered if this was the person they were looking for, but Sherlock pointed to her own fingers, neck, and ears and then put her hands together. *Everything matches, everything is silver,* the gesture clearly said. John nodded and they moved on.

They had peeped and peered and deduced, making it to the very front of first class, when tragedy almost occurred.

A baby began to murmur in her cot, mounted to the bulkhead at the front of the plane. Sherlock was absolutely ready to leg it, but John Watson stopped right in front of the babe. Without even a glance at the infant's sleeping parents, he whispered some silly song about a ticking clock, covered her with her rucked up blanket, and then gently placed her Indian flag-decorated dummy back in her mouth. It was only seconds before the babe was again asleep. Sherlock politely gawked at her friend, and then they *both* legged it back to economy before their luck ran out.

Reconvening aft of the plane, the children discussed how to proceed as they stuffed themselves with some of the nuts Sherlock had collected in what seemed hours ago.

While John picked carefully through his, giving Sherlock the almonds, and Sherlock shared the juice box lurking at the bottom of her big pockets – not much in the way of procedure emerged. They ate, they smiled gappy smiles at one another, until John Watson had an obvious and illuminating idea: 'Hey! Maybe we can figure out something if we look at the ring in the loo! It has lights!'

Quicker than the novel-reading flight attendant in the middle of a mighty yawn, the children slipped into one of the back toilets like very tiny cat burglars. Once the lock was engaged – 'Sshhh!' 'I am ssshhh!' – the light blazed, and after long seconds blinking away light blindness, each child finally fully saw the best friend each will ever have *ever.*

John Watson grinned at a short-haired girl a bit taller than him, with brown skin and eyes speaking of her Indian heritage, and crooked teeth that spoke of also being English. Her footy pyjamas were modelled off cricket whites, and their deep pockets appeared packed with stuff.

Sherlock Holmes grinned at a boy approximately three centimetres smaller and two kilos heavier than she, with auburn-brown hair the exact colour of Mycroft's guinea pig Hypatia. He had dark green eyes, pink cheeks, and white skin faintly dusted with freckles. His footy pyjamas were big on him and a bit faded, implying a sibling, while their tartan pattern, surfeit of square silver buttons, and faux sporran, strongly implied a Scottish heritage. He had a short scar on his left earlobe, two tiny moles at his hairline, a fading bruise between his collar bones, dimples at both corners of his mouth, and a gap of two missing teeth which she inferred behind a close-lipped smile. There was a small chocolate smear on his jaw.

If they weren't just very tiny people right now, each might have recognised that this, their first real meeting, was a momentous moment. Yet they weren't and so they didn't (though at least one person would remember today *for* them).

'Ready?' asked Sherlock by way of getting the adventure going again.

'Yes,' said John, and opened the box.

Both children stared at the ring inside.

'Wow, it's really pretty.'

'I've never seen a black ring before.'

'I think it's tungsten,' Sherlock said. 'It has a chemical number of 74 and its symbol is W. It's used in tools and magnets and lights and jewellery and even *rockets.*'

John Watson replied with a flurry of blinks, so impressed by his new friend's knowledge that he simply handed her his treasure.

Now in Sherlock's small hands they looked at the ring again. Its high gloss tungsten carbide exterior was more of a reflective grey than black and, like its box, the ring was lushly inset with green-blue abalone.

For a while both kids did what people always do before beauty: they admired. They took turns touching it, turning it, smiling first at it and then each other, before at last Sherlock said, 'Oh, there's writing on the inside.'

'I can't read yet,' John said, a little shy. 'Can you?'

Here's the thing: Sherlock Holmes' mummy works for the University of London as a research chemist and her daddy used to be one at Nizam College. That is to say that Sherlock Holmes' parents are clever.

When he was just under three years old, her brother Mycroft once used an old Meccano set, a broken abacus, and a toy truck to build a block-and-tackle system which not only got him up and out of the lounge room window of their holiday home, but also doubled as a tiny scooter. By the time Mycroft was found, he was a half kilometre from their rental and about to merge onto the M1. Directly after this daddy retired from full-time university work to full-time child minding. By the time Sherlock came along four years later, both parents recognised this as the best decision they had ever made.

That is to say that Sherlock Holmes comes from a particularly bright family, and has an ego which encourages her to keep up with them, and so she cleared her throat and read the inside of the ring with the solemn respect the message deserved. 'Eli. Every moment my love, all over again. Tejul.'

John Watson is a steadfast child but not quite as precocious as his friend. He was confused. 'What does that mean?'

'Well,' Sherlock said, 'my Auntie Sherlock bought my Uncle Aabhi a ring last year and proposed to him again on account of you have to keep your marriage fresh. I think this is like that.' John blink-blinked, so Sherlock added, 'He's not here though on account of you also need time away from each other to keep your marriage fresh. It's just me and am'ma and pinni – that means mummy and auntie in Telugu which is the fourteenth most spoken language in the world and we all just went to a Test Match in Hyderabad because Sherlock auntie used to be a famous cricket player and I'm named after her.'

Sherlock gestured to her cricket white footy pyjamas. At John's unexpected grimace, Sherlock looked down.

Oh ugh.

Crawling under airline seats was not a clean business and her whites were in fact quite grey. It was fine though, daddy was used to this sort of thing and had found a very good laundry detergen–

Sherlock stood so straight so suddenly she bonked her head on the door behind her, but it didn't stop her from closing the ring box and then *sniffing*.

Snort!

Sniff!

Deep. Big. Deep. Big. *Again. Again. Again.*

With each indrawn breath and noisy exhale her brow arched higher, her smile grew wider, until she whooshed out a great gust and said, 'I can smell laundry soap!'

This…was not the revelation John Watson was expecting.

In a household of the exceptionally articulate, clever, and bright, Sherlock always found her four year old fascinations with books, clues, and crime not only indulged but encouraged. So *she* encouraged by holding the box up to John's nose. 'Sniff.'

He did, and said nothing. Sherlock's expectant gaze said volumes, and then so did she.

'It was in the pocket of someone's trousers or jacket which was clearly freshly washed as this smells exactly like eco-friendly, concentrated, biological Clia Coconut Care Laundry Soap. It's very expensive because it's good for if you're like my brother Mycroft and have contact demmer-dimmer'

'Dermatitis? My brother has that.'

'Yeth!' Throat clear. 'Yes! So anyway, this smells like that and so it's one very good clue!'

'But why?'

'Cause maybe everything the person wears smells like that. All my clothes got washed before we left India so maybe theirs did too, including their *socks*. We can find them by their *feet* John!'

It all sounded kind of…logical, though the only thing John could think to add was, 'You should smell my brother's feet.'

Sherlock did not, in fact, smell John's brother's feet, but she did smell many others, whether woman, man, or child. There were feet that smelled of nail varnish, others of bleach. There was the scent of grass and baby powder, chlorine, rubber, and dogs, tar, mint, and cigarettes. A surprising number smelled of woodsmoke, a few of cinnamon. One smelled of coffee, another of toast, and when Sherlock came across a pair of feet with the scent of her am'mam'ma's camphor foot cream, she almost started to cry; she missed Grandma already and she'd only just left her ten hours ago.

On their journey they collected more unopened nut packets, returned two stuffed animals to the arms of their sleeping owners, and replaced a passport into the back pocket of the sleeping guy whose butt was mostly hanging off his seat.

Beneath seats 49 C and D they found a child of three quietly adding toys into her father's Flipkart e-basket and paused to share some peanuts with her. They weighed in on whether the Life Size Human Skull With Magnetic Remov-A-Top was worth it, all three children voting yes, then stifling their giggles as big, bare feet passed them on the way to the toilet.

For Sherlock, it was beginning to feel as if elbow-crawling with John in the land under the airline seats was the only life she'd ever known, and this was a comfort. So much so that she encouraged three separate diversions on their quest, including a twenty-minute pause to test out all the properties of one life vest, and fifteen minutes trying to deduce a particularly shocking carpet stain.

Yet time does not stand still, not for big people nor small, so Sherlock Holmes, new to friendship and all the more besotted for that, accepted that their journey must continue. And then just as quickly it ended for, as is the way of things, they were three rows from Sherlock's own seat when it happened.

Just ahead: an empty pair of Converse trainers which smelled so strongly of Coconut Care they caught the scent two metres off. Crawling close, Sherlock elbowed one of the shoes toward John, who sniffed delicately, then grinned so wide she could see he was actually missing *four* teeth. With silent nods to one another which would be exact echoes of their wordless agreements twenty-five years from now (when John and Sherlock are regularly jumping off bridges or busting open doors) they crept-crawled ever-so-slowly forward and peeked *up,* hoping no one was looking down.

Someone, in fact, was.

Sort of. Had his eyes not been closed he'd have seen the children instantly, but instead O'Cain Tejul Raju Rao was smiling in some secret reverie while he brushed at the hair of the man whose head rested in his lap.

That man, Eli O'Cain, was sound asleep, curled up across three seats, and drooling on the thigh of the man to whom he has been married nearly ten years. Sleeping Eli wore grey track pants, green socks, and on his left arm a black myoelectric prosthesis from shoulder to fingertip. From the inside of the prosthetic's wireframe, a green-blue light shone low, just barely illuminating the prosthetic's thick ring finger, on which there was a silver wedding band bearing the wear-and-tear of a life lived large. Tejul was taking his husband from their Hyderabad home to Glasgow, where they will restate their wedding vows at the foggy edge of the Conachair Cliffs, four hundred of their nearest and dearest in attendance.

This is all to say that when Tejul, more in love after a decade than when he started, opened his eyes to find two children gazing up at him, a very recognisable ring box he hadn't even realised he'd lost resting in the tiny palm of one, he responded in the only way he could: he cried.

Solemn in the face of the man's joy, Sherlock Holmes handed the ring up to him. She is only small, so when he clutched it to his chest she could not read on his joyful face all the things that face said. About a man whose smile illuminated Tejul's life, how impossible it was they'd found one another by the simple accident of sitting together in the same railway car.

If they weren't children and he wasn't getting all mucusy, Tejul could have told them right to their little upturned faces that the ring was not even as beautiful as Eli's smile, as gorgeous as the light emanating from his prosthetic, or as vibrant as his love lived each moment. And if the universe asked Tejul to live these ten years again, from the pains of their at-first long-distance romance, to last year's car wreck and Eli's amputation, to the joyful chaos of their dual-continent lives, he would, he'd tell them, oh he'd live–

…every moment my love, all over again…

Instead, he wiped at his running nose with the back of his hand and covered all his bases by whispering thank you to the children in Telugu, English, and Scots Gaelic as the little girl and boy returned his heart to him with toothy grins.

For her part, Sherlock Holmes will remember this day all *her* days, as it's the one where she discovered that finding clues wasn't the adventure, but finding the purpose *in the clues* was. While John? He was just glad he'd found Sherlock.

With a wave of their small hands the children elbow-crawled back into the shadows – like tiny assassins Tejul will tell Eli later, embellishing until his one true love is nauseous with laughter, the story soon growing with each telling, until on the Conachair Cliffs a few days from now, a little brown girl with bright eyes and a little white boy with missing teeth will become the small heroes in one of the many, many recountings of Tejul's and Eli's love story.

Sherlock and John knew that for now their adventure was over. And not. They were a little bit solemn but as they slowly meandered their way away from and then back toward Sherlock's am'ma and pinni – 'that means mummy and auntie and akka means older sister and tam'mudu means younger brother and' – she taught her new friend words in the language of her family, and learned the ones that John knew in Gaelic, and they discussed where they lived in London and neither knew you could say how much you'd miss someone you only just met and finally there they were, just inches from the big feet of Sherlock's auntie Sherlock, the tap-tap-tapping of her ever moving toes clearly showing she was awake.

Sherlock nodded at John, who waited until she'd crawled forward, made some sort of complex gesture to the owner of the fiddling feet, then turned back to look at him. If his footy pyjamas had a collar he'd have straightened it. Instead, the small child elbow-crawled his way to a spot beside his friend, beamed up with a gap-toothed grin at the grown-up and whispered, 'Hello Sherlock garu,' for little Sherlock had told him to whom those big feet belonged, and how to say hi respectfully. 'I'm John and I found a ring and Sherlock found the man who it belonged to and his husband has a shiny robot arm and we made him cry because he was happy.'

Nadella Sherlock Rama, looked serenely down at the pale little boy. A brown-skinned woman, with short black hair fringed with grey, a sharp nose and eyes, her arched brow and smile were exact echoes of those John had seen on his new friend's face about eighty-four times in the last two hours. He felt that she knew everything about him instantly and, as with his new friend, this was comforting.

Young Mr Watson was not wrong, for Nadella Sherlock Rama was very good at deducing people. A woman the sports press had dubbed The Detective a double dozen years ago, Sherlock could faultlessly look at her opposition, and find and make use of their every weakness, for cricket at the elite level was for her a game of mind as much as physical mettle, and as an all-rounder and Test captain, Rama – Sherlock to her friends – has played since she could walk unaided.

Sherlock garu knew her namesake had these same skills, only she suspected the child would put them to different use. This pleased her. What pleased her more was the light in the little girl's eyes, something Sherlock knew had to do with the small friend beside her akka's little girl.

With only a grinning gaze and a lifted chin, Nadella Sherlock Rama told her sweet namesake that *the plane doesn't land for another five hours, mēnakōḍalu, and I suspect your am'ma will sleep for every one of those. Go find adventure little one. We'll be here for you.*

With an answering smile the little girl took the hand of the small boy beside her and they disappeared into the dark in search of adventure.

It would be the habit of a lifetime.

WHAT YOU THINK THEY MEAN

Verity Burns

'*And I've never been attracted to boys.*'

Sherlock held the words suspended before her so as to examine each one more precisely, but they could not possibly mean what her startled heart wanted to think they meant.

She glanced across at John, but he was staring fixedly out the window.

No. She shook her head. Impossible for her to have missed something so momentous. She was Sherlock Holmes. And she saw everything.

She saw things she didn't want to see. Saw them every hour of every day. Each time someone clocked her voice as a little too low, her shoulders as a little too broad, anything about her that wouldn't fit into the rigid little box they wanted to shove her into, until she couldn't breathe, couldn't live, couldn't *bear*…she saw it all.

So something she'd dreamed of, had tried desperately not to hope for…she wouldn't have missed that. Couldn't have.

She sighed.

And that sigh pulled John's head around to face her at last, his eyebrows slowly rising as they stared at each other, and she didn't know what her face was doing but it certainly wasn't playing poker.

And proving once again that John Watson would always, always, be braver than her, he stretched out a hand. His fingers curling around hers felt like the very definition of belonging.

The Case of the Man Who Wasn't Dead

Dannye Chase

SHERLOCK HOLMES WAS NOT A FAN OF ZOOM. PEOPLE ON THE other end of the camera always wanted to look past Sherlock's face and beg a guided tour of her collection of souvenirs from crimes she'd solved. She had complained about it more than once to Jane, and Jane had suggested that Sherlock keep a blog narrating her adventures, illustrated with photos. But Sherlock didn't have the energy for that, and it wasn't like Jane could do it.

'How on earth did you link several hundred-year-old murders across two different countries?' At the moment, Sherlock was in the middle of a Zoom interview about her latest case. From the reporter's appearance Sherlock could tell she was a recently divorced vegetarian who owned two cats.

'Well, the crimes clearly align,' Sherlock said. 'They're all near train tracks, and the victims were all killed with the blunt side of axes. Other investigators had gotten that far, but no farther. So I simply had to consider what to do with an unsolvable series of random attacks. And the answer is that you must deny one of those primary assumptions.'

The reporter grinned, excited, and from her teeth Sherlock could see she'd been raised in the Eastern United States. 'You deny that they are unsolvable!'

'No, no, there will always be unsolvable crimes.' Sherlock couldn't say that without a glance at Jane, who was sitting at the kitchen table beside her. 'Especially as we get farther away from the time when they occurred. But in this case, we deny that the crimes are random. Now, these killings were certainly meant to look like opportunistic murders by a serial killer. But a bit of research showed they were all connected by a lawsuit filed thirty years before. Someone was carrying out a grudge against every family who benefited from the settlement. It's quite obvious, really.'

'Maybe to you, but that's why you're so famous.' The reporter leaned toward the camera, as if that would help her see better. 'I hear you found the actual axe handle in the attic of one of the victims' descendants.'

'Yes, I collected one of the murder weapons. The type of wood used, and manufacturing marks helped identify the hired killer's hometown.'

'So, could I get a picture for the article?'

'Sorry, no.' Sherlock clicked the box to leave the meeting.

'You don't have to be so rude,' Jane said. The light from the kitchen window didn't affect her, didn't set her red curls aglow or brighten her pale skin. But she was unfailingly lovely all the same, in that white sundress, with her hair swept back from her face and her lips bright red. If Jane were alive today, Sherlock thought, she'd probably be a fan of glitter lipstick, going around looking like she'd kissed one of Dorothy's ruby slippers.

Sherlock did attempt not to make a habit of thinking about Jane Watson kissing things.

'How is the waiting room?' Sherlock asked. 'Lots of victims in this last case, should have cleared out some space.'

Jane smiled. 'Yes, twenty-three spirits moved on this morning, thanks to you. Their murders solved, their attachment to Earth dissolved. I'm afraid the waiting room never gets very empty, though. Are you up for your next case?'

'Got nothing planned.'

'Do you want a historical or a recent murder this time?'

'Surprise me.'

After Jane vanished from the table, Sherlock drifted into the kitchen, putting fresh water in the coffee pot, washing her dishes from the night before: one plate, one fork. She took a few minutes to put up her hair, twisting it into a thick braid and winding it around itself at the crown of her head. Sherlock had thick enough hair that it took quite a few pins to put it up, but Jane had once remarked that she liked it that way, and Sherlock had been unable to forget that. She was actually unable to forget most of the details she observed each day, but at least that one was pleasant.

After that, Sherlock Holmes sat at her computer and logged into Twitter.

When Jane reappeared, she was sitting on the edge of Sherlock's desk, her legs crossed at the ankle, and a disapproving look on her face. 'You know, it doesn't matter how much smarter you are than everyone else on that web-net thing of yours, people don't like to be told about it.'

'I'm not telling them, I'm showing them. People are actually debating the usefulness of science in modern life–' Sherlock broke off. 'What happened to you? You look tense. Is someone on the other side being rude to *you?*'

'Someone is very distressed.'

'Ah. Recently dead.'

'No.' Jane frowned. 'Well, yes, but this one wasn't murdered.'

'Not murdered?' Sherlock asked. 'Then she should have moved on. You can't stay in the waiting room unless your death is unresolved.'

'Well, she refuses to go. It seems she can't find her brother. He was lost at sea twenty years ago as a young man and she's been looking forward to seeing him again on the other side.'

Sherlock took a drink of lukewarm coffee and frowned at her cup. 'I know the filing system is a bit haphazard up there, but how on earth does she expect me to solve a missing persons case in the afterworld? You can come here, but I certainly can't go there.'

'Sherlock, no, listen. This woman spent her life mourning the only family she ever really had, and all this time he wasn't here.'

Sherlock looked up, coffee forgotten. 'What, you mean he's still alive?'

'He must be. But he never contacted her after the ship accident. She's terribly worried about him, and I don't know how much longer she'll be able to stay in the waiting room when she should be moving on. Please?'

Sherlock waved a hand magnanimously. 'You're the supernatural secretary.'

'*Spirit guide,*' Jane said, fondly exasperated.

The Case of the Man Who Wasn't Dead

At the time of her death in 1944, Jane Watson had been a twenty-seven-year-old nurse in a World War II field hospital, risking her life to protect young men from the worst of what the world could do to them. Many years later, Jane had stepped in to protect a child named Sherlock from the overwhelming crowds of despairing murdered souls who were drawn to her.

Sherlock had seen Jane in her dreams as a child, sweet and soft, always standing in front of a closed door. And Jane was the one who explained things to Sherlock at the age of sixteen, appearing for the first time outside of a dream, sitting at the kitchen table with that sweet smile. Sherlock had many gifts, Jane had said, and the murdered dead could tell, they knew she would be able to see and hear them, and they hoped she would be able to solve their crimes. It was they who were on the other side of that door.

Jane herself had died by the hand of an unknown man in a dirty alley, a murderer who'd taken the sunny, sweet soul that had been Jane Watson away from the world, leaving just that much more darkness in the middle of a war. But finding herself in the waiting room full of spirits with a door that led into a child's mind, Jane hadn't bothered about her own case. Instead, somehow, she'd managed to lock that door and keep the only key.

With Jane's permission, the new spirit appeared on the couch in Sherlock's living room. She had dark eyes and a slight build, and she seemed to waver in and out a bit, as if Sherlock's eyes couldn't quite focus on her. Most spirits were far more solid, but this one clearly had a weaker grasp on the world that she was supposed to be leaving behind.

'This is Piper Sullivan,' Jane said, as she took her usual wing chair. 'Piper, Sherlock Holmes.'

Sherlock could tell quite a few things about Piper on seeing her: she'd died of cancer around the age of forty, after chemotherapy had been unsuccessful. She'd lived on the west coast for most of her adult life, but she'd grown up in Iowa, probably on or near a farm. She loved dogs. She'd never been married. Her favourite colour was yellow.

'Tell me about your brother,' Sherlock said.

It was not a happy story. Piper's brother Robin was seven years older. Like Robin, Piper had been a surprise to their parents, and neither of them had been described as welcome surprises. Eventually, the parents had moved on, and from the age of eighteen, Robin had raised his sister, working two jobs to pay for a tiny apartment in a small Iowa town.

One day when Piper was sixteen, Robin abruptly announced that he'd gotten a new job, somewhere far from winter snow and summer swelter. He'd be working on a small ship that did day cruises out of a sweet little California town all covered in flowers. Piper would be able to visit the beach every day.

And for a while, their life was exactly that. A year or more of blue California skies, cold waves, and hot beaches. But eventually, Robin began to get very stressed again, like he had in Iowa before the move, watching his back, peering into shadows, jumping at noises. And then one day his ship went out and did not come back. The captain had been drinking and steered into a rock. In the confusion, several people were lost, including Robin.

'Piper, what did you do after that?' Sherlock asked. 'After you graduated from high school in California? I can't see much sign of a career on you.'

Piper looked a little surprised, but said, 'Oh, I bounced around a bit, but after a couple of years, there was the settlement from the ship touring company. It was very generous. I lived on that the rest of my life.'

'You stayed in California.'

'I guess I always stupidly thought that maybe Robin would come back. I knew he was dead. I *knew* it. Until I died a month ago, and I still can't find him.'

Jane moved to the couch and put an arm around Piper, who had tears in her eyes. Sherlock tried not to stare at the spot where Jane's hand met Piper's shoulder. Did Jane's touch feel warm? Sherlock wondered. Surely Jane's hands were soft, and she probably smelled of roses or spiced oranges. But no matter how much Sherlock longed for it, those answers lay on the other side of an impassable barrier, the line between the living and the dead.

'Piper, what was in your will? Where did your possessions go?' Sherlock asked.

'I had no family, so I left it to charity. There was an animal shelter that I volunteered at, and they have an account at a consignment shop. I gave all my things to that shop to be sold for the shelter.' Piper looked uncertain. 'Is that really helpful in finding my brother?'

'Very helpful,' Sherlock said. 'Jane, we're going to California.'

There was a friendly woman at the shop in California. From her appearance, Sherlock gleaned that she had two sons who were taller than she was, and she collected salt and pepper shakers, which was either a very advantageous or a very dangerous hobby when one worked in a second-hand shop.

'What can I help you with?' the woman asked, all smiles.

It was a beautiful day, and the shop smelled faintly of sunscreen. 'Oh, I'm not much for – stuff,' Sherlock said, awkwardly.

Beside her, Jane made a rather rude snorting noise. 'You are the *worst* pack rat.'

'The things I have are useful,' Sherlock told her.

'I'm sorry?' asked Annoying Shop Lady, who of course could not see or hear Jane.

Sherlock waved a hand. 'Just talking to my not-imaginary friend. What do you have of Piper Sullivan's?'

Shop Lady gave Sherlock the look one gives people who talk to invisible friends, but she was clearly still hoping to make a sale. 'Oh, yes, such a nice woman to entrust her things to our care. We have some lovely crockery, and there's furniture in good condition.'

'Was there anything Piper might have been emotionally attached to?' Sherlock asked.

'Who are you asking?' Jane asked, peering at a set of pink champagne flutes.

'Both of you.'

Shop Lady frowned. 'I, ah, I didn't know Ms Sullivan personally, so I'm not sure I can–'

'Piper says just the jewellery,' Jane said.

'What jewellery?'

'Oh, well, we have some jewellery over there,' Shop Lady said, pointing. Then she fled back to the counter, seeming happier to observe Sherlock from afar.

Sherlock wasn't much for jewellery, except for stud earrings in unusual shapes. Today she was wearing one violin and one smoking pipe. And she'd put up her hair again the way Jane liked it.

'Piper says she had a black stone pendant,' Jane said, pointing. 'That must be it there.'

Sherlock picked up the pendant, which was a stylish cut of what looked like onyx, on a gold background with chipped diamonds surrounding it.

'Someone left her this.'

Jane was kind enough to show her surprise at Sherlock's deduction. Then she turned in a way that showed she was listening to someone. 'Piper says yes, her aunt. She didn't even know she had an aunt until that was left to her.'

'And did anything go with it?'

'Those.'

Sherlock picked up a set of gold dangling earrings. They were light, and partially damaged. One was a cat whose legs had gotten bent at strange angles, and the other a mouse with ears twisted to the side. 'These don't go with the pendant,' Sherlock said. 'Look how cheaply they were made.'

Shop Lady had drifted close again, sensing a sale. 'Find something you like?'

'I'll take the earrings,' Sherlock said. 'Not the pendant, but neither should you sell it. I think you'll find it's worth quite a bit more than you think, and that it's been stolen. You and the animal shelter may be able to split the reward.'

It had taken Sherlock six hours to drive from her home in Oregon to a Northern California beach town, and as she walked out onto the boardwalk, she felt quite at home among the cliffs and rocks, the cold water, cries of gulls, and threat of fog.

Sherlock travelled quite a bit for her work, everywhere from big-city police stations to tiny historical museums, houses of retired detectives, forgotten roads to overgrown graveyards, and even the dementia wards of nursing homes, speaking to people who believed themselves to exist in the past. Sherlock was not sure just where she herself existed, always working on past crimes for passed people, travelling endlessly through the real world while being focused on a world she could not see, ignoring the people she met to talk to a woman who wasn't really there.

Jane, standing beside Sherlock in her white sundress, looked made for a beach with bright sun, an endless horizon, and sand unbroken by rocks. In Southern California, Sherlock thought, Jane would smell of coconut oil, and brine, and eat saltwater taffy.

'Can you bring Piper out?' Sherlock asked.

When Piper appeared, she looked out at the ocean with a fond expression. 'This was one of my favourite spots.'

'You're sure you had no other family,' Sherlock said. 'No wealthy friends?'

'No, just my brother and my aunt.'

Jane frowned. 'I couldn't find an aunt in the filing system. But of course, we don't know her name—'

'There never was an aunt,' Sherlock said. 'Piper's brother, however, I believe is quite well, although perhaps not living a life on the right side of the law.'

Piper looked both intrigued and dismayed. 'Why do you say that?'

'Because someone's been taking care of you from afar. There was no settlement from the ship company. I searched yesterday and couldn't find one. Now, if it was just the money, I imagine your brother could have earned it honestly.'

'But he sent the stolen pendant,' Jane said.

Sherlock nodded. 'Precisely, Jane. I think we can assume that Robin has fallen in with thieves.'

'But how did he survive the sea?' Piper asked. 'And why not just contact me? Where is he?'

'When the time comes, that last one will be easy,' Sherlock assured her.

'Why?'

'Because, Piper, I'm certain you already know where he is. You just don't know that you know.'

That evening, Sherlock found an episode of some *Star Trek* series on the hotel TV. She was not really a fan of *Star Trek*, but Jane liked it very much, and whenever Sherlock would tune in an episode, Jane would show up to watch. And then she'd always give her warning: 'Don't you dare tell me how it ends.'

'I haven't seen this one before,' Sherlock objected, in her PJs with a bowl of popcorn in her lap and a glass of wine in her hand. Wine and popcorn were part of Sherlock's travel kit, along with her own pillow from home and a set of ear plugs.

'Yes, but that won't stop you from giving it away as soon as you figure it out,' Jane said.

Sherlock, who had already figured it out, put on an innocent expression. Jane was not fooled. She put a finger to her lips and shook her head.

Sherlock fell asleep before the end of the episode anyway, probably because of the glass of wine. Jane was good enough to wake her and remind her that she'd be more comfortable in the bed with her ergonomic pillow.

The next morning, Sherlock spent some time looking over shipping charts on her laptop. 'He'd have drifted here,' she said to Jane, pointing to the map.

Jane had been gone for a bit and she glanced around the slightly messy hotel room with distaste. 'Did you eat lunch? Or breakfast?'

'There was some leftover popcorn. You know, it wouldn't have been that odd to have Robin get picked up out of the ocean, honestly. It was near to shore, and in a crowded area, relatively speaking. If he'd been holding onto a piece of wreckage, it's possible someone would have found him within an hour or two and taken him ashore.'

'At least have a glass of water,' Jane scolded.

Sherlock acquiesced, filling up a little hotel glass from the bathroom sink. 'This morning in town I found a couple of shady characters who remembered Robin, and not fondly.' Sherlock leaned against the TV bureau, gesturing with the glass. 'I suspect Robin turned to crime to support his sister from the very beginning, starting in Iowa. But he made someone there very angry, and that was the reason for the sudden move to California. Then he got into trouble here too, but this time, there was a novel solution to his problem: everyone suddenly believed he was dead.

'So Robin had two choices: tell his sister he was still alive, and then have to immediately uproot her and move again, or let everyone continue to believe he was dead, which is what he chose to do. He'd had two experiences with being a criminal, and both had gone poorly. But this time, he got it right. He found more upscale thieves and made enough with them to send Piper the money, disguised as a settlement from the ship accident.'

'He really just left Piper behind like that?' Jane asked. 'That's a very cruel thing to do, even if it was in her best interest.'

'I don't think that was ever the plan. I think Robin sent Piper a message, telling her he was alive and how to find him.'

'Do you mean the jewellery?'

Sherlock nodded. 'Robin was Piper's only family, and so the gift of a pendant from an unknown dead family member was meant to tell her he was alive. And that he was a thief, thus explaining the reason for his secrecy. As for his location, I believe the answer lies in these.' Sherlock picked up the earrings from the table. 'A broken cat and mouse.'

'Well, the siblings have bird names,' Jane mused. 'Lots of animals in this case.'

'Robin and Piper,' Sherlock said slowly. She felt herself begin to smile. 'They're more than animals, Jane. Will you please get Piper?'

When Piper reappeared, Sherlock had her take a seat on the couch.

'Piper, I wonder if you are familiar with the nursery rhyme of the Crooked Man? It goes like this: *There was a crooked man, and he went a crooked mile. He found a crooked sixpence against a crooked stile. He bought a crooked cat, which caught a crooked mouse, and they all lived together in a little crooked house.*'

Sherlock held out Piper's earrings. 'Your parents named you and your brother for nursery rhymes, intentionally or not. *Peter Piper* and *Robin Redbreast.*'

'Oh, yes,' Piper said. 'We used to recite those as children, each of us with our own poem.'

'And that's how your brother is communicating with you. These earrings aren't broken, they're bent. On purpose. He sent you a crooked cat and a crooked mouse, because Robin, the jewel thief, is the crooked man. So,' Sherlock smiled at Piper, feeling the answer within reach now. 'Where is the crooked house?'

Piper was staring at Sherlock. Jane was too, looking rather proud. 'There was a farmhouse,' Piper said. 'When we were little, back in Iowa, there was a farm family that moved to a big city. Well, big for Iowa. Uh- Dubuque. They put their house up on blocks and towed it a couple of miles down the road and left it in a field. But then their money ran out, and the house just sat there, year after year, out in the weather, with no one keeping it up. It leaned terribly to one side, and we would see it every time we drove that way. We called it the Crooked House.'

Sherlock clapped her hands together sharply. 'Jane, we're going to Iowa.'

It was a little incongruous to see Jane Watson walking around in a white sundress when there was snow on the ground. Sherlock had stuffed a coat into her carry-on and she put it on as they left the airport.

'Well,' said Sherlock, 'this is Dubuque. Only an hour from where

Piper grew up. She stayed in California to wait for Robin, while he went home. Well, as close to home as he could get without being noticed by the people in their hometown, who presumably still held a grudge.'

'You know, Robin could have just sent Piper a letter explaining everything,' Jane said.

'Ah, yes, but remember, Piper Sullivan lived on stolen money her whole life. If she didn't know about it, she could maintain some distance from it. But a letter from her brother could have been used as evidence to convict her of profiting from stolen goods.'

'But instead, Robin's message was too vague,' Jane said. 'It didn't work. They never met up again.'

'They still might,' Sherlock said casually, averting her gaze.

Jane stopped walking. It looked like she was standing in an icy puddle of water, but her shoes remained dry. 'Absolutely not,' she said. 'No channelling, Sherlock. We've discussed this.'

Sherlock kept walking, looking at her phone now. 'If Robin wanted to be found by Piper, I think he'd have been willing to be a little foolish. Thieves usually work with fences, but I bet he'd want to cut out the middleman so he'd be sure to meet Piper himself if she came looking. There's an antique mall on the riverfront. Oh, they have an aquarium next door! With an octopus!'

Jane was not in the habit of throwing fits. Sherlock only ever knew Jane was truly upset when she vanished, which she did now. Jane did not reappear until Sherlock was standing inside the slightly musty antique mall, looking at a posted list of all the stalls.

'Sherlock,' Jane said quietly. 'Look at this one. *Blake Shepherd's Lost and Found.*'

'Another animal nursery rhyme pun!' Sherlock said, smiling, though Jane was still too put out to smile back. 'Blake Shepherd, the black sheep. Lost and now finally found. Jane, you'd better get Piper.'

Of course, it was rather heartbreaking to watch Piper watch her brother, invisible and unheard. Sherlock could tell that Robin was a jewel thief by looking at him, and that he had two cats, played the piano, and liked to dress as a zombie on Halloween. That one was a little on the nose, Sherlock thought, for a reanimated dead man.

'Jane, look at her,' Sherlock said. 'All this time, all this effort, and the message went wrong. She didn't understand it until it was too late. And Robin's healthy, he'll live another thirty years—'

'Thirty years is not that long,' Jane objected.

'And she's about to get kicked out of the waiting room, even I can see that, look how she's fading in and out.'

'Sherlock, channelling the dead is dangerous. Letting another spirit into yourself, allowing it to control your body, could kill you. I won't allow it.'

'Well, I'm hardly afraid to die,' Sherlock said quietly, watching Jane from the corner of her eye. 'It's not like I don't know what will happen.'

Jane looked livid. 'It is not your time!'

'Okay,' Sherlock said. 'But I'm doing it anyway. Hey, Piper! Come here.'

Sherlock woke up in a white room with no windows. She knew she hadn't been sleeping because she was standing up. And she wasn't alone in the quite disorienting space, thankfully. Jane was standing nearby, just in front of a closed door.

'Did I die?' Sherlock asked. 'Did it go wrong?'

Jane had her arms crossed. 'No, you idiot. But you still could, if something happens while you're getting your body back from Piper.' Jane went on lecturing, but Sherlock had stopped listening.

Jane smelled like roses.

Sherlock had always been able to tell a lot about Jane from her appearance and the way she talked, and Jane had told her about her life, of course. But now there was more, Sherlock found, as she slowly walked closer to Jane, the scent of roses, and beneath it a few other things. 'You drove an old car. You helped clean the hospital. And the night you died, someone had burned dinner. Jane, why didn't you tell me that channelling the dead would put me in the waiting room with you?'

'Because it's *dangerous*,' Jane said, distressed. 'I can't ask you to risk your life because of what I – what I might want.'

'What about what I want?' Sherlock asked. 'What if we both...'

'We don't have long,' Jane whispered, and so Sherlock kissed her.

Jane tasted like coffee, not the good stuff, but something overcooked by tired personnel in a field hospital. Jane felt like heaven, soft and sweet, short enough that Sherlock could pull her into her arms. And Jane kissed like she had to make it last.

Sherlock had seen kisses like this on old movie reels, between lovers about to be separated. But at the same time, it was a kiss of lovers united after a long time apart. It was a first kiss and probably an only kiss, and Sherlock, who felt so detached from the world, was finally fully present in one place for the first time in her life. And she wasn't alone there.

Jane's sundress was light and slightly rough under Sherlock's hands, and Jane's hair was smooth where it brushed against Sherlock's cheek. Everything was familiar and at the same time novel, a new conversation between old friends, lips and mouths moving as always, but finally together and without sound.

When Sherlock woke up again in the antique mall, she could still taste coffee and smell roses. There was red lipstick on her cheek. Sherlock didn't wipe it away.

Piper was gone. Moved on, Jane said. They had dinner with Robin to answer his questions, not that Jane ate anything, of course, and then Sherlock found a hotel overlooking the river.

They didn't talk about the kiss. But Jane had a faint blush to her cheeks that had lasted all through dinner, and Sherlock didn't imagine that she was much better off herself.

Sherlock had the TV remote in her hand, but she hadn't turned on the set yet to look for a show that Jane might like. 'Is it uncomfortable for spirits there?' Sherlock asked. 'In the waiting room, in limbo?'

Jane frowned slightly. 'For some. But you know you're helping with that, Sherlock. As soon as the spirits know who was responsible for their murder, they're drawn away into the next world, where I'm told it's quite nice.'

Sherlock looked down to where the couch was dipping slightly under her weight. It didn't do that where Jane was sitting. 'You know, your case wasn't unsolvable,' she said quietly. 'Jane, I do know who killed you.'

There was a hint of surprise on Jane's face that quickly faded to fondness. Then Jane put her finger to her ruby lips and shook her head.

So for the first and only time, Sherlock Holmes kept the solution to herself.

A MOTHER'S REPUTATION

Stacy Noe

MISS SHERLOCK HOLMES FIXED HER BONNET SECURELY OVER HER dark hair, then was certain to slam the door to her room as she left. She was a tall, sturdy girl, her white skin unfashionably tanned, and hair not quite where it belonged. She planted her heeled boots solidly against the wood floor as she made the landing, and descended to the house entry.

She preferred to be known for her noisy entrances and exits, so that no one would suspect her quiet ones.

Her landlady, Mrs Hudson, was by the front door, looking through the cards that had been delivered. Sherlock frowned, knowing the cards were for the other young ladies of the house. Her room was directly above, she heard everyone at the door.

'Really dear, where are you going in such a clatter?' Mrs Hudson asked, without looking up. She was an imposing lady, her greying blonde hair done up fashionably, if a bit severely, and her pale blue gown bringing out the starkness of her eyes. Her complexion was flawless, even if it was pale as a ghost's.

'Out,' Sherlock announced flatly. She had been shunted about to various landladies who were supposed to turn her into a proper young lady, since her mother's giving up hope on managing it herself. Mother had described Mrs Hudson as, 'A very upright and capable landlady. One who will prevent any sort of shenanigans.' Sherlock was set on squaring off with her sooner, rather than later.

Mrs Hudson glanced up briefly; Sherlock gave her a perfunctory, soulless smile. She returned her eyes to the cards, a slight upturn in the corners of her mouth. Finally, tossing the cards back onto the plate, she said, 'Just do be careful dear. We are supposed to be upholding an image, after all.'

Unfortunately, the anticipated stand-off was interrupted by the front door opening. In blew another young lady, like a rush of leaves caught by a breeze. She slammed the door behind her, a thick, black braid settling over her shoulder. She was taller even than Sherlock, with dark skin, and eyes lined with thick, black lashes. She seemed to share Sherlock's views on fashion – as free as possible with no cage, and only one petticoat and a crinoline.

'And just where have you been?' Mrs Hudson asked, turning to take the new girl in. 'And is that blood on your hem?'

Sherlock's eyes were immediately drawn. Sure enough, right above her buttoned-up boots, were droplets of blood.

The new girl laughed. 'It is. My last patient was a husband. He thought that he would drink until the sun came up this morning, and the sun has yet to come up. His wife vehemently disagreed when he finally deigned to come home. I had to stitch his head where it met with her bottle.'

'Oh, dear,' sighed Mrs Hudson. 'I don't suppose the end of days truly has arrived?'

Sherlock stared. Never had she heard such an announcement, and certainly not seen such a one met so calmly. Still, she couldn't help but automatically correct Mrs Hudson's response. 'While the aurora has certainly been unusual for us, and probably unusually bright, it is simply an atmospheric phenomenon. Although, this would not be the first time that man has misinterpreted such things as catastrophic.'

Both women turned to her, looking amused. 'Yes dear, thank you,' said Mrs Hudson, wryly. Before Sherlock could continue, she said, 'Allow me to introduce my daughter, Miss Joahana Watson. Joahana, this is Miss Sherlock Holmes, our newest guest.' Turning archly to her daughter, Mrs Hudson added, 'So odd, how you never seem available for appointments with families.'

Joahana smiled widely, 'Yes, how strange that there's always a conflict.'

Sherlock frowned, looking between the mother and daughter. Then, seeing no reason to completely abandon her manners, she brusquely offered her hand to Joahana. 'A pleasure to make your acquaintance.'

Joahana shook enthusiastically. 'And you, Miss Holmes. Please, call me Joahana.'

Uncertain how to respond, Sherlock simply bowed her head.

As if she had been met with equal zeal, Joahana replied, 'You were leaving, Miss Holmes?'

'Yes, to send a telegram.'

'Then I shall accompany you!' Before Sherlock could protest, Joahana opened the door and stepped out. Below, the sounds of the city in chaos filled the house.

'Do be careful, dears,' Mrs Hudson called after. 'End of times or no, London is not in her usual temper.'

The pavement and streets were filled. Joahana pulled Sherlock off the bottom step with her, linking their arms. Sherlock chafed, but there was no room to pull away. She also recognised that two bodies pushed their way through the throng more effectively than one. From the street corners, men shouted about sinners and the wrath of God.

The sky was an odd, reddish colour. It was a cloudy daytime, but the night had been no darker. Sherlock had read the papers from the light of her window. London, and beyond, was in an uproar.

Squeezing her arm, Joahana asked, 'Do you truly not believe in the end of days?'

'Of course not. There's a perfectly sound, scientific explanation for all of this.'

Joahana spoke directly into Sherlock's ear over the din. 'Do continue.'

'Solar flares, of course.'

'You mean flames from the sun? Wouldn't that simply light the world on fire?'

Sherlock looked at Joahana as they reached the corner. 'I would think you ignorant, but I should hope the Ladies Auxiliary is better than that.'

Joahana laughed loudly and pulled them across the street. They dodged people and carriages alike.

Reaching the other side, Joahana continued pulling them along. 'Why would you think I'm a member of such a group?'

'Please don't insult me.' Sherlock sniffed. 'I know they operate in this area, and you just admitted to your own mother your activities.'

'Yes, I'll admit it,' Joahana smiled broadly. 'I'm one of those rogue, female doctors.'

'Not a proper doctor,' Sherlock pointed out.

Joahana's nose wrinkled, and she admitted, 'Not an official doctor. No medical school for me. Mother does have her reputation to maintain.'

'Nonetheless,' Sherlock said, 'I should like to be a doctor, as well.'

'Oh no, doctoring is not something you just do, my dear Miss Holmes. I was trained up, at my dear, departed father's knee for many years. But it is something you may observe.'

Sherlock's face, having darkened at being told no, brightened. 'Oh, I do like to observe.' They walked in silence for a moment, dodging people hurrying by, others arguing loudly on the pavement. 'But why shouldn't you have gone to medical school? There are lady doctors.'

'There are, the lucky things. But Mother's reputation was the obstacle.' When Sherlock's face darkened again, Joahana flew to her absent mother's defence. 'Do not blame her, please! My mother is a very intelligent woman, but she was not given my advantages. No training in anything, and now she runs a boarding house.'

'I can only conclude then, that your mother is a liar,' Sherlock stated flatly.

Joahana gave a dramatic gasp, but when Sherlock looked at her sharply, she was smiling. 'Not very tactful, are you?' Joahana chided.

'Neither is lying.'

'On the contrary, my mother is extremely tactful. And underhanded. Don't these two things go hand in hand? And how exactly did you conclude that?'

Sherlock pulled them between two men arguing. 'She convinced my mother she was a lady of good breeding.' She looked at Joahana. 'Not that I'm implying she isn't.'

'Of course not.'

'And that she ran a household that would tame me. She implied there were other young ladies in the house with the same behaviours as mine, and that they were well under her control.'

'Aren't you shocked?'

'I'm impressed.' Sherlock was enthralled by the idea of someone lying to her own parents' faces. Tricking them, even. 'But how does she explain your continued absence?'

'More lies, of course. Mother tells people I'm working in a soup kitchen, which is frightening enough. Or studying to become a nun, which is absolutely terrifying. No one will ever figure it out because they quickly regret asking, and enquire no further. Either is unladylike, though mostly socially acceptable. But no one wishes to risk getting ensnared in that conversation.'

Sherlock found herself even more impressed. 'She truly is an accomplished liar. But she would have to be. My mother is very discerning.'

'Mother is, and it's young ladies like us that benefit.'

'I know. There are at least two other young ladies in the house that are in your Auxiliary. Another seems to be a scientist of some type; a young man was enquiring about some caustic chemicals. And I believe another to be a sort of political radical.'

Joahana looked impressed. 'How do you know all this? You've barely lived in the house a week.'

'My room is directly above the front door.'

'Ah, yes. Sound does travel.'

'I suppose Mrs Hudson heard about my mother's trials, and my mother's maid was directed to put a good word into her ear?'

Joahana laughed. 'Nothing quite so simple. But yes.'

The crowds streamed around them as they stopped on the next corner, the men loud with their signs declaring the end of times. A bobby stood in the road, whistle blowing endlessly, trying to direct some of the chaos.

'Good morning, Officer Lestrade!' Joahana pulled Sherlock across the street, dodging the traffic, and Lestrade's admonishments.

'Young ladies would be better off at home, at a time like this!' he shouted behind them. The rest was lost, as his distraction dissolved the meagre control he had achieved.

'My mother's house offers you an opportunity,' Joahana continued as they reached the relative safety of the opposite corner. 'It is up to you if you wish to take it.'

Sherlock was so quiet that Joahana pulled them out of the crowd, into an alcove. Cautiously Sherlock asked her, 'Just like that? With no expectations in return?'

'We require your discretion, regardless of your decision. If you choose to stay, you must not make too large of a spectacle. And we ask that you remain as safe as possible. If you will be wandering into shady spaces, as I suspect you will,' Joahana gave Sherlock a smug wink, 'then take one of us with you.'

'You, or your mother?'

'Heavens no!' Joahana pulled them back into the fray. 'Mother stays home and plays her part. Myself, or my stepfather, perhaps. He may look aged and stodgy, but he was a pugilist in his youth.' Joahana turned the last corner. 'You could even ask Miss Moriarty.'

'And who is Miss Moriarty?'

'Second floor, back room. She has her own knife.' Before Sherlock could respond, Joahana continued. 'Your mother and my mother are very alike.'

'I sincerely doubt that.'

'Indeed, they are,' Joahana insisted. 'Your mother does not truly care what mischief you get up to. She cares that word of it does not get around. Her reputation is what she cares about.'

Reflexively, Sherlock opened her mouth to disagree. Before the words passed her lips, she realised Joahana must be correct.

With a dramatic flourish, Joahana announced, 'And I have delivered you, safely to your destination!'

Sure enough, the telegraph office stood before them. The ladies nodded politely as a gentleman opened the door for them, leading him inside. He tipped his tall hat.

In stark contrast to the chaos outside, the telegraph office was nearly silent.

A knot of men stood around the cage; all concentration trained upon something in particular. There was a hushed murmuring, and no one looked up as they came in.

'What's this then?' cheerfully called the man that had opened the door for them.

Sombre faces turned to them. 'It's Mr Abernathy. He's dead, poor man.'

Sherlock craned her head to catch a view, the knot opening just wide enough to show poor Mr Abernathy slumped over his desk, and to spit out the harried office manager, Mr Downs.

'My dears,' the fatherly, greyed man bustled towards them. 'This is no place for young ladies right now. The office is closed.' He shooed them out, practically slamming the door behind them. He smartly turned the sign and pulled the shade with a snap.

'Well! That was rather rude.' She turned to Sherlock. 'It seems as though your errand must be delayed.' She offered her arm again.

Sherlock stared. 'Don't you want to know what happened?'

Joahana sighed. 'Poor Mr Abernathy was quite dead; past any help I could offer, I'm afraid. Now I only dread having to go back and tell Mother the sad news. She always did like Mr Abernathy.'

Sherlock's mind whirled. She stood silently for so long that Joahana spoke again. 'Sherlock, are you quite all right? The sight of Mr Abernathy didn't upset you, did it?'

The use of her Christian name caught Sherlock's attention. She chafed at it momentarily, then realised it only bothered her because it was something her mother would criticise. Instead, she said, 'I know what happened.'

Joahana's eyes brightened. 'Do you? Didn't he simply have a heart attack? He was old, and his heart has never been strong.'

'Yes,' Sherlock agreed, 'but it wasn't from natural causes.'

'Surely, you're not suggesting someone killed Mr Abernathy. He didn't have an enemy in the world!' Joahana's expression was more interested than horrified.

'No, not murder. But he was killed nonetheless.' She scrabbled at the ladies' bag that hung from her wrist. Pulling out a handful of telegraph paper, she pushed them at Joahana. 'I've been in contact with a gentleman, an astronomer.'

Joahana raised an eyebrow but took the papers. She sifted through them, amusement turning to confusion. 'Is this about the solar flames?'

'Flares,' Sherlock corrected, reflexively. 'He hadn't thought the effects would reach us for days, but it was less than twenty-four hours before the aurora overtook us. The electricity must have overtaken the circuits.'

'He was electrocuted?' Joahana's eyes grew large.

'I believe so, I only got a glimpse of him. But it appeared his left fingers were blackened.'

Joahana was nodding, 'Yes, yes. He always worked the telegraph with his left hand, so he could write with his proper hand.' After a moment she asked, 'Are you going to go tell them?'

Sherlock shook herself. 'Why? They wouldn't listen to me. It would sound ridiculous to them.'

'Why would that matter? You would be proven correct by the papers, in just a day or two. They would know then.' When Sherlock didn't answer right away, she held the telegraph papers out to her. 'You live in my mother's house now. What are you going to do?'

Sherlock took the papers thoughtfully. She nodded, then turned smartly back to the door. Ignoring the closed sign and uninviting shade, she opened it and marched in, Joahana on her heels.

'Gentlemen, I believe I can shed some light on this matter.'

The Curse of the Amethyst Society

Katya de Becerra

FAMED BIOLOGIST FOUND DEAD IN HER OFFICE

The Red Gazette, 2 May 1995

This week, Moscow State University's Biology Department is farewelling one of its brightest stars. Professor Vera Klimova (38) was found unresponsive in her office by a Zoology Department colleague on Monday. Moscow Department of Criminal Investigations has ruled out foul play, declaring a heart attack as the cause of death.

Professor Klimova had won multiple prestigious awards, including the USSR State Prize and Russian Federation National Award, for her ground-breaking research into animal toxins. A debilitating ophidiophobia resulting from a frightening early childhood incident with a northern viper ignited Klimova's lifelong passion for this work. In a cruel stroke of irony, while Klimova's regular office was undergoing renovations, she was issued a temporary working space in the Zoology Department adjacent to the serpentarium. This proximity was causing Klimova a great deal of stress, revealed a source close to the deceased.

Professor Klimova is remembered by her parents, siblings, and the Ladies of the Amethyst Society.

MOSCOW, NEAR PATRIARCH'S PONDS

5 May, 1995

'Your real name is Sherlock?' Valentina Vatska was trying not to laugh as she copied the unusual name from her flatmate's passport into their joint PI license application form. Valentina wondered if she'd read it wrong, the letters twisting in the dancing candlelight. But no, there it was: *Sherlock Arturovna Holmesova*.

Bureaucrats at the licensing office would have a field day with "Marina" Holmesova's legal name, which sounded so definitively not Russian it was sure to attract additional scrutiny the girls didn't want or need.

'Killing shadows,' Marina – or was it *Sherlock*? – replied. As if it explained things.

Valentina gave her flatmate an inquiring look. Even after a year of them studying at the MSU and sharing an apartment, Valentina's co-investigator, friend, and – *she hoped* – one day something more, was still full of surprises.

The young woman in question sat in the armchair on the other side of the scratched-up coffee table. In the near dark, she was a mysterious presence, her skin radiant. A violin was pressed against her right shoulder, a delicate bow paused in mid-air.

With Yeltsin's antics front and centre and the rouble in trouble again, addressing the power blackouts was the last thing on the government's to-do list. That meant tonight, like on most nights, the district's electricity was out. But that didn't deter Marina. She could play with her eyes closed.

'I beg your pardon?' Valentina asked when Marina didn't elaborate.

'*Killing Shadows*. My parents are fans of the book,' Marina said. 'They met at the Doyle Morland fan club in Saratov.'

'I've heard of a provincial town named Saratov,' Valentina teased. 'But the rest of it sounds like Martian to me.'

Marina sighed. 'Doyle Morland was an English writer. *Killing Shadows* was his breakout book. Sherlock is its main character. My parents named me after him, but unless I have to produce my documentation,' – that earned Valentina an evocative look – 'I go by "Marina".'

'Sherlock! How bourgeoisie of your parents, anti-Soviet even,' Valentina noted, hiding a laugh. 'And it sounds like a boy's name.'

'That's a rude thing to say, Comrade Vatska,' Marina deadpanned, but a ghost of a smile warmed the edge of her lips.

'We're not called comrades anymore, Sherlock,' Valentina parried.

'What are we then?'

'Who knows? Only time will tell. So what should I call you now? Marina or Sherlock?'

'Only my parents call me Sherlock.'

'Marina, it is.'

As the evening unfurled, a furious storm whipping lilacs in the nearby Patriarch's Ponds park into a frenzy, Valentina's mood soured. She remembered their endless shopping list and all the repairs their leaky, crumbling apartment urgently needed. She thought after solving their first murder case, with Marina mentioned by name in two news articles, they'd be swimming in fee-paying clients with mysteries to solve, but alas. To make their already miserable finances even more dire, Valentina had recently blown a small fortune on photocopying flyers for their yet-to-be-licensed investigative agency. Those were dutifully plastered all over campus and surrounds, but nobody had come calling yet. If the girls didn't come into some roubles soon, they'd be sitting in total darkness, drinking unboiled water for dinner.

There came a deafening roar of thunder, concealing all other sound in the apartment. Valentina took a moment to realise someone was knocking on their front door. A nervous rap at first, then a pounding.

A glance at the ancient pendulum clock's phosphorous face revealed it was past midnight.

Late hour brings foul guests, Valentina's grandmother used to say.

Sherlock "Marina" Holmesova felt a certain gratitude for the blackout-induced dark, for the privacy it afforded. Because their neighbours were surely awake now, congregating by the spyholes, hoping for a glimpse of the late-night visitor.

But who came calling at this hour? *Improper, impolite*, Marina's provincial intelligentsia mother would say. Could it be the dreaded authorities, coming to make an arrest for some unknown crime? Valentina definitely looked spooked – spooked enough for Marina to consider ignoring whoever was knocking so insistently. But then…Marina had a feeling about this, her senses tingling. She set her violin aside, picked up the candle and headed for the shadowed hallway.

Out there, on the dark staircase, she found a well-dressed but visibly shaken woman. Instead of a greeting, the stranger gasped and proceeded to wrestle her way inside, where she promptly collapsed into Marina's arms.

'What on earth is going on!' Valentina rushed to help.

Together, the girls led their swaying guest into the living room, where the woman flopped down on the couch. The stranger had no purse on her, but in her right hand she clutched a city-circle metro card. Her hair and clothes were damp from the rain and she was breathing heavily. Marina took a discreet sniff, detecting no smell of alcohol. The visitor's state was likely caused by stress and fright.

'I'm Polikova... Alexandra Ivanovna Polikova,' the strange woman managed to say. 'I need your h-help.'

'You're safe here, Alexandra Ivanovna.' Marina drew out the woman's proper name as a way of grounding her. When Marina found Valentina's gaze in the near dark, their fleeting contact communicated faster than words could.

'I'll put on a kettle,' Valentina said and disappeared into the kitchen.

With the storm reluctantly easing up, the night clouds were beginning to part, allowing milky moonlight to peek through. From the living room, Marina watched her flatmate's outline as Valentina moved around the kitchen, pouring water, striking a match.

Waiting for Alexandra Polikova to come to her senses, Marina relaxed into an armchair and studied the woman in the limited light of the candle. Alexandra must have been in her early forties. Her clothing, conservative and stylish, was likely tailored to order. A good seamstress wasn't easy to find, even harder to keep. Alexandra's look implied she was well connected and had some disposable income. Her shoes were lacquered flats, a layer of mud concealing their colour. What extravagant footwear for such terrible weather! Alexandra must've left in a hurry, having had no time to change into gumboots.

'You are tenured at the MSU, aren't you?' Marina addressed Alexandra, just as Valentina returned carrying a tray piled with cups and plates of sugar cubes and sliced lemon.

'Correct!' Alexandra exclaimed, reaching for a cup. 'But how did you know?'

'Strawberry in Chocolate,' Marina said. 'Your lipstick.'

Alexandra's hand flew to her mouth but didn't touch it.

'I believe that particular shade is all the rage on campus right now,' Marina went on. 'Since the campus pharmacy is the only location within the city bounds that sells it at a heavily discounted price.'

Alexandra seemed impressed, but Marina wasn't done.

'And then there's your necklace,' Marina said.

'What about it?' Alexandra's brows arched and her expression turned guarded.

The necklace in question circled Alexandra's neck like a noose. The unusual design featured a two-headed snake and a pair of scarabs crowding the central gem that had a purple tinge.

'That's an amethyst, isn't it?' Marina said. 'The other day, a newspaper article mentioned a certain organisation called the Amethyst Society in connection to a famous MSU biologist who had been recently found dead on campus…'

'Vera Klimova!' Alexandra exclaimed. 'Poor, poor Verochka. She's the reason I'm here!' Alexandra pulled a crumpled piece of paper from inside her cardigan. It was one of their photocopied ads.

Marina didn't need to see her flatmate's face to know Valentina was grinning ear to ear right now. Those costly ads worked after all!

'You must be Marina Holmesova. It appears you are indeed quite good,' Alexandra said. 'I have a case for you, which I hope you will accept.'

From the seemingly endless depths of her cardigan, Alexandra produced a small plastic folder, which she placed on the table next to the nearly melted candle.

'A deposit. Yours to keep, regardless of the outcome of your investigation. I will pay you the same amount after.'

'You don't believe Vera Klimova's death was an accident,' Marina said, a statement rather than a question.

Alexandra's shoulders sagged. She nodded. 'The detectives dismissed the very idea of murder. But it gets worse, much worse…'

'You're next on the killer's list,' Marina said. 'And it all has to do with that amethyst necklace you wear.'

Of all the secret clubs and associations operating on the MSU's sprawling campus, the Amethyst Society had to be the most secretive. So secretive, in fact, that Valentina had never even heard of it until Alexandra Polikova wrestled her way into their apartment. Even Marina, who tended to be a step ahead where most mysteries were concerned, had no knowledge of the Amethyst Society beyond the fact that it existed.

As Alexandra relayed her wild tale, her nervous fingers bothering the amethyst necklace that wrapped around her throat, a tight knot of disquiet formed in Valentina's chest and wouldn't let go.

'Earlier this month, Vera Klimova was elected as our Society's new High Priestess. She was dead the next day,' Alexandra said as she slurped her tea.

Sensing Marina's unspoken questions, Alexandra launched into an explanation. 'Every seven years, we must choose our new leader, the prime guardian of the amethyst. This year marked one such occasion. Lady Vera was to lead us into the new decade, but she was killed before the transfer of power could take place. There were no signs of an attack, no blood, no wounds. It was as if she was visited by a murderous ghost!'

'Ghosts can't murder anyone,' Valentina said. *Given how they don't exist,* she held back from adding. Having grown up in a household that effortlessly mixed religion and superstition, it went against her nature to bring up ghosts this late into the night. Even if she personally didn't believe in them. So, instead she asked, 'What exactly made you suspect Vera's death was unnatural?'

'Arina Makeeva, our outgoing Head Priestess – she was the one to find poor Vera – told us Vera's face carried a twisted look of fright.' Alexandra pulled again at the chain of her necklace. 'Arina said she only ever saw Vera terrified like that once before, during her Fearless Initiation ceremony, while seeking to join the Society many years ago.'

That jolted Marina out of her contemplation. 'Fearless Initiation?'

Alexandra nodded. 'Every prospective member must undergo it. During the ceremony we face our deepest fear.'

'Initiation...' Marina said, not addressing anyone in particular but rather thinking out loud. 'A way for a secret society to test their neophytes' mettle...' She met Alexandra's eyes. 'And how many people knew Vera's deepest fear?'

Alexandra sat up straighter and set her empty tea cup on the table with a little too much force. 'The Society's inner circle knew, of course, myself included. But Vera's dislike of snakes wasn't exactly a secret – she spoke of her phobia openly. What exactly are you implying?'

'Nothing. For now,' Marina said, unbothered. 'Earlier, when I said you were next on the killer's list, you didn't contradict me. Why?'

Alexandra pulled in a laboured breath, exhaled. 'Because I'm the next in line to become the High Priestess. And today someone tried to kill me. They sent me this.'

She showed the girls a piece of paper, which contained a hand-written code: *E1 5/3 20:00*

'Today's date. But E1? A grid location?' Marina said. 'Somewhere on campus?'

'Yes, it's the Observatory, MSU's tallest building,' Alexandra confirmed. 'I assumed the note came from a…client. I run a Mycology Lab, and it overproduces specimen, you see, so I sell some of it, leaving perfectly enough for science. It's not legal, yet I harm no one. I couldn't come with this to the police. I'd lose my job. Or worse. You know how these things are.'

Valentina knew exactly how these things were, and so did Marina. With the rouble unstable, when people got paid at all, often it was in what their employer produced. Milk, homeware, toys, bricks. Some things were easier to sell on the market than others. University staff, evidently, had to get creative. The local police would hardly be understanding about it.

Alexandra's well-off appearance made more sense now. Her clothes weren't tailored on a professor's salary.

'What happened when you arrived at the Observatory?' Marina urged.

'Further instructions were left at the entrance, directing me to the roof. Once I got there, someone shoved me toward the edge. I have a terrible fear of heights, you see. I screamed and held on to the railing! They ran away before they could finish the job. I didn't see them.'

'With you gone, who would benefit?' Marina asked. 'Other Society members, perhaps?'

Alexandra flinched. 'Sasha Brodskaya and Vika Kozub, the next two in line for the Head Priestess position. The role attracts a sizeable honorarium.' She seemed loathe to share the latter detail, as if the idea of her fellow Society Ladies pursuing enrichment, even willing to kill for it, was debasing.

'I'd like to meet them,' Marina said, 'and the current Head Priestess, too. Would it also be possible to get a copy of the Society's by-laws?'

'The latter is easily arranged,' Alexandra replied. 'As for meeting what's left of the inner circle… After Vera's death, Sasha and Vika have been keeping a low profile. The current Head Priestess… Professor Makeeva is an enigmatic figure, even by the Society's standards. She is not easy to pin down on a normal day. But let me see what I can do. Come tomorrow at 6pm to the Society's headquarters, the Belltower.'

She stood up, ready to leave.

'One more question, if you please?' Marina asked. The candle had long burned away, but the moonlight brought some relief from the dark. 'What exactly is the purpose of your Society?'

With Alexandra's shoulders pulled back, her impressive height towered over the girls. 'We guard the world from an evil, cursed object.' She tapped a finger against her necklace. 'This is a replica, of course. We all wear it, to remind us of our duty, of the cross we bear, but also to protect us from the real amethyst's vile influence. For as long as we live, we're never to take it off unless absolutely necessary. Which reminds me… Our poor Vera wasn't wearing hers the day she died; the clasp had been damaged so her necklace was off for repairs. But don't look so sceptical, dear,' Alexandra addressed Valentina, whose eyebrows formed a quizzical arch. 'The cursed amethyst's influence is far-reaching; it penetrates even the most logical of minds. You'll see what I mean soon enough.'

Having issued her sinister pronouncement, Alexandra walked out of the apartment, to brave the night and the mysterious danger lurking in the shadows.

Marina slept poorly that night.

The rain returned after Alexandra's departure, and its incessant whispering leaked into Marina's dreams, turning them dark and urgent. A blur of chasing feet, a frightened scream, a heartbeat's rapid drum… and the snakes. Terrible, hissing shapes slithering out from every corner. A sleek, brown body of a northern viper tightened around Marina's throat. And above it all, like some cursed sun, reigned the wicked amethyst, bathing the world in its unholy light.

Morning brought reprieve, but Marina remained on high alert. Being hired for a new case may have boosted her confidence, but what if she failed? And what if she endangered Valentina in the process? There was a killer on the loose, exploiting their victim's deepest fears. Vera Klimova appeared to have been frightened to death, and the same method was pursued with Alexandra, albeit unsuccessfully.

But what if Alexandra was lying? As the next in line to lead this mysterious Amethyst Society, she'd come into a certain deal of power, as well as the honorarium. Everyone struggled financially these days, though Alexandra seemed to be doing well, selling her illegal mushrooms on the side.

Marina needed more information.

'And where do you think you're going?' Valentina demanded when she caught Marina sneaking out.

'I thought I'd have a look at Vera's office. If her death is being treated as non-suspicious, surely they missed something, a clue.'

'Wait up. I'm coming with you.'

Marina sighed but didn't attempt to leave on her own. If she did, she'd never hear the end of it.

'I'm ready. Let's go!' When Valentina reappeared from the depths of the apartment, she was carrying two pairs of gumboots, recently cleaned. The drizzle outside appeared innocent, but their walk to the nearest metro station tracked through a bulldozed sidewalk, full of muddy puddles. Unlike Alexandra, they couldn't afford to ruin their shoes.

Twenty minutes later, the gloomy underpass spat them back out, and soon they were entering the campus grounds. On a Sunday, all was empty and unmoving, aside from a street sweeper melancholically swinging his broom.

'Do you know where we're going?' Valentina asked.

'That article about Klimova's death mentioned her temporary office was near the serpentarium. There's only one serpentarium on campus.'

'Lots of snakes, right? Goody!'

'You're not afraid, are you?' Marina teased.

'I actually like snakes.' Valentina shrugged. 'My brother used to keep a pet natrix, a harmless, well-natured creature.'

'I doubt Vera Klimova would agree with that assessment.'

Marina was the first to spot the serpentarium, and the unremarkable whitebrick building next to it. Her recently acquired master key proved worthy of its exorbitant price when it opened the whitebrick's service door for them.

It was uncharacteristically warm inside and the stale air carried a hint of mildew. The near sweltering conditions were likely a consequence of the building sharing a circulation system with the serpentarium. Sweating, the girls followed the slippery cement stairs to the second floor, where one of the offices still had bits of a police seal stuck over the keyhole.

The first one in, Marina headed straight for the desk that claimed nearly half of the small room. She produced a loupe from her messenger bag and proceeded to study the desk's surface.

'A shard of glass on an otherwise clean desk,' Marina noted, using a plastic bag to pick up a small pebble-sized object lodged amid the grooves of the cracked wood. '*Purple* glass,' she added, studying the uneven fragment through her loupe.

'What makes you think it's glass and not, let's say, quartz?' Valentina asked, coming closer.

Valentina smelled of vanilla and wild peppermint, a scent so undeniably attractive that Marina had to fight an inexplicable pull to lean in for a lungful of Valentina's hair.

'Quartz doesn't have bubbles trapped in it,' Marina said, winking at Valentina to conceal her inner turmoil.

'That makes sense.' Valentina looked a little peeved, perhaps because she hadn't thought of it herself. Her eyes were alert and bright. She was taken by the case, by the thrill of deduction. 'Alexandra did mention her necklace was a replica. Perhaps, the Amethyst Ladies can only afford to produce glass copies for its members? Or maybe it's symbolic – only the original is made with an amethyst, and the replicas have glass?'

'Perhaps, perhaps.' Marina waited for Valentina to reach the necessary conclusions herself.

'So, what happened here, in addition to a dead body, resulted in a broken glass necklace – likely, the type of necklace all the Ladies of the Amethyst wear. And Alexandra mentioned that Vera's necklace was off for repairs, meaning…it wasn't her necklace that broke!' Valentina's face was flushed with the excitement of deduction. She and Marina exchanged a meaningful look, both reaching the same explanation: the fragment of glass Marina found had to have come from the murderer's necklace.

'She was killed by a fellow Lady of the Amethyst,' Valentina said, grimly.

'Yes, but which one?' Marina replied. 'Let's finish having a look around,' she said next, coming to crouch by the air duct not far from the desk. Squinting against the smelly air blowing from the duct, she produced another plastic bag and used it to peel off some debris from the widely spaced metal grille.

A hiss drifted from the duct, but Marina was lost in the task, not paying attention.

'What do you know,' she said, looking up sideways at Valentina, who stepped away to study the bookshelves. 'A piece of reptilian skin stuck to the grille! It appears foul air is not the only thing that can travel between these buildings, but creatures too. And I bet this particular creature was helped on its journey!'

'Watch out!' Valentina screamed, pointing at something behind Marina.

Everything slowed down. Marina turned just in time to see a brown viper emerge from the duct.

The snake launched itself at her.

Valentina rushed to Marina's aid, but the snake didn't waste any time. It slithered up, up, up, toward its victim's throat.

Marina's hands slid against the reptile's body, seeking purchase.

Close enough to see the detailed pattern of the snake's skin, Valentina exhaled the tense breath she was holding. When she reached for the snake, Marina slapped her hand away.

'It'll bite you,' Marina cried out. 'I won't let it hurt you!'

'It's perfectly harmless,' Valentina assured her. While she was no snake expert, her brother's pet had taught her a valuable lesson long ago. She knew how to tell the harmless natrix from the poisonous northern viper, the two local breeds often mistaken for one another.

'Someone made its skin look more threatening.' Valentina pointed out where the paint was peeling off in parts. 'The poor snake must be scared out of its mind!' She lifted the natrix from Marina's shoulders and let it curl around her arm.

'It's a good thing I don't have ophidiophobia,' Marina said, studying the snake. 'If I did, I'd likely be dead from a heart attack. Just like Vera Klimova.'

After entrusting the snake to the hands of the serpentarium's befuddled weekend attendant, the girls headed for the Belltower, only making a brief stop while Marina used a public phone to reach out to a trusted contact at her local police office. The painted state of the snake's skin was evidence of foul play. That meant Klimova's case would need to be reopened.

But even though Marina now was one step closer to solving the mystery, could she identify the killer before another Lady of the Amethyst Society had to die?

The Belltower's southern gate was unlocked. Inside, a carpet stretched the length of the narrow hallway, disappearing into shadows. Indentations in the walls indicated where windows once stood before some dedicated mason filled them in with bricks and cement. Mounted torches bathed everything in a medieval glow.

The temperature dropped. Marina's breath left her in white puffs.

The cursed amethyst is near.

The thought shocked her. She didn't believe in curses, but a part of her couldn't resist the dark pull of the idea.

As they proceeded deeper in, countless eyes tracked their progress. Portraits, photographs, claiming the walls. The Society's notable members, all women, with faces proud and stern, eyes weighted down, as if by a heavy burden. Each and every one of them had the familiar necklace caging their throats, the purple gem guarded by a pair of beetles and a snake.

'The first recorded ownership of this cursed amethyst is attributed to Edward Heron-Allen, an English writer, polymath, and a practitioner of chiromancy...' Valentina read out loud from the plaque mounted next to an ornate vault.

'Likely looted by the British colonialists during the Indian Mutiny in 1855, the amethyst was brought to England... A trail of troubles, destitution and suicide followed the mysterious stone as it changed possession several times before ending up in the hands of Heron-Allen in 1890 – shortly after, he too started to experience terrible events.'

Marina grew entranced by Valentina's voice, the sound of it echoing in the cavernous space. Marina shivered, but not because she was spooked. Her flatmate was...beautiful, Marina realised with a start, soaking up every bit of Valentina's spirited reading.

'Heron-Allen attempted on several occasions to get rid of the stone,' Valentina went on, oblivious to her flatmate's gaze. 'He threw it into a river, he tried burning it, he even left it buried in the ground far from his residence. But each time, the accursed amethyst was returned to him, culminating in a desperate plan to keep the stone in a specially designed box behind seven levels of protection. Heron-Allen also commissioned a jeweller to surround the amethyst with protective charms – a double-headed snake on one end and a pair of scarabs of Queen Hatasu of Thebes on the other. After Heron-Allen's death, the amethyst was given to his bank for safekeeping, with instructions not to open the box until three and thirty years had passed after his death. While its current locality is kept from the public, protecting the world from the amethyst's terrible influence…'

'…has been the sole duty of the Ladies of the Amethyst Society,' concluded Alexandra Polikova as she joined the girls by the vault. 'I'm glad to see you here,' she said, looking at Marina. 'I was worried you might've changed your mind.'

'I can't imagine ever changing my mind about a case so intriguing,' Marina said. 'The Amethyst Society sure has a fascinating history. It is odd, however, that I couldn't find any record of it in the public domain.'

'We thrive on secrecy,' Alexandra replied. 'Keeping a low profile is a must, considering the object we guard. Whenever the amethyst ventured out into the world, misery and death soon followed.'

'Perhaps it was the object's bloody colonial history that haunted its colonialist owners,' Marina said. 'And the misfortunes that befell the amethyst's past owners were but a symbol of their suppressed guilt.'

'The curse is quite real, my dear,' said Alexandra gravely. 'It befalls *everyone*, colonialist or not. Take our poor Lady Vera, for instance.'

'I don't think it was the curse that took her,' Marina said, pressing a possessive hand against her messenger bag, which contained two pieces of evidence from the office of the deceased.

'What have you found?' Alexandra asked, voice trembling. As if a light switch was flipped, Marina could see tangible signs of Alexandra's anxiety. The dark half-moons under her eyes, the bitten pulp of her lips.

'Enough to say that Professor Klimova's death was an inside job.'

'A Society member?' Alexandra cried out. 'We take great care to only admit those with a strong enough will to guard the accursed amethyst. Perhaps someone unworthy slipped through…'

'Is that the Society's by-laws? May I?' Marina changed the topic, indicating the leather-bound book in Alexandra's hands. The dark purple cover of the volume carried a hexagon shaped stamp.

'Yes, indeed.' Alexandra offered the book to Marina. 'You can read all about the cursed amethyst in here.'

'Speaking of curses, would it be possible to see the amethyst itself?' Valentina asked.

Alexandra's face darkened. 'I suppose.'

She produced a heavy keychain from a hidden niche in the wall. The chain held seven elaborate keys. Alexandra started to unlock one door of the vault at a time. There was a certain pomp to the way she went about the task. Perhaps there was some ceremonial significance even behind the simple act of unlocking.

As the vault's seventh door was pulled open, Alexandra's haunted gasp reverberated through the room.

Inside the vault was a plinth. On it rested a broken necklace, purple stone cracked in the middle and missing a piece.

'The amethyst!' Alexandra took a swaying step away from the vault. The keychain fell from her grip with a loud clink.

'Not likely,' Marina said under her breath as she kneeled to pick up the keys. She studied them with interest. 'They all appear to be the same? All but one, I see,' she added after a moment. 'Who besides you has access to the vault?'

'*Officially*, only the Head Priestess. Professor Makeeva keeps her two keys in her office,' Alexandra said, growing red in visible discomfort. 'But these seven keys' – she took the rattling keychain from Marina – 'are ceremonial. They're always kept next to the vault, and all the inner circle Ladies know about it. The niche where the keys are stored is not even locked. In the Society, we trust each other completely.'

'Perhaps you shouldn't,' Marina said, producing a plastic glove from her pocket and reaching inside the vault to pick up the shattered necklace.

'Don't!' Alexandra warned. 'The plinth is wired with a weight sensor alarm. It's activated if the necklace is removed for longer than five seconds.'

'Interesting…' Marina said under her nose as she replaced the plastic glove with her loupe, aiming it at the broken necklace. 'Just like I thought,' she said after studying the necklace for a few seconds. 'The broken pieces are smooth and even-coloured. There're barely any striations and streaks on their surface. This is definitely glass, not amethyst.'

'A replica?' Alexandra whispered in shock, tugging at her own identical necklace in panic. 'But where is the original?'

Meeting Valentina's eyes, Marina knew that her partner had reached the same conclusion that blazed through Marina's mind like a comet: *the murderer must be in the possession of the original.*

Given the evidence they'd discovered in the late Professor Klimova's office, after the killer's own glass necklace had been smashed, procuring the original from the vault had to be their only, or at least the fastest, way to ensure the killer had an unbroken necklace in their possession before its absence drew attention. And with the alarm-wired plinth, the killer had to leave their own shattered necklace in the vault. Perhaps the plan was to remove it later. The killer hadn't counted on Marina being brought in to solve the case.

'If the alarm is triggered, who is notified?' Marina asked, putting the loupe away.

Alexandra looked down. 'Nobody. It just rings very loudly in the building. We can't afford anything more than that. Our funding is based on private donations and we don't charge membership fees. But if it did ring, we'd hear it – there's always someone present in the Belltower, in the offices upstairs.'

'I believe I've seen and heard enough here,' Marina said after a pause. 'But I'm yet to talk to those in the Society's inner circle. The current Head Priestess and the two remaining candidates – where can I find them?'

'The only way to get them to come out of hiding now would be to... No, it is too risky!' Alexandra said. '*All* current Society members must attend the Fearless Initiation for the neophytes. Our next scheduled ceremony was meant to be this week, but it had to be put on hold after Vera's death.'

'You must go ahead with the Initiation,' Marina said after tense contemplation. 'It is the only way to catch Vera's killer and prevent more deaths.'

As the night of the Initiation approached, Valentina busied herself with altering the robes they would wear during the ceremony, posing as neophytes. The silky robes' purple tint contrasted with the deathly white masks completing the look. In the meantime, Marina pored over the Society's by-laws, releasing an occasional 'a-ha' at her discoveries, a habit Valentina found endearing.

Later, they found themselves on the desolate campus, the Belltower dark and impenetrable, its spire piercing the gossamer mist into ribbons. With their robes and masks on, Marina and Valentina joined a short line of the Society's members-to-be, a group of girls enrolled at MSU who were handpicked by the current Ladies of the Amethyst and invited to pledge. It seemed the recent death of the Society's leader did little to dissuade the new members from joining. Valentina was mystified by that. Danger aside, she wondered what the appeal was. Only the Head

Priestess was paid for her duties. The rest of the members dedicated their time and energy free of charge. Perhaps Valentina had yet things to learn about human motivation.

Alexandra led the procession. Her face wasn't hidden behind a mask. Neophytes, on the other hand, had to earn the right to remove their masks once they had conquered their biggest fear. Before that, their identities didn't matter. This was specified in the Society's by-laws, alongside many other rules and regulations the Ladies of the Amethyst followed.

Deep inside the dark heart of the Belltower, the neophytes gathered around the vault. The members of the Society's inner circle stood facing them, lining the wall – all the suspects in one place.

Next to Alexandra stood two other candidates for the High Priestess position. Sasha Brodskaya and Vika Kozub were nothing alike, and yet there was an eerie symmetry to their jumpy body language. They mimicked Alexandra's preoccupation with her necklace, tight chains digging into the skin. The Society's rules regulated even how tight the chains had to be, as they were to serve as a constant reminder of the responsibility the Ladies of the Amethyst carried. Valentina followed Marina's gaze to Sasha's neck, then to Vika's, but she wasn't sure what exactly Marina was looking for. Could Marina tell if someone had the real cursed amethyst necklace wrapped around their necks just by looking? Was one of them Vera's murderer?

And then there was the current Head Priestess, Professor Arina Makeeva. She had an aquiline nose and a confident mouth, but her eyes seemed haunted. When Head Priestess Makeeva readjusted her amethyst necklace, Marina's observant gaze lingered on her throat.

Head Priestess Makeeva directed Alexandra to distribute a trayful of steaming cups among the neophytes. The aroma from the brew was earthy, herbaceous. Not tea. What then? Alexandra's hands shook as she put the empty tray away.

'Drink up and fight your fear!' Head Priestess Makeeva's voice carried effortlessly inside the Belltower. It was easy to see how she came to lead this group. Everything about her manner and appearance emitted power. She practically glowed with it, feeding on the admiration mixed with fear in the eyes of her audience.

As the neophytes brought the drinks to their mouths, Valentina felt Marina's hand wrap around her fingers. 'Hallucinogenic mushrooms!' Marina murmured. 'Don't...'

Valentina tipped her cup upside down, aiming for the darker front of her robes, hoping the liquid wouldn't end up on the floor. As the still-warm brew drenched her chest, she crossed her arms and started swaying, in imitation of the increasingly erratic moves of the drugged neophytes.

'Let your fear take you…' Head Priestess Makeeva crooned, a distorted singsong.

And so the Fearless Initiation began.

The fumes of the drink alone were enough to slightly alter her reality, Marina realised. Her head grew light and hollow.

One of the neophytes collapsed to her knees. Her hood fell away from her head as she pulled at her hair and sobbed. 'It's falling out! My hair! My skin!'

'She's not worthy!' Head Priestess Makeeva pronounced, glaring at the frightened girl with distaste. 'How can anyone guard the cursed amethyst if they can't overcome their basic fears and phobias?' She looked away from the failed neophyte, her withering gaze briefly trained on Alexandra.

Another neophyte gave in to her fear. She screamed and broke into a run, flinging her hands as if to protect herself from an attack from above.

The remaining girls stood their ground, allowing only an occasional low whimper or a sniffle. When Marina checked on Valentina, she was relieved to find her blending in with the successful neophytes. Marina didn't need to drink hallucinogenic potion to know what her biggest fear was: losing Valentina.

'Look at those two! They haven't drunk the brew!' The accusation came from Sasha, one of the Head Priestess candidates. She was pointing a finger at the discolouration on Marina's robes. The damned drink must've reacted against the cheap material, washing out the dye. To her horror, Marina saw a similar stain blooming on Valentina's attire.

Before Marina could grab her partner and flee, the nearest Belltower gate was busted open, admitting a squad of stern-faced uniformed officers. Yekaterina Gorodets, Marina's contact with the force, was leading them.

Ahead of the Initiation Ceremony, Yekaterina had listened with great interest to Marina's plan to flush out Vera Klimova's killer. If the squad had arrived at the Belltower even a minute later, Marina and Valentina would have been in deep trouble. The Society's by-laws didn't specify how impostors were to be punished, only that any outsider found attempting infiltration was to meet *the wrath of the amethyst's curse.*

'It's over,' Marina said as she removed her hood and mask.

'What is going on in here? Who the hell are you?' The Head Priestess gave Marina a vicious look.

'I'm Sherlock Holmesova, and I'm here to solve a crime,' Marina replied.

'You're just a girl! I don't have to tolerate this.' Head Priestess headed for the nearest exit but was stopped by Yekaterina's squad.

'Before you leave us, Professor Makeeva, let's listen to what this *girl* has to say,' said Yekaterina, then gave Marina an encouraging look.

Letting her robe fall away from her shoulders, Marina walked up to the vault. She met the Head Priestess's eyes, then Alexandra's, lastly acknowledging the two remaining senior Society members.

'A few days ago I was approached by one of your own and asked to solve Vera Klimova's murder.'

Marina's words provoked a collective sound of indignation.

'Yes, murder. And Vera's murderer is in this room with us now,' Marina went on, ignoring another gasp from the audience. 'Allow me to lay out the facts of the case. Your society's dogma, we know, centres on fear; specifically, on overcoming it. Professor Klimova was found with a grimace of horror upon her face. What did the deceased fear in life? She was terrified of snakes. Her fellow Ladies of the Amethyst, the inner circle, knew this all too well. In Klimova's temporary office, I came across the murder weapon itself – a harmless natrix, disguised to look like a deadly viper, a breed Vera Klimova feared after a childhood incident. Her likely cause of death? A heart attack brought on by fright. While it's yet to become clear whether Klimova's temporary office relocation was part of the murderer's plan, only someone linked to the Zoology Department would have had easy access to the snake.'

'Pure conjecture,' protested Sasha Brodskaya. 'At least three of us have connections to the Zoology Department.'

'True,' Marina allowed. 'But the natrix is not the only thing I found in Klimova's office.'

'With the snake unleashed, was Vera's fate sealed?' Marina went on, 'The impatient murderer went to the victim's office to check, only to find poor Vera suffering a heart attack. In her death throes, Vera must've snapped her murderer's necklace, the glass imitation of the amethyst breaking in the process. The murderer cleared the room of the evidence, but missed a shard of glass that had become embedded in the desk, as well as a piece of painted snake skin stuck to the grille of the duct. Marina produced her two plastic bags of evidence, which she handed over to Senior Officer Gorodets.

'The killer then rushed to rid herself of the destroyed necklace. Since Vera's necklace was off for repairs, the only undamaged one the killer could get on short notice was the real one – the cursed amethyst itself. The killer stole it from the vault, leaving the broken replica in its place not to trigger the alarm.

'With Vera out of the way, the remaining High Priestess candidates became the murderer's next targets, starting with Alexandra Polikova. Even though the plan to have Polikova fall to her death failed, the murderer still came closer to achieving her ultimate goal. Because, you see, with the remaining candidates too scared to go on with the election process, the current Head Priestess gets to keep the position – and the power and privilege that come with it – for seven more years. That leaves us with our murderer, the High Priestess herself.'

'You have no proof!' Professor Arina Makeeva's commanding voice soared to the heights of the Belltower, as she took a careful step away from her accuser. But her fellow Ladies of the Amethyst closed ranks around her, cutting off her escape.

'But I do,' said Marina. 'While the gold used in the original amethyst necklace was produced in the 1880s outside of the Russian Empire, all the replica necklaces were made locally and relatively recently. Despite the cheap glass replacing the amethyst, the replicas are all made of gold. Only it's a different type of gold, this recent mixture containing 58.3% of Au, the remainder filled with other metals designed to keep the gold from tarnishing. Older, darker, gold tends to leave a stain upon the skin. Just like the necklace around your neck, Professor Makeeva, Lady High Priestess.'

Everyone's eyes zeroed in on the slight dark imprint the cursed amethyst necklace had left around the murderer's throat.

In the ensuing clamour, High Priestess Makeeva broke through the crowd, but she didn't make it far, tripping over Marina's strategically placed foot, only to be tackled by Yekaterina's men shortly after.

TWO MSU STUDENTS OPEN FIRST-EVER ALL-WOMEN PI AGENCY

The Red Gazette, 15 July 1995

Following the incredible unmasking of the Amethyst Society Killer last May, two MSU students have opened a private investigative agency in Moscow, the first agency of its kind in Russia to be fully operated by women. Sherlock "Marina" Holmesova (22) is a Criminology student and a freelance psychological profiler who gained celebrity after helping catch the killer of the American dissident director Michael Rottner.

Holmesova's partner is Valentina Vatska (21), a chemistry student. Despite the women's youth, they now have two high-profile cases to their name, the latest of which saw Arina Makeeva arrested for the murder of Vera Klimova. Both women were members of the Amethyst Society. Klimova was murdered after challenging Makeeva's leadership status. Makeeva believed that Klimova – as well as other candidates for Makeeva's replacement – were not worthy to lead the Society as they could never fully overcome their fears.

In addition to Klimova's murder, Makeeva is also facing charges for the attempted murder of another Society member. Clandestine societies of this kind are not uncommon on university campuses, with leadership roles often attracting an enviable honorarium in addition to prestige.

Coincidentally, police seized a stockpile of hallucinogenic *mukhomor* mushrooms from the MSU's Mycology Lab, with the case currently under investigation.

The BOOK for the PAGE

Verity Burns

'But HOW?' Sherlock exploded, before John was even halfway done revelling in the feel of her thumb stroking over his knuckles. God, he wanted her hands all over him. And vice very much versa.

'How did I not see this?' she demanded, her genuine concern reaching him as it always would, and he shifted across the seat until he could raise a hand to her beloved face.

Sherlock leant into it, still frowning. 'I always thought I could read you like a book,' she said plaintively.

John tugged gently, closing the distance between them. 'Not when you're all that's on the page.'

The cabbie smiled as the traffic inched forward, thinking of his favourite niece. Dana put a lot more effort into her appearance than the woman currently getting the life snogged out of her in the back of his taxi, but they shared the same difficulty – puberty was a one way street and a voice once broken was broken for good.

Her sister, his least favourite niece, wouldn't leave the house if she had a spot on her nose, but Dana went out every day knowing she'd be judged as soon as she opened her mouth. Every single day.

Oh, he got plenty of tough guys in his cab. No shortage of bravado. But that...now that was bravery.

A TASTE FOR SKULLS
Tansy Rayner Roberts

I RETURNED FROM THE WAR UNDER UNFORTUNATE CIRCUMSTANCES, with my career in ashes, and a magical curse burning its way through the upper muscle of my right thigh.

The city of Lyceum, tall and full of wonders, should have felt like a warm, familiar embrace. Instead, it felt like a prison.

I had a family home in Gramercy Street, and relatives who would be happy to take me in. Instead, mindful of the curse and my own disgrace, I took up residence at the Criterion Hotel, to ponder my options.

It was there, as I lunched with an old friend, Imogen Cartwell, that I first became acquainted with the most extraordinary person I have ever met: Sherlock Holmes, consulting detective.

She was a tall, angular woman in tweed trousers and a swinging jacket at least a decade out of style. Her long hair was pinned up in a fashion belonging to a previous era, and her concentration was entirely devoted to an enormous, spiky green plant.

I should say: Miss Holmes was at the time occupying the garden atrium in the centre of the hotel restaurant. I watched her capering about for most of my lunch, all the way through to coffee and dessert. She appeared to be testing, or torturing, the various large botanical wonders that filled the glass-walled garden.

It was Imogen, amused, who told me the name of that odd person, and sent me into the garden with a message while she herself ordered a second cup of coffee with chocolate shortbreads, and read the newspaper.

As soon as I entered the atrium, Miss Holmes began to speak: 'You see, it's such a marvellous specimen of vampire rose, and if I am correct, the sap of the moon-lily in conjunction with the powdered thorns of the rose should form the base of the first ever universal antidote of poisons!' She spoke as if I were an old friend rather than a person she had never met.

'That sounds terribly useful,' I remarked.

She turned suddenly, and gripped me with her piercing stare. 'Are you a botanist?'

'I am not.'

'Good. They're all thieves. Hold this.' She thrust a handful of rose stems at me, which I was certain she had not been given permission to remove from the restaurant. The roses, sensing the nearness of my human skin, hissed and entwined themselves towards my heart. I held them at arm's length, a little awkwardly because I relied so heavily on my walking stick. 'I must perform the final tests in my laboratory to be certain of clear results,' Miss Holmes went on. 'Though of course, I am currently between laboratories.'

Imogen had told me a little of Miss Holmes' troubles. 'That's why I came to meet you,' I said. 'We have a mutual acquaintance in Miss Cartwell.'

'So we have.' Miss Holmes produced a small trowel from her voluminous pockets and began digging rootstock out of a simply enormous fern. 'Are you a spy?'

'Not yet.'

'She's recruiting you. She does that.'

'She's trying!'

Our friend Miss Cartwell was the Director of Domestic Intelligence in Lyceum, and had long considered me a potential addition of value to her department. I had so far avoided all attempts to pin me down. But beggars could not be choosers, and my income was going to run thin for as long as I resisted falling upon the erratic fortunes of my family.

My answer was interesting enough that Miss Holmes stopped what she was doing, stood to her full height, and gave me a proper look, as if deciding to pay attention to me as someone other than a short-term botanical assistant. I was mesmerised by the probing intensity of her dark eyes. It was as though she could see past my clothes and skin to the bones beneath.

Her face softened a little. 'How goes the war?'

'No one's winning,' I said bitterly. 'How did you know?'

'It leaves its mark.' Her gaze swept down to the curse-burned thigh beneath my linen trousers. 'Literally, in your case.'

'Are *you* a spy?' I blurted out. 'Or a curse-breaker?'

Miss Holmes' face broke into a smile, as if she knew exactly how odd it was that I should ask that of her, given my background. But of course, she knew nothing about me. It did not matter that the name Hathaway was synonymous with the delicate art of curse-breaking; I had left that name behind me in the ruins of my career.

'Sadly, neither of those fascinating professions has ever appealed to me,' she went on, 'though Imogen has tried her best to recruit me. I am, in fact, a consulting detective. Or I will be, once I have secured a particular set of rooms in Baker Street.'

'That's why I came to meet you,' I told her. 'Imogen said you were looking for someone to share the cost of rooms. I need somewhere to live.' Baker Street, I knew, was on the opposite side of the city to Gramercy Street, the one place I wanted more than any other to avoid.

'Name?' the detective asked of me.

'Jeanne Watson.' I'd borrowed it from a book, and had been practising it for days, so that it came out smoothly and without hesitation.

Miss Holmes tilted her head at me. 'No, that's not it.' She snapped her fingers and shouted: 'Hemlock!' She knelt down, savaging more of the hotel's greenery with an elegant antique pocket knife. 'An essential component of the antidote,' she threw at me. 'Though why it should be growing in such quantities in an ornamental garden is a question best put to the hotel manager…or the local constabulary. Are you sure you wish to room with me? I have been told I am an acquired taste.'

She sounded uncertain with that last line, her head still down so that I could not see her face.

'Everyone I know is eccentric,' I assured her. 'Perhaps we could room together on a trial basis, to see if we suit? You might not like *me*.'

Miss Holmes got to her feet, arms full of frothy green hemlock fronds. They looked remarkably like parsley. She heaped the plants into my own arms, providing something of a buffer between myself and the sinister rose stems which even now were making an attempt for my throat. 'Born to an academic family,' she murmured. 'Though it was no act of rebellion when you chose a path of adventure. I suspect you have several relatives who went the same way. Most recently you have spent time in Balvoria, as well as Malakeen – hence my question about the war. Not a soldier. Something involving typewriter ribbons and copious numbers of ballpoint pens. Reporter, I assume. You must be exceptional, or Imogen wouldn't be trying to recruit you. For some reason you wish to stay anonymous in this city despite having loved ones nearby. I suspect that has something to do with pride, and the dark curse currently lodged in your right leg. Do I need to know more than that, to determine whether or not I like you?'

I blinked rapidly. 'How the devil did you deduce all that?'

'Didn't I say, my dear? I'm a *very good* consulting detective.' She patted me on the shoulder. 'There are curse-breakers in the city. Would you like me to recommend one?'

'No, thank you. I can handle the matter myself.'

'Well, then. Let us proceed to Baker Street. I have to put these cuttings somewhere. I think you should call me Sherlock, if we're to be friends. Personally, I've always thought of friendship as a distracting and frivolous intimacy, but I have been assured by others it is a worthwhile pursuit on occasion. One should experiment on oneself from time to time, don't you think?'

I assumed this was an entirely rhetorical statement and indeed, could think of no way of responding to it other than to introduce myself.

'You can call me…' I began, and hesitated.

'Jeanne for now,' Sherlock said with a winning smile. 'Of course.'

Imogen met me by the hotel doors. Sherlock was distracted, explaining to the hotel manager exactly why they should be concerned that the new chef had suddenly chosen to add 'parsley soup' to the menu, on the same weekend that the chef's mother-in-law had chosen this very hotel for her Ruby Wedding Anniversary.

I stood there, arms full of someone else's homicidal plant cuttings, allowing myself to be smirked at by the deputy head of the Bureau of Domestic Intelligence.

'Did you tell her anything about me?' I accused.

'Me, volunteer information to the great Holmes? I wouldn't dare.' Imogen kissed me on the cheek as she left. 'You'll be good for each other,' she assured me. 'Let me know if you change your mind about a job.'

'I have a job.'

'Sulking isn't a job, *Jeanne*.'

I could do this. I could be Jeanne Watson, a perfectly ordinary name for a perfectly ordinary person. I could avoid my family long enough to sort out my dirty laundry, up to and including the curse in my leg. I could do it all while sharing digs with an uncommonly perceptive detective.

Piece of cake.

'It's all about skulls,' Sherlock Holmes told me, four days later, over crumpets and tea.

I turned the toasting fork over to properly brown the other side of my crumpet over the fire. 'What's all about skulls, Sherlock?'

'Your curse,' she said, as she spread jam directly onto a crumpet, forgoing the butter. I would never understand her. 'I'm sorry, did you think I had forgotten?'

'You have been rather busy, with the Case of the Avaricious Wallpaper, and the Mysterious Death at Shropbury Heights,' I reminded her. 'Besides, my curse is not your mystery to solve. I told you, I have it handled.'

'If that were true, you would already have a growing skull collection on that table over there,' Sherlock said, pointing to the only piece of furniture in our already-cluttered rooms that was not laden with her experiments, books, or random vials of poison. 'But you do not. I will have to manage it myself.'

It was on the tip of my tongue to tell her that I had forgotten more about curses than she could possibly ever learn, but given I was still operating under a name that was not attached to my real family, it was better to remain silent.

Also, I was genuinely curious where she was heading with this.

'Tell me more,' I said, slathering the appropriate amount of butter on to my crumpet, 'about skulls.'

Sherlock shook her head, as if explaining was too much trouble. This, from a person who had spent two hours that same day explaining to me (with hand-drawn diagrams) why it was that the other nine of the top ten magical forensics experts in the city were all idiots. 'Better that I show you,' she said, and promptly changed the subject to the Failings of Urban Pathology, Part Two.

I allowed myself to forget about that conversation until three days later, when I returned from the market to find our apartment full of skulls.

You may think from my phrasing that a merely large number of skulls were dotted about the apartment.

Let me repeat: *full of skulls*. There were crates piled upon crates. Those that had already been unloaded from crates were sorted into themed piles, like morbid little pyramids dotted around the Apollonian rug.

Bird skulls here, rat skulls there, and…oh, on the nearly-new sofa: a heap of skulls that were *clearly of human origin*.

'Sherlock,' I said in a voice that was heroically calm, under the circumstances. 'What in hellfire have you done?'

'There you are!' my friend remarked happily, breezing in from the other room with a plateful of sardines on toast. 'I was worried you'd return before I was ready, but you've been *ages*.'

'Ready to hold two hundred funerals?' I ventured.

'Two hundred,' Sherlock scoffed. 'As if two hundred skulls would do the trick. Really, Jeanne, I'm disappointed in you for thinking I would contribute such a paltry effort. This is a life or death situation.'

I gazed around the room. Now that I had recovered from the initial shock, I was able to notice other details. The expensive midnight-black wax candles set up in a loose circle around Sherlock's armchair, and the towering stack of books on the coffee table, surrounded by a great wall of dried-out beaks and smooth white craniums.

The book at the top of the stack was *Curse-breaking With A Vengeance*, by Charlotte Hathaway. I knew that book upside down and inside out. The author used to babysit me as a child. (Aunt C's sequel, *Curse-breaking Best Served Cold*, was personally dedicated to me and my sisters. I spotted it now, four books down in the stack, partially concealed by a simply enormous skull that must have belonged to a large dog or possibly a wolf.)

The title that caught my eye, though, of all the spines in the teetering stack of research, was *Age Old Tales of the Spirits*, a book I remembered not because a family member had written it, but because it was a favourite of my elder sister Charity's when we were little. It sounded charming enough, but was packed full of the kind of spine-tingling, eldritch horror stories she adored. No wonder she had married into the aristocracy.

Now I realised why the sight of so many grotesque heaps of skulls had sparked an old but familiar memory in me. 'Sherlock,' I said steadily, 'is it possible you think I was cursed by the Bone Witch?'

Her piercing eyes held mine for a moment, and then released me. 'Are you saying you were not cursed by a witch made out of bones?'

I huffed in impatience. 'I don't know who cursed me. But I'm fairly sure it was not a mythic creature from ancient times.'

Sherlock blinked, as if no one had ever told her she was wrong before.

I desperately wanted to collapse on the sofa, but it was covered in human remains. Instead, I let Sherlock have it: the truth.

'I was on the trail of a war profiteering scandal that implicated at least three very powerful families in Balvoria, four in Malakeen, and a couple right here in Lyceum,' I told her, settling in to share my tale. 'Any one of those families might have taken the hit out on me. It was at night. I was attacked a few streets from my digs. No witnesses, even myself. I remember a bright bolt of blue light in the darkness, and when I awoke, I had lost ten minutes of memory. I compounded my own ruin by not disclosing the curse to my newspaper. I didn't want them to take me off the story, not when I was so close. But trying to keep a secret from your own newspaper is like trying to keep ink inside a bottle made of blotting paper.'

As is often the case, it was not the curse itself that was my undoing so much as the lies I told to conceal my condition from my employers. I thought I had it under control, with enough knowledge from my curse-breaking family to brew potions, cobble together a talisman or two to keep the worst symptoms at bay. The pain, the dark dreams and night sweats, the strange instances of missing memory…

Then it turned out that during those mystery blackouts – the ones I had hidden from my colleagues and editor – I had been apparently writing letters to other newspapers, sharing all manner of confidential information and sources. The war-profiteering story fell apart, and several of those terribly important families brought lawsuits against my paper.

'I'm now blacklisted in the newspaper industry, across a dozen countries,' I concluded unhappily. 'That's it. That's my tale. All terribly mundane and lacking in magical glamour.'

Sherlock was unmoved. 'I know all that.'

Fury overtook me. 'How could you possibly know all that?' Sherlock had told me from the beginning that she was a very good consulting detective; in my innocence I had never realised she considered me an open case. 'I didn't *consult* you, Sherlock. I didn't ask you to poke your nose into my business. And I certainly did not ask you to fill our living space with hundreds of skulls.' I looked around the room again, my heart sinking. More than two hundred, of course. 'At a guess, three hundred and thirty three?'

'A splendid deduction, my dear Jeanne,' said Sherlock, proud of me.

'Exactly the number of skulls required to summon the Bone Witch,' I sighed. 'Sherlock, she is a fairy tale. Do you even have any experience at mystic conjuration?'

'None whatsoever!' she declared. 'Though I suspect I shall experience it more often in future. Once one has sacrificed a certain amount of floor space in one's brain-attic to absorb a specific form of knowledge, it is a waste not to make regular use of it. This is why I avoid astronomy lectures and trivia nights.'

A waste, not to use your knowledge. My aunt once said something similar to me, when I walked away from an apprenticeship with her.

'What was the point of it all, if you're not going to use what you know to help others?' she demanded at the time. Aunt Charlotte was a lot like Sherlock, now I came to think of it. She could not imagine anyone not wanting to spend their lives dedicated to the art of curse-breaking.

Aunt Charlotte was dead now. Six months ago, my expert aunt had been struck down in the course of her work by an ancient curse. She was the best in the world at what she did, and her life was over in a single unlucky instant. Perhaps, if I'd been with her, I might have saved her life.

(She would be beyond furious to discover how little incentive I had felt in recent weeks to save myself.)

'Fine,' I said in resignation. 'But put those midnight candles back in the hamper. You can return them later to the outrageously overpriced boutique from which you bought them. Plain kitchen candles are perfectly serviceable. You'll find six in the drawer behind you. Fish out the ball of string as well, and a bottle of apple cider vinegar. It's better than chalk for drawing circles.'

'You sound like you know what you are doing,' remarked Sherlock, wide-eyed.

'Don't make fun of me,' I snapped. 'I know you know everything about me, including *what I know*.'

'I do,' she agreed. 'Candles, you say?'

Twelve minutes later, we stood within a more robust and reliable form of summoning circle, surrounded by a complex and terrifyingly elegant pattern of skulls.

(I had yet to discover how Sherlock, perennially short on funds, had sourced them all, and was not sure I wanted that information in my "brain-attic" anytime soon.)

Together, we summoned the darkest of fairy tale creatures from beyond the shadow realm.

The Bone Witch.

We heard the crunching first. A snapping of an invisible jaw, the powdering of skull between fierce teeth. An ominous sound. One rat skull disappeared into thin air, one bite at a time, and then the next, and then the next.

A hand appeared, and then an arm.

The Bone Witch bit and crunched her way through skull after skull, her body becoming a little more visible with each tasty treat. It was one of the most unsettling experiences of my life, watching her appear.

Finally, with half the skulls consumed, she was whole and visible: a bent old woman in a tattered gown from a previous century, the fabric as faded and grey as her skin. Her long white hair fell in clumped, matted weeds from her scalp to her waist.

'Why have you called me from my centuries of endless slumber?' she croaked, picking fragments of bone from her teeth.

Sherlock leaned forward, eyes alert. 'That's rather misleading, is it not, madam? I believe you have in fact been freely roaming the streets of Balvoria in recent weeks. You laid a rather vicious curse on my friend here, at the behest of the–' she consulted her notes, '–Norwindian family. Miss Watson isn't the first of your recent victims. You were also responsible for the death of the Princess Carlion of Lachesis, the assassination of the Archduke Fenrir of Apollonia, and the slow, wasting death of the Prime Minister of Galvestri. Were you not?'

I gave Sherlock a sidelong look, wondering if all that was true. 'The death of the Prime Minister of Galvestri was eighty years ago,' I said.

Sherlock was unmoved. 'Obviously the word "recent" has a different meaning when one is addressing an ancient being of immense power who has lived in the shadow realm for millennia. Or so you would like us to believe, madam.'

The Bone Witch gave Sherlock an impatient, frustrated look. 'What is that supposed to mean?' she demanded, baring her teeth.

A nearby skull – a human one – flew from the sofa into the Bone Witch's hand. She bit into it, sending explosive shard fragments into the air like crumbs from a freshly-bitten croissant. Did I imagine a little colour staining her cheeks rosier in the same instant?

'Obviously, you're a fraud,' said the consulting detective, as if this was a matter of public record.

Three more skulls flew past our faces, into the hands of the crone.

'Are you suggesting I am not the Bone Witch of ancient lore?' she demanded.

'*A* bone witch, perhaps,' said Sherlock. 'But you're hardly the scourge of the Lost Continents, are you?'

The creature's eyes glowed red. She grew a little in stature, bearing down upon us. My cursed leg flared in pain, and I felt its dark magic claw more deeply into my veins. 'Sherlock,' I gasped. 'Be nice.'

Sherlock looked hurt at the suggestion. 'How would that help? Let me begin by outlining what I know of your activities over the last century, madam. And then we shall discuss you releasing my friend.'

'Do your worst,' the Bone Witch challenged her, chomping on another human skull as if it was a ripe melon.

I shivered. The tales of the Bone Witch always ended in tragedy – for the summoners, once she ran out of skulls to eat. I hoped very much that Sherlock's research included a plan for what to do next.

What followed was a most extraordinary presentation by my friend Sherlock Holmes. I had seen her grandstanding performances before. It was hard to avoid, given that she used our rooms to greet clients. Her ability to conjure inviolable facts out of the air thanks to observations no one else might ever have made had always struck me as deeply uncanny.

As she spoke now, I found myself caught between awe and annoyance. This was not curse-breaking, as I knew it. It was a wholly new occupation.

Theatre of revelations.

I longed for a typewriter, so I might capture some of it for posterity. Never mind all those newspapers that turned their backs on me; I would paper walls with the tale of Sherlock and the Bone Witch, to share it with the world. I would embroider it on a *cushion* if I had to.

'You were born Victoria Adams, one hundred and twenty years ago, in the slums of Caerdocia,' said Sherlock to our guest, naming a town on the coast of Galvestri, a small island country that had sided with Balvoria in the most recent war. 'An actress by trade, you made a decent enough living until your path crossed with that of a young politician, who made you his mistress. You lived in comfort and style at his expense until you disappeared without trace, shortly before the election that made him Prime Minister.'

'I had no idea you had an interest in political history, Sherlock,' I said, impressed.

'Political history is hardly worth my time,' she said with a wave of her hand. 'I have, however, examined every missing person case and grisly murder of the last century. The behaviour of human beings around dark and mysterious crimes is the only subject worthy of academic interest, or indeed bedtime reading.'

'Go on,' snarled the Bone Witch. Snap, crunch, gone.

'I believe your family sold your soul to a minor demon,' Sherlock continued. 'I've narrowed it down to Azeriad, or Chalmzos.'

'Of the eighty minor demons in the pantheon,' I muttered.

'Rare to hear tales of people selling souls other than their own, but in this instance, your family's fortunes rose, and you became a monstrous creature, beholden to generation after generation of the Family Norwindian. I have tracked your various assassinations, minor and major – there's a chart over on the piano. It's my understanding that each member of the family is allowed a single – favour, let us say, of the family ghoul. And you perform them. Every murder, every curse, every cruel trick asked of you. Using the mask of a far more ancient fairy tale…'

Sherlock continued in her pronouncements, but I was already limping towards the piano to peer at the chart. The *Norwindians*. I hadn't considered that they might be involved – a wealthy family with shipping interests around to the world, to be sure, as well as dozens of other businesses. But they had not even slightly been implicated in the war profiteering story, not once in all of my research. I had no idea what I might have done to inspire one of them to have me cursed in the first place.

Behind me, the crunching continued.

I scanned the document, taking particular note of the younger Norwindian generation, the nephews and nieces who might by accident of marriage bear another name…

And then I saw him. Jacob Norwindian Manitob. Jake Manitob and I had shared half a desk in the Lyceum office years ago, before we were both sent into the field. I liked him. After I was cast out from the newspaper, I heard he got the promotion we had both been gunning for, and I had felt *pleased* that it was him who snapped it up, and not Dorcas Shandiboot, or Elias Twint.

'Bastard,' I said aloud. 'That–! He used up his one go on a family curse to get me out of the way of his career? Couldn't he just bad-mouth me to our colleagues like a normal person?'

I wanted to reach back through time and hit him with my typewriter. He hadn't just ruined my career. The curse still lodged in my thigh was likely to be the death of me, if I couldn't rid myself of it. My dreams had been getting darker, my pain more intense at nights.

The best curse-breaker I knew was dead. And I'd been pretending that it didn't matter, that I could handle it. I hadn't even tried to rid myself of it. After my life fell apart, I suppose part of me thought I deserved this fate.

It would be nice to tell myself that the curse was self-protecting, that these dark thoughts came from the magic burning me from the inside out. But I'd always had an unhealthy tendency towards self-sabotage. Why else would I set up house with a woman like Sherlock, becoming a shadowy supporting character in her dramatic life?

Crunch. Crunch.

I spun around. Barely any skulls were left, now. Just a small heap of tiny bird craniums, going down the Bone Witch's gullet like strawberries in summer, one after the other.

'Sherlock,' I said. 'We're going to have to kill her.'

My friend's face froze. She tore her eyes away from her fascination with the creature on our rug. 'What?'

'She's a demon talisman. Barely even a person any more. Certainly not an ancient mythic witch.' As long as her life force continued, my curse would continue to drain me.

Sherlock's face brightened. 'I've researched demon talismans. I read fourteen books on the subject last Wednesday.'

'Of course you did.'

Crunch, snap.

'If anyone,' Sherlock went on, 'any single person outside the host family, learns of the secret of the talisman, then she can't cast further curses. We have her trapped!'

'Yes,' I said calmly. 'But once she finishes eating those skulls, she can start on ours. In the unlikely event that we survive her, all of the

Norwindians will come for us. Their family's special ability to ruin lives will be restored to them the second you and I both die.'

Sherlock blinked at me. 'If only you had a platform by which information could be spread to an impossibly large number of people in a hurry.'

I blinked back at her. 'Are you thinking about newspapers?'

'Jeanne, don't pretend you're not always thinking about newspapers.'

Five bird skulls remained. Bite, crunch, chomp. Four left.

'If we kill her right now,' I said. 'My curse unwinds. My death sentence unravels.'

'We can't kill her,' Sherlock said firmly. 'I'm a consulting detective, not the city hangman. I have standards, Jeanne.'

'I don't. This creature is a curse. And my family knows exactly what to do with curses.'

Crunch, crunch.

The Bone Witch – the Talisman – had one bird skull remaining. It sat on the palm of her hand.

'She will kill us both,' I said desperately, hoping to convince Sherlock before it was too late. I didn't think I could murder this creature without my friend's assistance. 'The second she eats that final skull, Sherlock. We have to do it *now*.'

Sherlock looked unbothered, remarkably cool given the circumstances. 'My dear Watson, you said you had this handled.'

The Bone Witch's mouth opened wide. She placed the bird cranium between her teeth, and bit down…

Killing the Bone Witch would solve so many of my problems. And yet…there was always more than one way to break a curse. Sherlock's declaration had reminded me of another, more risky method.

When in doubt, my Aunt Charlotte had taught me when I was very small, only just beginning to absorb the first steps of curse-breaking. *Remember that a curse is a weapon. And the best, worst thing about weapons is how often they cause terrible accidents to those who would wield them.*

Time slowed. I breathed. I reached inside my thigh.

I could not have done this before. It wasn't a magic one could produce casually over crumpets and tea. It required ritual. It required the presence of the wielder of the curse, the victim of the curse, and, crucially, the opposite of an executioner: a person who had refused to kill another.

Ritual was everything in the business of curse-breaking. I hated that about it. Magical rituals were tricksy and tangled, a mass of rules and conditions and the history of people messing them up by forgetting a single crucial detail. I might as well take up contract law. I was not going to make a habit of this.

I would never be a curse-breaker.

But curse-breaking was in my blood. In my brain-attic, as Sherlock might say.

I reached into my thigh, and felt the dark threads of pain and fire and darkness spreading through my muscle. I ripped it out, bringing blood and flesh along with the horrible, poisoned magic.

'Return,' I commanded. I let go of the cursed wet gobbets of me, of my rage and fire.

The curse snapped back into the body of the Bone Witch who was not the Bone Witch, like a missile flicked by rubber band. She screamed, and her teeth crunched down…

Light blazed from the perfectly ordinary candles. Steam and the scent of apple cider vinegar billowed in the air.

A single, unmarked bird skull fell on to the ornate carpet. Its eye sockets briefly glowed dark, and then emptied.

'Where is she?' asked Sherlock.

'You tell me,' I sniped in return. 'You're the consulting detective who knows everything.'

She reached out gently to lift the skull as if she knew (of course she knew, she had read fourteen books on the subject) that a live creature was trapped inside it, her magic neutralised, her consciousness…let us say asleep. 'In this particular case,' Sherlock said thoughtfully. 'I believed the best solution was: curse-breaker, heal thyself.'

'Are you absolutely sure you weren't just making it up as you went along?' I demanded.

'Miss Watson, how dare you! Sherlock Holmes always has a plan.'

'My name's not Watson,' I said softly.

'I know,' said Sherlock. She crossed the room in long strides, placing the final bird skull in pride of place on our shared mantlepiece, over the fireplace. 'Are you ready to share your other name with me yet?'

'Not yet. Do you think – are there bandages? I'm bleeding quite a lot.'

'Oh, don't get it on the rug!' Sherlock scooped up a vintage tablecloth and brought it to me. 'Haven't you made a mess!'

'Says the woman who filled our rooms with skulls.'

My friend laughed gently and I, allowing my bleeding, curse-free leg to be bound securely in antique lace, laughed in return.

I have never wanted to kiss someone so much in my life. A dizzying moment later, I realised that there was nothing preventing me from doing so.

As it turns out, it is quite possible to distract a consulting detective with the pursuit of frivolous intimacy, if you catch her at the right moment. For us, apparently, the right moment was swooning on a rug scattered with bone fragments.

Start as you mean to go on, and all that.

Three days later, I lunched with Imogen Cartwell at the Criterion Hotel, where I informed her I was ready to consider an offer of employment. An office job, nothing involving much in the way of travel or heavy lifting. My leg, I suspected, was unlikely to heal well enough for me to run about after criminals and the like. Domestic intelligence seemed like an interesting enough field. I could contribute to society, and it would keep me out from under Sherlock's feet during the days.

For the first time since my life fell apart, I had plans for my future. I had begun work on a book detailing the various fascinating exploits of Sherlock Holmes, consulting detective. Perhaps there might be the occasional opportunity to help her out in the more interesting cases. But for now, a day job was necessary to pay our shared rent and weekly crumpet bill. Sherlock's consulting fees were far too cheap, and her work-related expenses terrifyingly high. The credit request covering the supply of all those skulls still brought me out in a cold sweat.

'I have one condition,' I added.

'Is it to keep working under an alias instead of your perfectly decent family name with all its useful connections?' Imogen sighed.

I bit into a toasted tea cake. 'I have two conditions.'

She raised both eyebrows. 'Is it sanctioned vengeance against a certain reporter related to a certain internationally noteworthy family who hold many significant business interests directly relevant to Lyceum's thriving economy?'

I raised my finger and thumb a little way apart. 'A small amount of sanctioned vengeance. It comes along with the necessary public exposure of the history of a certain curse-wielder over the centuries, in connection with the Norwindian family.'

'We'll see.' Imogen looked unamused, but not unfriendly. 'Sherlock asked for the same thing, you know.'

'Sherlock accepted your offer?' Now I was surprised.

'Not at all. Apparently she already has a job as a consulting detective.'

I smiled. 'Yes. I've heard that.'

'But she did offer to trade certain information on a certain internationally noteworthy family and their history of malicious curse-working, in return for getting one of their junior relatives fired from his newspaper job and publicly exposed for his crimes.'

'Oh, in that case,' I brightened my smile, 'we can move on to salary negotiations. I have everything else that I need.'

Imogen raised her eyebrows. 'You're bedding each other, I suppose. Wildly in love, and all that rot. I knew you'd be marvellous for each other.'

'Miss Cartwell!' I replied, pretending to be shocked. 'What a thing to suggest.'

Three days after that, I found myself standing on Gramercy Street, staring at the family home I had been avoiding all this time.

Aunt Charlotte's house. My aunt, who had reached out and helped me from beyond the grave. My aunt, who taught me everything I knew and loved and rejected. My aunt, who must have been so disappointed in me.

'I've never met anyone's family before,' Sherlock said. She was holding a pineapple, for no reason I could discern. Either it was intended as a host gift, or she was halfway through fathoming out The Case of the Poisoned Pineapple, and at some point in the afternoon would scream, 'I've got it!' and run away at high speed.

'It's not all that intimidating, as families go,' I said, eyes on the big red door. 'One sister abroad, one at home. A handful of ghosts. A houseful of dangerous artefacts. That sort of thing.'

'I hope you don't expect me to make small talk,' Sherlock said.

I took her hand. 'Dear heart, I can't wait to find out what your idea of small talk even looks like. You don't need to be afraid of my family.' Wildly in love, and all that rot. Oh yes. My sisters were going to adore her. Pineapple and all.

'Then, why are you trembling?' she asked.

Sherlock Holmes, always with the incisive questions.

'I don't know,' I said. 'But I'm as ready as I'll ever be.'

'I may have to leave early,' she warned as we approached the front door, 'to solve a murder.'

I smiled again. I would be smiling when my sister opened the door. 'My dear Holmes, I would expect nothing else.'

The Conductor's Last Overture
JD Cadmon

As the final cadence rang out in Reichenbach Hall, master conductor Rupert Martin dropped his hands and fell dead on the podium.

The National Junior Honour Orchestra, made of the best high school musicians in the country, had finished its penultimate piece with only the Mahler finale yet to play. Absent a conductor, both the young musicians and the audience were stunned into momentary silence before chaos and disorder ripped the concert hall apart.

Teens cried out in shock, then pulled out phones that had been explicitly forbidden from the performance. Parents raced to the stage to get to their children. The stage manager and several of the stagehands shouted into phones for emergency services. Rupert Martin's business agent paced the wings like a caged panther ready to maul anyone at the slightest provocation.

The picture of calm in the storm around her, Sherlock Holmes gracefully took her violin from under her chin and stared at the body. Martin's stage makeup was melting and dripping on the floor. The skin tone underneath was a peculiar green Holmes had seen in meat gone bad.

Rupert Martin had been an unusual choice for the festival conductor of a teen ensemble. The reputation that preceded him was not that of a kind educator, but of a temperamental genius who could guide his usually adult orchestras to dizzying heights of excellence. To Sherlock, he was capable enough, but he'd made mistakes and got lost in the score a time or two.

The maestro's gaffes hadn't hindered Sherlock. She came into any situation as well-prepared as possible and had learned the parts for both the first and the second violins. Sherlock was the leader of the second violins because she preferred to observe everything without the pressure of being the principal violin. Her position at the front of her section included witnessing a slight tremor in Martin's hand and all the bottles with a particularly elaborate seal on them that he'd been drinking through rehearsals.

Martin hadn't been kind to many of the students or festival staff, but he had taken a shine to Sherlock's best friend since elementary school, Jennifer Watson. She had perfected a tuba solo for the last piece that would have gone a long way to convince Jenny's mother, Dr Mary Watson, that Jenny's chosen path was music, not medicine. Unfortunately for the younger Watson, the conductor's sudden death upstaged the solo in the Mahler.

According to the rumour mill, of which Jenny kept Sherlock well apprised, Martin and his wife, movie actress Cecily Baron, were going through a bitter divorce, with accusations of cheating on both sides. Earlier, during the lunchtime rehearsal break, Sherlock and others had overheard the couple bickering, but then Baron ran out of the hall claiming to be late to an appointment. Sherlock hadn't seen her return, though she'd been present during the other rehearsal days.

The stage manager barked at one of the stagehands in the wings to close the curtain and deny the audience any further chance at observing the horror on stage. The students were told to remain in their seats, but as soon as the orchestra was hidden, Jenny ran over from the low brass section to squat by Holmes in the violins.

'Can you believe this?' Jenny shook her head sadly. 'No one likes conductors, but I wouldn't have wished him this kind of death.'

'I don't know,' Sherlock said with a tone intended only for Jenny. 'It's a very fitting way for a conductor to die. Very dramatic.'

Watson harrumphed, and Sherlock pointed to the drops of melting makeup on the stage. 'What do you suppose he was hiding?'

'The same things anyone else does, I suspect. His imperfections.'

That was a logical deduction, especially in light of the conductor's widely publicised divorce. Martin would want to appear impeccable and beyond reproach in the court of public opinion before he went into a real court to settle his divorce.

'Astute observation, Watson,' Sherlock replied in a posh tone, bumping shoulders playfully with her best friend.

Cecily Baron finally made an appearance, running across the stage to her husband's body. She threw herself over him and wailed with the kind of pain that left the listener feeling the prick of secondhand grief.

The actress had cultivated a persona as a beautiful blonde with a gift for comedy. As Baron cried over her husband, her face looked red and puffy with tears, and there was slight bruising around her eyes that might have been a sign of many sleepless nights covered up with makeup. Her emotions seemed too real to be a display of acting prowess.

The police and the ambulance crew arrived back-to-back. They whispered to each other about what to do with Martin's body while shooting Holmes and Watson looks, since the teens were sitting so close they could be in the same conversation circle. After confirming no signs of life, the EMTs loaded Rupert Martin's body to take to the hospital, which had a morgue under the supervision of Dr Mary Watson.

The new widow stood alone on stage and was approached by a pair of uniformed police officers. 'We'd like to ask you a few questions about your husband.'

It took her a few seconds to speak. 'Of course. Anything.'

'We can use the stage manager's office for privacy,' one officer suggested, with a hand near Baron's elbow and the other with his palm out to show the way.

Cecily Baron schooled her features and with red carpet poise walked off the stage with the officers.

Sherlock snapped her violin case closed, ready to follow her curiosity after them. 'Let's find out what they're saying.'

'I can't leave my tuba!' Jenny hissed.

'Then put it away and come find me. Quietly.'

Jenny whispered, 'You're going up on the catwalk to spy on them, aren't you?'

Sherlock nodded and took out her phone, ready to record what she heard in case she needed to review the details later. Then she sprinted away, avoiding the people loitering or trying to gain entrance to the stage.

When Sherlock got into her hidden position with a bird's eye view of the stage manager's office, the widow was nursing a cup of coffee. The lead officer opened his notepad, but it was too far away for Sherlock to see what he was writing, even with the help of a camera.

'Mrs Martin,' the officer said, making Cecily Baron flinch.

'That's Ms Baron,' she replied icily.

'Apologies. What can you tell us about your husband's health? Did he have any chronic conditions or known allergens?'

'As far as I know, he was fine,' she said. 'He hadn't told me about any history of disease.'

'You and your husband were in the middle of a divorce, weren't you? His death certainly sped up the end of your marriage.'

The actress hissed. 'Are you implying something? Do I need to call my lawyer?'

'I'm not implying anything, Ms Baron, but spouses are often the first suspects in a wrongful death.'

'I didn't kill my husband.' Gesticulating with her cup of coffee, she said, 'I was gone all afternoon. If I'd killed him, what reason would I have to come back?'

'Do you have an alibi for your whereabouts this afternoon?'

Cecily Baron pressed her lips together. 'I do, but that information is of a private, sensitive nature. I won't be telling you anything else without my lawyer present.'

While the officer told Baron she needed to stay close in case the police had further questions, Sherlock backed up from her hiding place to find Jenny right behind her.

'We need to inspect Martin's dressing room before the scene is disturbed, in case there are any clues there.'

'Like what?' Jenny whispered as Sherlock leapt forward to get there post-haste.

'I don't know yet,' she said over her shoulder, 'but we'll recognise it when we see it. Martin was a creature of habit. We'll look for something different, no matter how mundane.'

When she got to where she was going, Sherlock moved a ceiling tile aside to reveal the conductor's dressing room below. She was skinny, like her violin bow, and could make a direct route into the room. With catlike grace, she dropped from the ceiling while Jenny hissed at her not to do something that could get them in trouble.

Once on the floor, Sherlock pressed her ear to the door to hear if anyone was coming. Satisfied she was alone, she quickly looked around the dressing room. A low table by a sofa was piled high with a working set of scores for the pieces the orchestra had performed. It was the most orderly spot in the room.

Food and alcohol gifts littered the rest of the space, and several empty bottles of Martin's special drink filled the trash. Sherlock snapped a photo of one of the bottle labels and then sniffed it. The odour reminded her of rancid kiwi and not at all alcoholic, as some of the other students had guessed. There were no traces of the almond scent that sometimes disguised poisons, and nothing else in the trash was particularly revealing.

Though she was trying to be quick, Sherlock was not fast enough. The door of the dressing room swung open, and Rupert Martin's agent stepped in.

'What are you doing here?'

Decisively stepping toward the low table, Sherlock scooped up the stack of scores. 'The music librarian told me to get these. She didn't want them to get lost in the commotion. The festival is already losing enough money without the scandal of Rupert Martin's death.'

He grumbled his agreement before poking a hole in her excuse. 'How come she didn't get it herself?'

Sherlock shrugged. 'That's why you have teenagers to boss around.'

He stared at her and then waved her away, muttering how it was all a disaster.

Taking the opportunity she had, Sherlock asked, 'What do you think the conductor died of?'

He sighed. 'No clue, but Ripper was worried about declining performance.'

That was a surprisingly candid statement. Clutching the manuscripts to her chest and curling her shoulders demurely, Sherlock asked, 'What specifically do you think it was? He seemed in control of the music, though he missed a few cues in rehearsals. Not that anyone questioned him on it.'

The agent narrowed his eyes at Sherlock and pressed his lips together. 'That's none of your business!'

'It's okay if you don't know,' she replied with bland friendliness.

Sherlock glanced up to the hole in the ceiling where Jenny, silently watching them, jerked her head for Sherlock to get out of there. She ran out of the room, repeating her lie about taking the scores to the music librarian.

Hours later, after Jenny's tuba was safely retrieved and Dr Watson had taken both girls home for a sleepover, Sherlock sat in the window seat of Jenny's room. She toyed with a vape pen in her mouth, thinking about the facts of Rupert Martin's death as she knew them.

Jenny walked in wearing a T-shirt and sleep shorts, fluffing her damp hair after taking a shower. She pressed her plump lips together before unleashing a mild scolding.

'You shouldn't do that, Sherlock. My mother would never let you come back if she caught you vaping.'

'It helps me think,' Sherlock replied unapologetically, though she put the vape away.

Jenny stomped across her bedroom, took hold of the big stack of papers, and shook them. 'Too bad you weren't thinking when you grabbed these scores!'

As if sifting the lumps out of flour, a heavier item fell forward. Sherlock bounded over and snatched it before it could hit the floor. Martin had a letter-sized calendar planner. Sherlock opened it up to find extensive annotations of appointments.

Watson stood beside her, pointing out all the clinics he had written in. 'I knew he was an in-demand conductor, but that was one busy musician.'

'Some of the best orchestras in the world,' Sherlock said, pointing out famous places listed in Martin's calendar. His list included both major cities and regions with quality orchestras.

'But not there,' Watson said, pointing to the name of a small town in Switzerland. 'Maybe he was forming a new ensemble there. Or cheating on his wife like all the gossip sites suggest.'

Sherlock wasn't completely misanthropic, but she was more likely to believe the latter. Infidelity was a solid motive for murder, and Cecily Baron could have poisoned Martin to speed up the end of their marriage. The conductor had looked clammy and discoloured under his stage makeup.

After a big yawn, Watson crawled into bed and covered herself with the duvet. 'Turn the light off when you're done.'

'Good night,' Sherlock wished as she studied the dates and locations in the book. There was something curious here with a regular return to Switzerland.

Perhaps there was no murder at all. Sometimes people died suddenly with no foul play involved. Yet something about the grandeur of this death made it seem dramatically staged, whether by an actress or the conductor himself.

Watson, a sound sleeper, had already started gently snoring, so Sherlock followed her curiosity to study Swiss German with her phone through the dark hours of the night. It took very little time for her to find an interactive language app and immerse herself in the language. Her existing talent for music helped her master new languages, as each had a distinct music of its own. She had previously learned continental French and its Quebecois variant. Adding the Swiss dialect to the German she already knew would be a delightful challenge.

Through all of Sherlock's study, Watson slept peacefully. It was a blessing to have a best friend who wasn't bothered by her peculiar and often nocturnal habits.

Returning her thoughts back to music, Sherlock retrieved the scores she'd liberated from Rupert Martin's dressing room. The annotations in pencil began with a precise script and were copiously laid out. Some cueing notes looked unnecessarily basic. Even Watson wouldn't need to use some of those notes, and all she cared about was the tuba.

Putting the scores in performance order, Sherlock read them fast with her near-perfect eidetic memory. The pieces with more notes corresponded to the pieces Martin made the ensemble rehearse more. The places in the score that showed where the ensemble had struggled in rehearsal were also notated, but the handwriting had changed so significantly that a different person could have written it.

Watson passed gas in her sleep, and Sherlock shook her head. Though Holmes didn't rest many hours a night, it was still time to give the sandman his due. She turned out the light and climbed into bed.

The next morning, Sherlock stared at a plate of breakfast artfully arranged to look like a cadaver. Dr Watson didn't do much in the way of cooking, but she liked to add red dye to the scrambled eggs to make them look like viscera. The toast was cut in a Y incision with strips of bacon angled into the bread on the sides like ribs.

'Mom! Did you have to?'

'She could have dyed the eggs grey and made them look like brains,' Sherlock quipped at the headless and limbless creation.

'Don't give her any ideas,' Jenny whispered.

Tapping the fork against her lower lip, Sherlock thought again about Martin and the mystery of his sudden death. Some people were just ill of health, but she didn't trust that to be the whole story.

Dr Watson was on the same wavelength because she entered the breakfast nook and sat down beside Jenny. With her hands folded together apologetically, Dr Watson said, 'I have to go in this afternoon to perform Rupert Martin's autopsy.'

'Will you do it in the observation theatre?' Sherlock asked before taking a bite of the red-dyed eggs.

'I believe so. It was an unexpected death of a somewhat famous person. There will be questions and scrutiny.'

'Jenny and I would like to watch you do the autopsy.'

'What?!' the younger Watson protested, earning Sherlock's kick under the table.

'Jenny and I were talking last night, and now with the death of our conductor, she's rethinking her career path.'

The creative lie earned an incredulous look from the young tuba player and a look of delight from Dr Watson.

Clapping her hands together with more joy than was merited for the observation of an autopsy, Dr Watson said, 'Jenny! I'm so excited for you. Not that I would have wished for the death of your conductor to make you seriously consider medicine...'

'Yes, mother,' Jenny replied before shooting Sherlock a narrow-eyed gaze.

As soon as the doctor left the table to refill her coffee, Jenny hissed, 'You know I don't want to give my mother any hope that I'm going into medicine. Just for that, I'm going to stuff you in my tuba case, Sherlock!'

Watson's threat didn't bother Holmes one bit. Being thin and flexible, Sherlock had already spent significant time inside Jenny's tuba case to practise Houdini-inspired feats of escapism. She didn't mind more opportunities to practise.

'I want to observe the autopsy, so you can torture me about it later,' Sherlock promised.

'Oh, I will.' Jenny glowered and bit her cadaver-shaped toast with menace.

Sherlock didn't mind being trapped in the dark. Being curled up inside Jenny's tuba case with the Swiss German lessons playing in her ear was a good opportunity to organise her thoughts.

Dr Watson had completed Rupert Martin's autopsy two days ago but still awaited the definitive toxicology report from the lab. Her initial findings concluded that Martin had consumed a poisonous substance the afternoon of the festival performance, around the same time as his public argument with his wife. Cecily Baron was immediately taken into custody, preventing her from fulfilling the contractual obligations of her filming schedule.

Spouses could certainly commit crimes of passion against each other. To Sherlock, the clues didn't add up to murder, though. During the afternoon before the deadly performance, Cecily had visible signs of aging that no actress would want to show. Upon her return, the puffiness and dark circles around her eyes could have been signs of grief but might not have been. Watson had suggested cosmetic surgery. Baron could have easily completed an outpatient procedure between the times she left Martin's dressing room and returned to Reichenbach Hall.

What if the entire incident was rooted in vanity? The actress didn't want to appear aging, and the conductor wanted to cover up his waning skills. During the autopsy, Dr Watson had found lesions in Rupert Martin's frontal lobe and evidence of other possible brain injuries. Maybe that was the root cause of his conducting errors.

Sherlock let that idea simmer in one part of her mind while she finished the speaking part of her Swiss German lesson. When she was older and had more freedom to travel, she would enjoy visiting Switzerland, hopefully with Jenny at her side. At the conclusion of the lesson, Sherlock knocked in a specific rhythm on the case so Jenny would let her out.

Watson clicked open the locks and smirked as she gave Sherlock a hand to step out of the case. 'Did you master Swiss German while you were inside?'

'Enough for basic conversation,' Sherlock answered as she stretched. 'I'm not convinced Cecily Baron poisoned her husband. The answer might be in Martin's calendar. I've been thinking about this like a musician. What if the clinics on the calendar weren't for music engagements at all? Maybe they were for medical clinics.'

'Oh, that is a possibility,' Watson agreed. 'I'd also assumed music because that was Martin's job.'

'One he wasn't doing very well despite his reputation for excellence,' Sherlock said. 'Better than others, but not up to his personal best. You saw how he got distracted in the middle of a piece and miscued us. He laughed it off elegantly enough that some believed him.'

After Jenny confirmed what Sherlock already knew, Holmes declared, 'I believe he had some kind of neurological disorder.'

'That doesn't explain him dying on the podium when the cause of death was poisoning.'

'It is a stereotypically female way to kill someone,' Sherlock agreed and began pacing. 'Do you still have Martin's calendar?'

'In my room safely beside my autographed score of Jennifer Higdon's tuba concerto.'

'Excellent,' Sherlock said, taking the stairs by two and pulling the calendar out of its hiding place.

It might have been a by-product of her current fascination with Swiss German, but Sherlock kept coming back to Martin's clinics in that small Swiss town of no known musical value. The medical connection was tenuous at best with an individual treatment facility that advertised itself like a spa.

Jenny opened her laptop and did some searching for any likely businesses that might be located in the town. When she found it, she called out to Sherlock.

'Look at this. It has the seal that was on the bottles he'd been chugging all week. They came from the spa.'

Sherlock pulled out her phone to show Jenny she was exactly right. 'I sniffed the bottles in his dressing room. They weren't water, but they weren't alcohol, either. Interesting.'

'Definitely. This is the best place given the clues,' Jenny declared. 'Celebrities go to treatment facilities all the time when they don't want to admit they've been in rehab. It doesn't mean they're not serious medical institutions.'

'Spoken like a doctor's daughter,' Sherlock teased.

Jenny scoffed. 'Are you going to use the language skills you mastered while meditating in my tuba case and call them?'

It was still early enough that Sherlock could call the Swiss clinic during operating hours. Without fanfare, Holmes dialled, and when the call connected, she affected the persona of someone who'd been hired by Martin's lawyer to organise information in light of his recent death.

The receptionist quickly confirmed that Martin had been receiving regular treatments at the clinic. She politely expressed condolences over his death.

'Thank you. We need details about the condition you were treating. You can send them to the medical examiner who performed Rupert Martin's autopsy.'

Sherlock snapped at Jenny to write down the fax number for Dr Watson's office, and then she repeated it to the clinic.

'I will send it immediately.'

True to her word and reliable as a Swiss timepiece, the receptionist promptly sent a fax to Dr Watson's home office. It was there she found Sherlock and Jenny hours later.

'Captain, some new evidence has come to light on the death of Rupert Martin,' Dr Watson said, striding into the police station with the full gravitas of her position as medical examiner.

Convincing Jenny's mother of their conclusions after she'd got over her anger at finding them in her office had been one of the most challenging conversations Holmes had ever had. Dr Watson had vacillated between forbidding Sherlock and Jenny to see each other again, and wishing Sherlock herself would go into medicine since her own daughter clearly wouldn't. As pertained to the case, the medical examiner ultimately fell on the side of facts that cast doubt on Baron's guilt.

Sherlock and Jenny followed in Dr Watson's high-heeled wake as she approached the captain.

'My daughter Jennifer and her friend Sherlock were both members of the youth orchestra that Martin conducted that evening. They have done extensive research and put together a theory of the case that will interest you. It might help free an innocent woman.'

The captain made a show of looking around Dr Watson to assess the teenagers with her. He sighed as if already weary of any ideas they might try to sell him. 'You two girls don't listen to true crime podcasts, do you?'

The teens glanced at each other and answered him that they didn't.

'Who has time for that?' Jenny added.

'Sir, if I may,' Sherlock said, stepping out from behind Dr Watson's shoulder. 'I do not believe that Cecily Baron poisoned her husband Rupert Martin. I contend that Martin's death was caused by Martin himself.'

The Conductor's Last Overture

The captain sat back in his seat and laced his fingers together over his soft middle. 'Just because you're fans of Ms Baron's movies doesn't mean she's not guilty of killing the husband she was trying to divorce.'

'This is not about that!' Sherlock, who received most of her pop culture knowledge through Jenny rather than any effort of her own, had not expected the captain to compare them to fans who assume their favourite celebrity could do no wrong.

Dr Watson crossed her arms and levelled the captain a serious stare. 'You would do well to listen to these young women. I dare say they make excellent detectives.'

'You'll owe me one, Mary,' the captain said.

'No, sir. I think not. Their work speaks for itself. Jenny. Sherlock. Lay out the case for the captain as you have done for me.'

'Thanks, Mom,' Jenny said as she stepped forward to stand shoulder to shoulder with Sherlock. Then she started recounting the tale.

'Okay, so, the conductor and his wife were going through a divorce, and they both accused each other of cheating. They argued throughout festival rehearsals.'

Sherlock took up the next point. 'Cecily Baron had been busy doing outpatient cosmetic procedures, including one she went to the afternoon that Martin died.'

The captain sat forward in his seat. 'True, but we haven't released that fact to the public. How'd you guess that?'

'I observed her,' Sherlock said simply. 'I was near her several times during rehearsals, and Rupert Martin died a few feet away from me. I saw her weeping over the body. Her face was different.'

Jenny spoke again. 'Rupert Martin was failing as a conductor. Sherlock and I compared what we experienced to videos available on the internet. Yes, people can have bad days, but someone at his skill level shouldn't.'

Sherlock nodded beside her. 'He was making cueing mistakes only inexperienced conductors would make, and his obvious decline in performance coincides with a trip he made to Switzerland five years ago.'

'It's the same time rumours of him cheating on his wife started,' Jenny added.

The captain rubbed the middle of his forehead and groaned. 'Are you two sure you're teenagers? You don't talk like teenagers.'

'Yes, Captain,' Sherlock replied and paused before sharing her next piece of the puzzle. 'After the body was removed from the scene, I went to the conductor's dressing room to look for clues. I saw several bottles with a certain seal on them and Martin's calendar hidden amongst his practice scores.'

She opened the photo app on her phone and swiped to the picture she'd taken in Martin's dressing room. 'It looks like this.'

'Right!' Jenny said, excitedly pointing to the image. 'Martin's calendar shows a pattern of returning to Switzerland regularly, and that seal comes from a private therapeutic spa where he definitely had appointments.'

The captain locked eyes with Dr Watson before asking Sherlock and Jenny, 'Dare I ask how you know this? Did he talk about it during rehearsals?'

'No, sir. We had his records sent to Dr Watson as the medical examiner,' Sherlock said, feeling rather proud of how she'd navigated that language challenge.

Jenny handed the captain the folder of medical record printouts faxed over from the spa. 'These outline the nature of the treatments he'd been receiving for a brain injury, one that could have impacted Martin's performance and reputation as one of today's top conductors.'

Sputtering, the captain looked up at the teens. 'But how did you get these?'

'I asked. Politely,' Sherlock said with an unaffected shrug.

'Their findings match my autopsy report,' Dr Watson corroborated. 'The poison in Martin's system fits what we know about his treatment according to the spa files.'

'We don't know enough about Martin's state of mind to call it a suicide. Medically, though,' Jenny said, 'it was an overdose.'

'Precisely,' Sherlock said. 'This was not a murder. Cecily Baron should be released.'

The captain sighed and tapped the top of his desk reluctantly with his fingers. 'You two ladies could show my detectives a thing or two about observing clues and stringing a chain of events together. Perhaps you have law enforcement in your future.'

'Absolutely not,' Dr Watson said, putting her hand on Jenny's shoulder.

Sherlock hadn't considered it before, but she most definitely liked knowing things and righting wrongs. She shared a secret look with Jenny, who shrugged and bobbed her head like she was thinking about it. As lifelong best friends, they'd had many adventures together. Being detectives would allow room for both Jenny's and Sherlock's talents and curiosities. It was a winning idea to pursue after Dr Watson was reconciled that her daughter was definitely not going into medicine.

In the meantime, the best course was to remember polite manners.

'Thank you, Captain. Maybe I do have a future as an investigator,' Sherlock said. 'If Ms Baron is in holding, can we tell her that she's free to go?'

'Right this way,' the captain said with a groan and loudly popping joints as he led them out of his office and down to release the innocent woman.

SOMETHING BORROWED
Millie Billingsworth

A NEW ONE, HOW ABSURD. *SHE* IS THE QUEEN OF THIS HOUSEHOLD. Up until now she thought Mrs Hudson understood that. Sniffing the travel crate that's been brought into her domain Sherlock hisses, her black fur bristling at the thought of another in her home.

What betrayal!

'Be nice, Sherlock,' Mrs Hudson scolds, gently using her foot to move Sherlock from the room. 'The shelter said if no one gave John a home he'd be put down.'

Sherlock screams, no, she wails, standing at the closed bedroom door. How dare her caretaker deny her access?

It's her bed! *Hers!*

It's none of her concern what would happen to this new cat if no one took him in. She absolutely refuses to share her bed. If she was a street cat she'd urinate on the sofa in protest, but she isn't undignified. Unlike this new one.

Hours pass before the bedroom door is opened, *hours*. Outraged at the denial Sherlock darts through the gap before it closes again, Mrs Hudson calling her name.

Jumping up onto the bed Sherlock lays her ears back, ready to teach this upstart cat who owns the house. Yet, as she's faced with the three legged kitten staring at her with big blue eyes she has a realisation.

Her bed hasn't been stolen, it's only been borrowed.

THE CASE OF THE TOXIC TEACAKE

Karen J Carlisle

REMNANTS OF SOIL TRICKLED FROM MY FINGERS AND THUDDED ON the polished oak casket. John was dead. I was the one who'd been ill. He'd saved me. My heart knotted. It should have been me.

'My condolences, Mrs Watson.' Mrs Hudson stepped to my side, an imposing figure in black, though she stood almost a foot shorter than me. She pulled a crisp handkerchief from the purse on her chatelaine and offered it to me. 'Would you like to join Sherlock for afternoon tea?'

Sherlock Holmes stood alone, at the opposite end of the coffin. She stared into the grave, ignoring our fellow mourners.

Her gaze drifted upwards, catching mine for only a moment before returning to the grave. To her left, neighbours and patients bowed their heads in respect. A small retinue of officers from Scotland Yard, with shiny buttons and hats in hand, flanked her right. A young boy lurked behind the headstones, just beyond their eye-line.

A tall man with a rugged moustache edged away from the group. I recognised him – a former friend of John's, who'd left the army in disgrace.

Inspector Lestrade hovered beyond the mourners. His gaze darted over the assembly and settled on Sherlock. A wry smile flickered over his lips. He turned and strode to a waiting hansom cab.

The Case of the Toxic Teacake

Sherlock continued to avoid my gaze. She stared past the mourners, as if looking for a diversion. No emotion showed on her face. No slouch of shoulders. No flutter of eyelids to hold back tears.

The cape of her Ulster coat fluttered. A strong breeze breathed over the casket and tugged my veil, bringing with it the smell of damp, musty soil, wood stain, and resin.

Another flurry of wind showered soil onto the casket. A drop of rain thudded on my parasol and drizzled over the edge of the silk as the sun slipped behind grey clouds.

Thunder rumbled in the distance. The mourners fidgeted. Soil tumbled onto the casket as they filed past the grave and shuffled towards waiting carriages.

My heart pounded. My head ached. The world spun. Sherlock steadied me. Mrs Hudson supported me on the other side.

'Tell me this is one of John's dreadful jokes,' I whispered.

'That would be in poor jest, even for Watson.' Sherlock's voice was calm.

They bundled me into the hansom cab as heaven poured out its grief, providing no competition for my own tears.

A parcel wrapped in brown paper sat on the doorstep of 221B Baker Street, a note tucked under its string. Mrs Hudson picked it up.

A reporter jumped onto the bottom step.

'Do you have a statement, Miss Holmes?' He pressed his pencil to the paper, and waited. 'Do you still plan to make your announcement?'

Sherlock grunted and strode into the hall. Mrs Hudson closed the door and led me up the stairs.

The sitting room smelled of stale tobacco, musty socks, and old books. Mrs Hudson drew in a deep breath, frowned.

'It smells like something–' She caught herself. 'Some fresh air will do the trick.'

Sherlock fumbled with the jet buttons of her bodice, wriggled out of the narrow sleeves and let the jacket fall to the floor where she stood. She unhooked her mesh stays and trudged into the bedroom.

Mrs Hudson picked up the discarded clothes and draped them over a chair.

Sherlock re-emerged – a collarless shirt over her skirts – and dragged a smoking jacket onto her shoulders. She frowned and slumped into her usual armchair in front of the unlit fireplace. 'How did I not see it? I could have stopped it.'

Mrs Hudson abandoned the package and newspaper on the small table next to her, and opened the curtains. Light from two broad windows spilled across the carpet. She pushed up the sash window of the nearest.

Scientific papers fluttered on the walls. The desk near the door boasted an assortment of books and scattered notes. A violin case leaned against a nearby bookshelf. Another desk stood by the far window, stocked with racks of glass tubes. A tantalus and gasogene had pride of place on the small dining table by the open window.

'Perhaps you can coax her out of this malaise?' Mrs Hudson asked me.

A long silence settled over the room.

'Perhaps your guest would like to sit?' Mrs Hudson prodded Sherlock.

'Of course.' Sherlock motioned towards the chair opposite her.

Another uncomfortable silence.

'I wonder who sent the package?' I removed the note from under the string: '*A teacake, with condolences, from Detective Inspector Lestrade.* That's considerate of him.'

'Yes.' Mrs Hudson smirked. 'Wasn't it?'

Sherlock shrugged.

I unwrapped the parcel. A strong aroma of cinnamon and cocoa filled the room. Inside was a sponge cake, drizzled with chocolate icing. Sherlock inhaled deeply.

'That's not a teacake.' Mrs Hudson huffed and fetched two cake plates and a knife from the dining table. 'And who, in their right mind, would slather a cinnamon sponge with chocolate icing?'

I nudged the parcel towards Sherlock.

The corner of her lip twitched.

Mrs Hudson smiled. 'I'll put the kettle on. Coffee?' She raised an eyebrow. 'I'm told the powers of the mind increase proportionally to the quantity of coffee consumed.'

I wrinkled my nose. 'I never did acquire the taste.'

'Perhaps something else?' she asked. 'Hot cocoa? It clears the mind,' she lowered her voice, 'and lifts the mood.'

'Cocoa will be fine,' I said. 'Perhaps a touch of sugar to dull the bitterness.'

Mrs Hudson nodded and bustled out of the room.

'I hear cocoa is a traditional drink in the Central Americas,' I ventured.

'It's considered to have medicinal properties,' replied Sherlock.

I smiled – trivia was like catnip to her – and handed her the knife.

'The Aztecs used it in their ceremonies.' The knife swiped in the air. 'They cut the heart–' Her smile slipped.

She sliced the cinnamon "teacake" with precision, and offered me a piece. The smell was sickly sweet. My stomach churned.

'No, thank you. I've no appetite.'

Sherlock's hand hovered over her plate. Her stomach rumbled. I knew her habit of fasting for days, followed by insatiable appetite.

'Don't let me stop you.'

She took a large bite, followed by another.

'When did you last eat?' I asked.

'You sound like your husband.' She cut another piece of cake.

'Do you always avoid answering questions?'

'I had luncheon at The Langham, the day Watson–' She swallowed. 'The day he died.'

My stomach twisted. There it was. The admission: John was dead. I needed to breathe, to obliterate the pain.

'I won't tell Mrs Hudson,' I whispered.

Sherlock devoured the second piece of cake.

'How about a drink to honour the fallen?' I asked.

'A red burgundy, perhaps?'

'Do you have anything stronger?' I strolled to the dining table. 'I saw a gasogene on the table.'

'If only Watson shared your excellent powers of observation.'

I held back my tears.

'John loved a whisky with soda.' The soft clink of the crystal decanters was comforting. I poured two whiskies. The liquid swirled in the glass.

The window rattled. A gust of icy wind caught my hair, clearing my head. I leaned through the open section of window. Below was the spot John had died. Cold rain ran down my cheeks. I gulped down the liquid, poured another, and handed Sherlock her drink.

'To Watson.' Sherlock swigged a mouthful, loosened her cravat, and stared into the empty fireplace as if lost in a daydream. 'The carriage came out of nowhere.' She swallowed another mouthful of whisky. 'I should have seen it.' Her glass thunked on the table. 'I still have his bag.' She glanced towards the medical bag on the floor by the desk; a graze marred the leather and the handle drooped at an odd angle. 'It was left on the street.'

'It's not your fault.' I touched her shoulder. Her muscles tightened. 'He'd just lost a patient. He said it reminded him of an incident in India. He dashed out as soon as he got your message.'

Banging on the front door reverberated up the stairs.

Sherlock stretched her legs and fanned her flushed face.

'Miss Holmes, will you still make your announcement?' The voice drifted up from the street below.

I turned my back on the din and perched on the sill.

Sherlock unbuttoned her collar. A faint rash tracked up her neck.

'I should ask Mrs Hudson not to set a fire on such a...' Her gaze flicked in my direction. Her eyes seemed darker. They shifted again. Something wasn't right.

'Sherlock?' I went to her and placed my fingers on her wrist, as I'd seen John do a hundred times. Her pulse raced.

She flinched, staggered, and braced herself on the edge of the desk. 'Can you hear them?'

'Hear who?' I asked.

'They'll never give up.' She turned to face the door, swiped the air, and growled. 'I'll tell you when I'm ready.'

A desk drawer scraped open. She pulled out a pistol, and waved it wildly in the air – mumbling something about acrobats and reporters – and lunged towards the open window, knocking the remains of the food parcel to the floor.

My heart pounded. I heard John's calm voice: *with sudden symptoms look to comestibles*. I knelt by the mess on the carpet, and sniffed the remnants of "not-teacake": cinnamon and unsweetened cocoa, mixed with a faint smell of honeysuckle.

'They're coming for me.' Sherlock's breaths were fast and shallow. Her skin was red. She batted at her sleeves, ripped off her smoking jacket.

'Stand to, Watson! I need your assistance.' She stared, unfocused, in my direction. She struggled to keep her balance, squinted into the overcast sky, her free arm shielding her eyes, and shot the pistol wildly into the street. The weapon slipped from her fingers and clattered onto the desk. I tugged her away from the casement. Heat radiated from her skin.

My fingers were at her neck, searching for a pulse. It raced so fast I could barely discern one beat from another. At this rate, her heart would eventually fail.

Her body twitched.

'Mrs Hudson!' I snatched the gasogene from the table, wrenched open her shirt, and aimed the gasogene at her. The rash extended down her chest.

Mrs Hudson saw our predicament at once. She dropped the tray of steaming cocoa on the desk by the door, kicked the door closed behind her. 'Symptoms?'

I heard John's voice as I recited them: *Mad as a hatter. Red as a beet. Dry as a bone.*

'Hell's teeth!' Mrs Hudson pried open Sherlock's eyelids. Her pupils devoured the colour of her irises. Mrs Hudson pushed a linen handkerchief into my hand. 'Wet this. And keep it on her head.'

'What is it?'

'Atropine, most likely. Used for disguises. Makes the eyes look darker.' She loosened the bandages, pressed her ear to Sherlock's chest. 'There were a few miscalculations in her early experiments.'

'Atropine? That's in datura, isn't it?' I asked.

She shrugged.

'John's last patient had datura poisoning,' I said. 'There's an antidote.' I caught my breath; he hadn't restocked his bag before... I prayed there was still some left. 'Quick, the medical bag by the desk.'

Bottles clinked as Mrs Hudson rummaged through its contents.

'Look for *Calabar Bean*.' I wet the handkerchief and pressed it against Sherlock's forehead.

'There's nothing.'

'Try...' What had John called it? 'Eserine. A milky-white liquid, used for eyes. One-tenth of an ounce.'

Sherlock convulsed. I struggled to keep the handkerchief in place.

Mrs Hudson slipped a syringe into the bottle and drew out the liquid. She tapped the cylinder and pressed the plunger. Liquid dribbled from the tip.

'You've done this before?' I asked.

'Only when necessary,' she replied.

I held out my hand.

'Are you certain?' she asked.

'If it's datura, yes.'

She relinquished the syringe.

'Hold her still.'

The needle pierced the skin and found a vein. I said a silent prayer as the liquid emptied.

A shrill of police whistles drifted up from the street.

Sherlock gagged. I rolled her onto her side as she expelled the contents of her stomach onto the rug. The stench of whisky, and sickly-sweet honeysuckle flooded the room.

'They can't see her like this.' Mrs Hudson slipped her hands under Sherlock's arms. 'You take her feet.'

Mrs Hudson answered the door.

'I heard shots fired.' Inspector Lestrade pushed past her and removed his bowler. A constable followed.

'Shoes!' scolded Mrs Hudson.

He scraped his boots on the mat. The constable remained outside the door.

'Where's Holmes?' asked Lestrade. 'There's reporters everywhere. They're saying she's dead.'

'*Miss* Holmes is resting.' I pocketed the parcel's note; until its origin was confirmed, I couldn't trust him.

'We can't help it if that rabble below panicked.' Mrs Hudson edged towards the desk, retrieved Sherlock's pistol, and concealed it behind her back.

'Then, she's unharmed?' He nudged the teacake on the carpet with the toe of his boot. 'What happened here?'

Sherlock moaned in the bedroom.

Lestrade's ears pricked at the sound. 'Holmes? Are you in there?'

I cursed under my breath. Sherlock's visions were returning; she needed a second dose of Eserine and more time to recover.

He continued towards the bedroom. I stepped in front of him. 'You can't enter a lady's private chambers.'

'She's been poisoned,' said Mrs Hudson.

Lestrade caught his breath. 'Shall I fetch a doctor?'

'Mrs Watson has it in hand, as usual,' replied Mrs Hudson.

'Very well.' He stepped back. 'I trust your judgment. But I'll require a statement from both of you. At the station, as soon as possible.'

Another raucous din erupted from the street below.

'Can't you control them?' Mrs Hudson joined me.

'They're desperate for a story.' Lestrade turned slowly, surveying the room.

'As are you, it seems.' Her fingers clenched tighter around the pistol's handle.

'I'll post a constable outside until I return.' He tipped his hat and closed the door behind him.

'I don't trust that man,' hissed Mrs Hudson. 'His lackey will wait for us to leave so he can finish off Sherlock. One of us must remain with her at all times.' She returned the pistol to the desk.

Sherlock shuddered and rolled out of bed with a thump.

'Fetch the bag, Mrs Hudson,' I scooped Sherlock back onto the bed. 'She needs a second dose. Then you can open that bottle of red burgundy. We've got a long wait.'

The hubbub in the street below fizzled after Lestrade — not-so-politely — told the reporters to ignore Holmes' theatrics and find something newsworthy. One reporter remained, hovering near the edge of the streetlight below.

Mrs Hudson returned just after dawn, with a hearty Scottish breakfast and a strong pot of tea. I sat at the dining table, opposite her. The familiar aroma of cinnamon engulfed me as she filled my teacup, and added a dash of milk. *Just how John liked it.* I glanced out the window, hoping she wouldn't see the tear rimming my eyelid.

The reporter was still there, leaning against the building across the street, discarded cigarette ends scattered at his feet. He scrawled in his notebook, and lit another cigarette. Something moved in the shadows behind him. A boy dashed out of the alley, snatched his notebook and fled. The reporter flinched as the lit match burned his fingers. He cursed and took chase.

'He'll never see that again.' Mrs Hudson chuckled.

A clatter and a thud from the bedroom; we were both on our feet. I reached the door first.

Sherlock stood in the middle of the room, straddling the fallen washstand, a walking cane in one hand. Water from the ceramic jug seeped into the rug.

'You're back, Watson?' Her words were slightly slurred. 'Fetch your stick, and help me vanquish these ruffians.'

She swung her cane in a wide arc and toppled onto the bed. She sat up, threw her head forward, and vomited.

'Better out than in.' Mrs Hudson picked up the wash jug. 'I'll fill this up. Best get some clean linens.'

I screwed up my nose, stepped over the vomit, and opened a dresser drawer.

Sherlock stared into the washstand mirror on the floor.

'*En garde*. The blaggard's returned.' She lunged.

'Fetch some more sedative, Mrs Hudson.' I pushed Sherlock back onto the bed.

'Are you haunting me, Watson?' Sherlock's hand slapped my shoulder. 'Because I haven't told Mary I'm going to retire?'

My heart sank. I loved her visits to retell of their adventures – the mystery and excitement; a life I lacked the courage to pursue, and my regret that I couldn't share it with John.

'Is that your big announcement?' I lowered myself onto the chair beside the bed.

Her fingers slipped from my arm.

'Shh!' She lowered her voice. 'Mary will hear you.' She grabbed my arm, and shook me. 'She'll be devastated.'

'You can't retire. I...' A shaky breath escaped my lungs. 'Why?'

'I'm sorry, John. I'm sorry I failed you.' Her fingers dug into my skin.

I pried them off and clasped her hands in mine.

'I know I promised Mycroft,' she whispered. 'But I'd rather join you in death, than retire to endure society's expectations as a dutiful housewife.' She collapsed back onto the bed. 'Tell Mary I'm sorry.' Her hand twitched in mine. Her breaths slowed.

'Sherlock?' I checked her pulse: slow and rhythmic.

There was a scrape outside the door. I rushed into the sitting room.

'Mrs Hudson?' I opened the door to the staircase. A step creaked. The front door clicked shut.

Sherlock slept fitfully for the rest of the day. Mid-afternoon, her fever broke.

Mrs Hudson laid a delicious supper of roast beef, vegetables, and gravy on the table.

My eyelids drooped.

'You need rest, lass. Doctor Watson's old room is upstairs.' She poured a glass of Sherlock's port, picked up the evening paper and plumped the cushions on the chaise lounge. 'I'll keep watch.'

I woke to insistent chirping from the plane tree beneath the window. Sunlight had already filled the room. I dragged off the bedclothes. I'd slept too long; Sherlock's sedative would have worn off hours ago.

I trudged down the stairs and tapped on the sitting room door.

'Mrs Hudson?'

No answer. I knocked louder.

A key fidgeted in the lock. Mrs Hudson rubbed her eyes.

'Why did you lock the door?' I asked.

She frowned. 'I didn't.'

'Sherlock!' We raced to the bedroom.

The window facing Baker Street was open. The curtains flapped in the breeze.

Sherlock was gone.

Mrs Hudson leaned out the window, and sighed. 'At least she didn't fall to her death.'

I joined her at the window and scanned the street. A boy was talking with a man. The boy looked up at me, spoke to the man again, and ran off.

'That boy,' I said. 'He stole the reporter's notebook, and was at the funeral.'

The bedroom door creaked. I turned to speak to Mrs Hudson. On the other side of the room, the rear window curtain had been pulled aside. The sash was half-open and there were scuff marks on the sill.

Mrs Hudson was already gone.

As I followed her towards the stairs, the man I'd seen in the street strode into the sitting room.

'What's going on?' I asked. 'Who was that boy?'

'The boy's name is Wiggins.' The man removed a cropped wig.

'Sherlock?'

Sherlock removed a handful of pins from her braided hair.

'He was skulking around the funeral,' I said.

'I know.' She flung her jacket on a dining chair.

'How did you get past the constable?' I asked.

'A brother has a right to visit his ill sister.' Sherlock bowed. 'I look like him, do I not?'

'I meant when you left.'

'I had the back piping reinforced in case I had the occasion to slip out unseen and circle around. It may need fixing again.'

Mrs Hudson entered the room. 'And I shall be planting thorny roses beneath that window.' She grinned. 'You're feeling better?'

'Much improved.' Sherlock caught her breath, removed her shirt collar, and undid the top buttons of her shirt. A faint rash lingered on her neck and though her face was fashionably pale, her cheeks were flushed.

'You should be resting,' I said.

'Strong coffee, Mrs Hudson. There's much work to do.' She strode into the bedroom.

'Tea, Mrs Watson?' asked Mrs Hudson. 'You'll need it if you're to keep up.'

I nodded.

Sherlock re-emerged, wiping the last vestiges of make-up from her face.

'Why the disguise?' I asked.

Sherlock grinned, snatched up the newspaper from the chaise lounge, and thrust it in my direction. The headlines screamed:

HOLMES FEARED DEAD!
SCOTLAND YARD REMAINS SILENT

'I couldn't wander around London as myself, could I?' She filled a glass from the gasogene, guzzled the liquid, and refilled the glass.

'You still need rest.' I placed the back of my hand against her forehead. 'You're burning up.'

'I shall survive.' Sherlock shrugged away. 'Thanks to your observant eye and quick action.' She lowered herself onto a dining chair.

'What did the boy Wiggins say?' I asked.

Sherlock sipped another mouthful of soda water.

'Still avoiding questions?'

She narrowed her eyes as if to assess me. 'I'd forgotten how curious you can be.' She slid a leather-bound diary across the table. 'I wasn't the first case of datura poisoning.'

'John's diary?' I flipped through the pages and read the last entry. 'A valet?'

'Not just any valet.' Sherlock removed an oily clay pipe from her jacket pocket. 'This one was in the employ of Professor Attri, a botanist just returned from India.' She flipped open the newspaper and pointed below the fold. I scanned the page: *Queen Victoria Knights Botanist.* 'There's been whispers of a plot to assassinate the Queen.'

'There was something in the paper.'

'The Queen's to visit Attri.' Sherlock sniffed. 'I don't believe in coincidences, so I inspected the Professor's residence before dawn. There is no sign of Attri's family. There is, however, signs of a new resident. It seems our assassin is coercing the Professor and has assumed the role of his assistant, in place of the late valet, who had witnessed the removal of Attri's family. Such a position would allow the assassin to slip datura into Her food or drink.' Sherlock turned the pipe in hand. 'Hallucinations, erratic behaviour; a clever misdirection. It would appear as if the Queen had gone mad, like her uncle.'

'How horrible!' I replied. 'But there are more reliable poisons than datura.'

'Not many doctors in England would suspect it,' replied Sherlock.

'Unless they'd spent time in India.' My heart raced. 'John knew! The valet discovered the plot, so they poisoned him. And when the local doctor – my John – attended him, they couldn't risk the valet's ramblings hadn't revealed it to him. That's why John was killed, isn't it?' I tried to ignore the knot in my chest. 'And why they poisoned you. Because they thought he'd told you their plan or you'd deduce their plan when you discovered the identity of John's patient.'

Sherlock puffed on her pipe. 'The poison was in the cake?'

'How did you know?' I asked.

'The cocoa would have masked the taste, and neither you, nor Mrs Hudson, ate any.'

The door opened.

'We know who it was.' The smell of freshly brewed coffee trailed Mrs Hudson across the room. 'Lestrade's spy is still skulking downstairs.'

'No.' Sherlock shook her head. 'Lestrade is a friend.'

'I don't trust him.' Mrs Hudson placed a tray with two cups, a siphon pot, and a pot of tea on the table.

'I grant you he can be an imbecile, but he's learned a great deal since we've worked together. What do you think, Mary?'

'Well, he seemed concerned about you. But he did send the cake.' I handed Sherlock the note that had accompanied the parcel.

'The traitor must be someone close, who knows my habits,' she said.

'Well, it's not me.' Mrs Hudson raised an eyebrow.

'It could be almost anyone who's read John's stories about your exploits,' I said. 'They are popular.'

'I still don't trust him.' Mrs Hudson poured a cup of each, and left.

I sipped the tea. *Cinnamon*. My cup clinked on its saucer.

'Why are you going to retire?' I asked.

Sherlock choked on her coffee. 'How did you know?'

'You get chatty when you're delirious.' I opened the paper and skimmed the page.

'John and I made a formidable team.'

'I know,' I whispered.

'It's my fault he's dead. I thought the incident in India he meant to tell me was just another one of his army stories.' She avoided eye contact. 'I was too absorbed in my petty family problems.'

'Why didn't you tell me? I could've helped.'

'My dear brother is quite happy to remind society the great detective Sherlock Holmes is, after all, a woman,' she said. 'A fact not looked upon favourably by his precious Diogenes Club. They've threatened to rescind his membership, so he threatened to discredit John unless I promised I'd retire.'

I sucked a breath in through my teeth. 'Well, he'll have to deal with both of us now.'

Sherlock smiled.

'But first we must assure the world you are not dead.' I turned another page and examined the photograph of Professor Attri and an associate dining at the Langham Hotel. 'We have an assassination to–' I caught my breath. 'That man.'

'What of him?' asked Sherlock.

'I know this man. He was a captain. He served in India with John. Dishonourably discharged, and went to Australia in search of riches. I saw him at the funeral. He left just before the Inspector, and your Wiggins.'

Sherlock examined the image.

'You didn't notice him?' I asked.

'My wits were dulled by the loss of a good friend. It won't happen again.' Sherlock frowned. 'He was driving the carriage.' She looked me in the eye. 'He drove directly at Watson.'

'He murdered John?' Anger flared in my heart. The newspaper crumpled in my fingers. 'He's a dead man.'

'Let me do this, Watson.' She nudged my teacup closer to me.

A burst of cinnamon caught my nostrils, strengthening my resolve.

'You can't get rid of me that easily.'

'Drink your tea,' she said.

The Case of the Toxic Teacake

A door slammed downstairs. I leapt from my chair and snatched the pistol from the desk drawer.

'Bloody reporters are infesting the station, demanding answers.' Lestrade stormed into the sitting room, waving the morning newspaper. 'Are the rumours true?' His hand shook. 'You're to retire?'

Sherlock frowned. 'How did they—?'

'There *was* someone on the stair that night.' I hissed. 'That pesky reporter was listening at the door.'

The pistol shook in my hands.

Lestrade glared at the weapon I held. 'I demand you tell me what's going on.'

'I will, if *you* will, Lestrade,' I said.

'What?' He frowned.

'You sent the poisoned cake, Lestrade.' I indicated the parcel on the table between the armchairs.

'I did not.'

'You signed the card.' I clenched the pistol.

'Damn it, woman.' Lestrade snatched off his bowler and twisted the brim between his fingers. 'On my honour, Holmes, I did not poison you.

'I believe you.' Sherlock placed a gentle hand on my forearm. 'Besides, what motive does he have?'

Lestrade stopped torturing his hat.

'Are you sure, Sherlock?' I kept my finger close to the trigger. 'He's your rival?'

'We're friends, not enemies.' She lit her pipe and placed the parcel's note and sheet of paper, printed with Scotland Yard letterhead and signed by Lestrade, on the table. 'It's not Lestrade's handwriting. They don't match.' She lit her pipe.

Lestrade smiled.

'Then why the intrusion?' I asked.

'I hoped to convince you to reconsider retirement.' He avoided direct eye contact.

'You're just concerned for your own reputation,' I scoffed. 'Afraid Sherlock will no longer solve your impossible cases.'

'No, I—' His mouth gaped like a drowning fish.

'You'll miss me?' Sherlock leaned back in her chair and chewed her pipe.

Lestrade's cheeks flushed. His jaw clenched.

'I am concerned for the Queen's safety,' he replied.

'Why did you leave the funeral early?' I asked, remembering Sherlock's distrust of coincidences.

'I was following a suspect whose brother was arrested for sedition.'

'Hewett?' I asked.

'Yes, how did you know?'

Sherlock puffed her pipe and grinned.

Lestrade slid onto a dining chair.

'Cheer up, Inspector.' Sherlock poured him a whisky.

'Captain Hewett and Professor Attri are in cahoots,' I said.

'Not exactly.' Sherlock swigged the last of her coffee.

'They're acquainted?' Lestrade frowned.

'*Professor Attri has become a regular diner at the Langham while awaiting the arrival of his family from India.*' I tapped the newspaper article.

'Well spotted, Watson.'

I smiled. Twice now she'd used the endearment.

'Professor Attri's family is not in residence,' Sherlock continued. 'No doubt Hewett is holding them hostage to force the Professor's compliance until the assassination plot is complete.'

Lestrade's eyes widened.

'You'll find evidence datura was distilled for its poison at his residence.' said Sherlock. 'The handwriting on the parcel's card belongs to Captain Hewett.' She slid another paper across the table, a page from the Langham Hotel register. 'I made a quick detour on the way to the Attri residence.'

'You deduced all that from your sickbed?' asked Lestrade.

Sherlock leaned back in her chair and bit on her pipe.

'I think I'll defer my retirement.' Smoke curled from her lips. She sucked it back into her mouth.

'But the newspapers? Your announcement?'

Another puff of smoke coiled around her head. 'Tomorrow's headlines will read: *Scotland Yard Thwarts Plot to Assassinate Queen*. And below the fold: *Holmes' Secret Revealed as Ruse to Aid Scotland Yard*. All will be revealed in the next Sherlock Holmes adventure.'

'But who'll write it?' he asked.

'I have a new author.' She glanced in my direction.

Lestrade nodded.

'Most excellent.' He placed the note and scrap of paper in his pocket. 'Be sure to keep the rivalry between Holmes and the Yard's finest.' He smiled. 'It makes my life easier with the chaps at the Yard.' He slipped his bowler onto his head, and took his leave.

'Why me?' I asked.

'I can trust you. And Watson mentioned you helped him with his scribblings.'

'Just one last thing.' I laid the pistol on the table and sat opposite her. 'What made you think to check the Captain's handwriting on the note?'

'Elementary, Watson.' She poured two glasses of whisky with soda. 'The word "teacake".'

'But, it was a cinnamon sponge cake, not a teacake,' I said.

'Exactly.' She wrapped her hand around her glass. 'The Captain had recently returned from Australia, where it's often called a *teacake*.'

Author Bios

Atlin Merrick *(The Game is a Foot)* has written more short stories about Sherlock Holmes than Arthur Conan Doyle and is kinda sorta planning sequels to her *Sherlock Holmes and John Watson: The Day They Met* (written as Wendy C Fries), and *Sherlock Holmes and John Watson: The Night They Met* (written as Atlin Merrick). By day Atlin runs Improbable Press, a publishing company which never met a cryptid it didn't like, and is ever-keen on telling the stories of women, LGBTQIA+, disabled, BIPOC, and neurodiverse people. Some of Atlin's other anthologies include *Dark Cheer: Cryptids Emerging (Volumes Blue & Silver)*, as well as *Anna Karenina Isn't Dead*. Atlin hopes you read her recent non-fiction anthology *Spark: How Fanfiction and Fandom Can Set Your Creativity On Fire* of which she's very proud.

Dannye Chase *(The Case of the Man Who Wasn't Dead)* is a queer, married mom of three who lives in the US Pacific Northwest. She claims to write in many genres, but her oldest offspring suspects it all boils down to either romance or horror…or somehow both. Dannye's short fiction has appeared in magazines, anthologies, and podcasts. You can find her on Facebook as Dannye Chase, and at DannyeChase.com, where she gives weird writing prompts.

Eugen Bacon *(The Mystery of the Vanishing Echoes)* is an African Australian author of several novels and collections. She's a British Fantasy Award winner, a Victorian Premier's Literary Award finalist, a Foreword Indies Award winner, and a twice World Fantasy Award finalist. Eugen was announced in the honour list of the Otherwise Fellowships for 'doing exciting work in gender and speculative fiction'. *Danged Black Thing* made the Otherwise Award Honour List as a 'sharp collection of Afro-Surrealist work', and was a 2024 Philip K Dick Award nominee. Eugen's creative work has appeared worldwide, including in *Apex Magazine, Award Winning Australian Writing, Fantasy, Fantasy & Science Fiction*, and *Year's Best African Speculative Fiction*. Visit her at eugenbacon.com.

JD Cadmon *(The Conductor's Last Overture)* is a Louisiana-based writer and librarian who likes bringing romantic sci-fi and fantasy tales to life, usually with a humorous bent. Her stories often contain skilled musicians and people who speak multiple languages. While completing her bachelor's degree in music education, JD assisted several guest clinicians during various music festivals. With Sherlock being a violinist in canon, it was easy to imagine Holmes and Watson in a similar setting solving their first case. If you liked "The Conductor's Last Overture" and want to read more from JD Cadmon, try *A Feral Spark*, which features a werewolf violinist fluent in American Sign Language.

Karen J Carlisle *(The Case of the Toxic Teacake)* writes speculative fiction, favouring mysteries (not necessarily of the murderous kind). Her works range from light-hearted Victorian steampunk and alternate-history, Holmesian mysteries, and cosy(ish) fantasy mysteries set in Australia, to darker Gaslamp adventures. After obtaining a BAppSc, she moved to Adelaide, to live with her family and ghost of her ancient Devon Rex, and continue her long-term affairs with Doctor Who, fantasy fiction, tabletop role-playing, gardening, historical re-creation, and steampunk. Karen's stories have been short-listed by the 2013 Australian Literature Review, featured in the 2016 Adelaide Fringe, and published in Australian, US, and Canadian anthologies. She's always loved dark chocolate, rarely refuses a cup of tea, and is not keen on South Australian summers.

Katya de Becerra *(The Curse of the Amethyst Society)* was born in Russia, studied in California, lived in Peru, and then stayed in Australia long enough to become a local. She was going to be an Egyptologist when she grew up, but instead she earned a PhD in Anthropology. She is the author of horror-thrillers *When Ghosts Call Us Home*, *What The Woods Keep*, *Oasis*, and the forthcoming *They Watch From Below*. She is also co-editor of the *This Fresh Hell* anthology, which reimagines and subverts horror tropes in new and unexpected ways. Find Katya on Instagram as @katyadebecerra and check out her website www.katyadebecerra.com.

Kenzie Lappin *(The Case of the Love Affair)* is a writer with short stories in publications such as Wizards In Space Literary Magazine, Brigids Gate Press, Apex Magazine, WordFire Press, Air And Nothingness Press, and more. Check her out on Twitter at @KenzieLappin.

Millie Billingsworth *(Something Borrowed)* is approaching thirty-five, enjoying country life with her beloved cat. In her spare time she likes to write, doing it for fun over anything else.

Narrelle M Harris *(The Solitary Recyclist)* Narrelle's 80+ works include vampire novels, spy adventures, crime fiction, het and queer romance, and Holmes/Watson mysteries, as well as songs and poetry. Some of her works have won or been nominated for awards. Recent works include Grounded and Kitty and Cadaver and the re-release of her Vampires of Melbourne novels. She also edits anthologies: including Holmesian anthology The Only One in the World (2021) and Clamour and Mischief (2022); This Fresh Hell (2023) was co-edited with Katya de Becerra and Sherlock is a Girl's Name (2024) with Atlin Merrick. Her latest book is The She-Wolf of Baker Street (2024), a contemporary, paranormal take on the inhabitants of 221B Baker Street. https://narrellemharris.iwriter.com.au.

Sarah Tollok *(The Clothes Maketh the Man?)* lives in the beautiful Shenandoah Valley of Virginia with her husband and two sons. Her work can be found in anthologies with Improbable Press and Alan Squire Publishing, as well as numerous online literary journals. As a staff writer with Coffee House Writers, Sarah shares her thoughts about the magic of reading. *Bookstories*, the author's love letter to the world of books, debuted in 2024 with Balance of Seven. You can find out more about her work at SarahTollok.com.

Stacy Noe *(A Mother's Reputation)* lives in the foothills of the mountains and (when their child isn't inspiring them to write about Sherlock Holmes) enjoys writing rural, parafantasy about how magical it is. They have stories in Worm Moon Archive, and the anthologies 'Things Improbable' and 'Clarity' (2022 Queer SciFi). You can find them at StacyNoe.com and linktr.ee/stacynoeauthor.

Tansy Rayner Roberts *(A Taste for Skulls)* is a Tasmanian author and podcaster. Her many books include *Musketeer Space, Tea & Sympathetic Magic, Time of the Cat* and *Gorgons Deserve Nice Things*. She also writes cosy mysteries with murder and cake under the pen-name Livia Day. You can find Tansy on Patreon, Insta, Threads & Bluesky as @tansyrr and on her website at tansyrr.com.

Verity Burns *(Adjectives are Forever, What You Think They Mean, The Book for the Page)* has written four novel length Sherlock Holmes stories and several shorter works. She also met her beloved late husband, who happened to be transgender, through their shared passion for all things Sherlockian. Her contributions to *Sherlock is a Girl's Name* draw on all of this experience.

More from Clan Destine Press and Improbable Press

The Only One in the World
Edited by Narrelle M. Harris
CLAN DESTINE PRESS

What if Sherlock Holmes was Polish? What if he or John Watson were Indian or Irish or Australian or Japanese? How would their worlds look if one or both was from a completely different background?

In The Only One in the World, we asked a baker's dozen of writers to answer these questions, and the marvelous results are adventures in Ancient Egypt, Viking Iceland, and 17th century England; in 19th century Ireland, Germany, and Poland; in South Africa of the 1970s and New Orleans of the 1920s; and in contemporary Australia, USA, Russia, India and Portugal.

The stories and contributors taking a new look at our old friends, Sherlock Holmes and John Watson, include:

The Affair of the Purloined Rentboy by Greg Herren

S.H.E.R.L.O.C.K. by Atlin Merrick

The Path of Truth by Jack Fennell

Sharaku Homura and the Heart of Iron by Jason Franks

The Adventure of the Disappearing Village by Natalie Conyer

The Saga of the Hidden Treasure by Kerry Greenwood and David Greagg

The Problem of the Lying Author by Lisa Fessler

Mistress Islet and the General's Son by Lucy Sussex

A Scandalous Case of Poisoning by Katya de Becerra

The Adventure of the Fated Homecoming by Jayantika Ganguly

Prince Ha-mahes and the Adventure of the Stoned Mason by LJM Owen

The Enemy Within by Raymond Gates

A Study in Lavender by JM Redmann

Spark:
How Fanfiction and Fandom Can Set Your Creativity On Fire
Edited by Atlin Merrick
IMPROBABLE PRESS, AN IMPRINT OF CLAN DESTINE PRESS

Spark is all about encouragement, permission, it's about firing you up.

Spark: How Fanfiction and Fandom Can Set Your Creativity On Fire hopes to help you believe that your fandom writing, drawing, podficcing – whatever you're creating right now – is, was, and ever shall be legitimate, important, and a fantastic way to expand your community, develop your skills, and above all help you find your voice in the world.

Spark's more than forty essays and interviews from best-selling writers Anne Jamison, Claire O'Dell, Diane Duane, Henry Jenkins, KJ Charles, Lyndsay Faye, Sara Dobie Bauer and many others discuss, encourage, and shout about how fic and fandom in all their glories can absolutely inspire you, set your creativity on fire – and change your world.

With essays, interviews, and art including these contributors:

Adalisa Zarate, Amy Murphy, Andrea L Farley, Angela Nauss, Ann McClellan, Anne Jamison, Atlin Merrick, Audra McCauley, Bel Murphy, Camille Happert, Carman C Curton, Claire O'Dell, Colleen Veillon, Dannye Chase, Darcy Lindbergh, Darth Astris, Diandra Hollman, Diane Duane, Dimitra Stathopoulos, E C Foxglove, Elena Piatti, Emily Schmitt, George Ivanoff, Hannah S, Henry Jenkins, Hubblegleeflower, Janet Anderton, Jayantika Ganguly, K Caine, Kameo Llyn Douglas, Khorazir Anke Eissmann, KJ Charles, L.S., Lucy W, Lyndsay Faye, Margaret Walsh, May Shepard, Melissa Good, Meredith Spies, Merinda Brayfield, Monica Hotaru, Narrelle M. Harris, Natalie Conyer, Rosalyn Hunter, Sara Dobie Bauer, Sebastian Jack, Sherrinford Holmes, Stacey Cunningham, Tei, Verena Höhn, Wendy C Fries

Who Sleuthed It?
Edited by Lindy Cameron
CLAN DESTINE PRESS

Who Sleuthed It? is the book you want when you want a book about animals helping their animal friends – or their human sidekicks – solve a host of diabolical crimes and whimsical mysteries.

Why, let us tell you about it in rhyme:

Penguins and humans and dogs run by
Magpies, hawks, owls and pigs that fly…
Weredogs and cats and rats are why…
Dragonflies, starlings, and cockies flash by
Foxes and spiders and bats… oh my
Fingers and wings and paws, all solving…
Mysteries and crimes and…
Ectoplasm?
Good grief

This anthology from Clan Destine Press features a host of Australian, American, and Irish authors, including:

Atlin Merrick, Chuck McKenzie, CJ McGumbleberry, Craig Hilton, David Greagg, Elizabeth Ann Scarborough, Fin J Ross, GV Pearce, Jack Fennell, Kat Clay, Kerry Greenwood, Lindy Cameron, Livia Day, LJM Owen, Louisa Bennet, Meg Keneally, Narrelle M Harris, Tor Roxburgh, Vikki Petraitis

Milton Keynes UK
Ingram Content Group UK Ltd.
UKHW010642080724
445166UK00001B/39